Davidia and
THE PRINCE OF TRIPLOCK

Ken Spargo

About the Author

Ken lives in Vermont, Victoria, Australia.

During the 1970s he travelled overseas and lived in Austria, England, Papua New Guinea and New Zealand for six years. He spent three years as a European tour guide on camping tours. He is a practicing accountant and has managed his own business for  the past thirty years. His interest in travel, sports, theatre, literature and raising his two children led him to writing many short stories; his first crime novel – *Stumped*, and now his first fantasy novel – *Davidia and The Prince Of Triplock*.

Published in Australia by Sid Harta Publishers Pty Ltd,
ABN: 46 119 415 842

23 Stirling Crescent, Glen Waverley, Victoria 3150 Australia
Telephone: +61 3 9560 9920, Facsimile: +61 3 9545 1742
E-mail: author@sidharta.com.au

First published in Australia January 2012
This edition published January 2012
Copyright © Ken Spargo 2012
Cover design, typesetting: Chameleon Print Design

The right of Ken Spargo to be identified as the Author
of the Work has been asserted in accordance with the
Copyright, Designs and Patents Act 1988.

Spargo, Ken
Davidia and the Prince of Triplock
ISBN: 1-921829-11-7   EAN13: 978-1-921829-11-6
pp310

To my daughter, Sophie, who inspired me to enter a child's world to relive my childhood imagination.

CONTENTS

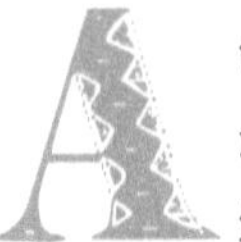t the time of the Great Split, unhappiness permeated the everyday life of all life forms in the ancient Valley of Triplock. A cataclysmic disagreement between the two most powerful life forms erupted into unbridled rage. Good was being held to ransom by evil. The two emotional sides could not agree on the raising of a small life form.

'He stays with me,' boomed the loud voice of the King.

'I will raise him how I feel,' boomed the very strong voice of the Queen.

'He is safer here than anywhere else.'

'We'll see.'

The Queen stormed off in a huff, unable to console her evil thoughts. Her head brimmed with an army of them. She couldn't ward off their evil attacks on her mind. She grumbled to herself that this young life form would not stand in her way. She thought that she was the future rightful ruler of Triplock and every other valley. No obstacle or hurdle would be foolish enough to bar her access to her perceived destiny.

The King sat dejectedly, eyes downcast, rueing the impasse he had to solve.

'Why is it so difficult to raise young life forms, when the valleys can accommodate all manner of things?' he mumbled to himself. The King was a fair and wise ruler; however, his

Queen had been mentally menaced by desires he knew nothing of. Evil wasn't a friend of his. It wasn't initially a friend of the Queen's either, but whisperings into her ears at a moment of low emotional resistance, allowed her mental landscape to alter and not for the better.

'We can rule together,' whispered the wind. A cold breeze enveloped the Queen. She shuddered.

'What do you mean?' she answered into the floating breeze.

'If we achieve my goals, then it's that simple.'

'Who are you?'

'I am an enemy of the King. He won't allow me into the Valley of Triplock, but with your help, I can succeed. I promise you will be installed as ruler of all the valleys.'

The Queen's smile spread across her face like a widening river gorge. It had been a while since her face had parted in such a manner. The view was pleasant, but the meaning was sinister. After that meeting, the Queen plotted the downfall of the King, with the assistance of her new "friend", The Murmur.

They hatched a plan to snatch the young Igloid before he came of age as an Iglood, when it would be too late for their plan to succeed.

In the Cave of Murm where The Murmur lived, a young life form that had been tricked to stray outside the palace walls was brought yelling and kicking.

'You snivelling, little life form, how dare I risk you to form into an Iglood and threaten me with the power and control of the Valleys. I curse you to be banished forever. You can't be killed, so this is the next worst thing that can happen. Say the curse, you windbag.'

The Murmur whispered in a cold, deep, throaty voice, 'Be gone oh yonder life form. May the Nettles of Neverness sting you, the Sprig of Spruce change your shape, may the Voice of

Vanishment snuff out your sounds and the Dirt of Disaster, send you to a life of Gloom.'

An explosive wind suddenly whirled around the caves, picked up the young Igloid and swallowed him whole.

What had happened to the small life form?

'Dad, can I play in the attic, please? Miss Percival needs to have her hair done. It's raining outside and I don't have anyone else to play with,' said Davidia, with her bottom lip pouting as if it was about to fall off.

Dad couldn't deny his beautiful twelve year old daughter's pleas. He was a sucker for a soft voice and angelic looks. Davidia lived with her parents and older brother, Dan. Their house was an old style Tudor house with painted wood angling in all directions, white rendered walls and an upstairs attic, which seemed to dominate the house. It was Davidia's favourite playing area. She and Miss Percival would often be found ferreting through old boxes of clothes her parents had stored. They played dress-ups and were like two sisters, even though one was a special doll.

One day, when mum and dad were out and she was in the care of Dan, a large, grey cloud hovered over the street, blacking out the power source. The air was moist with water vapour and a chill wind ran the length of the street. It felt like winter in the middle of summer.

'Dan, I'm going to play upstairs in the attic,' said Davidia, knowing that it was usually warmer than the rest of the house.

'Mum and dad will be home in an hour, so I suppose it's okay, but don't open any of the windows,' replied Dan. He often wondered what his little sister found so interesting in the attic. He was a fourteen-year-old grappling with his development as a teenager. The attic to him was old hat for amusement.

Davidia slowly climbed the attic stairs. A frightened spider scampered along its web, fearing it would be squashed if it had been seen. The door to the attic was closed. It was usually left slightly open. She pushed against it. Her young frame couldn't make it budge.

'You have to turn me,' said a voice.

'Turn what?' answered Davidia amazed to hear the comment.

'The doorknob.'

'Is that the dented, round thing poking out?'

'Yes it is. I am very useful. You can't come in unless you turn me. Go on, give it a try.'

Davidia gave the rounded brass fitting a solid twist. It didn't move.

'I can't open it.'

'Yes you can. Push me in first, and then twist me anti-clockwise,' the doorknob directed.

'What's an anti-clock thingamy?' asked Davidia.

'You turn me in that particular way.' The doorknob seemed to move slowly, hinting at the correct procedure.

Davidia, who was as sharp as a tack, quickly grabbed the doorknob and gave it a solid push and twist. It opened instantly.

'That wasn't fair,' whined the doorknob, who was now left alone to hang silently until someone else wanted entrance.

'That stupid doorknob! It's my daddy's and mummy's house and I can go where I like,' said Davidia to herself. 'Miss Percival, we shall play over there today behind those boxes.' Davidia went to the far corner of the attic, where many boxes were stacked. She began to remove them one by one. She left the heavy ones where they sat. One particularly large box caught her attention. It was tied up with a pink ribbon. A label was written in red ink and read, "Split Personality. If you have one, dare to open me."

Davidia didn't quite understand what that was, but she was an adventurous young girl so she untied the ribbon. It was a magical moment. As soon as the ribbon was undone, the sides of the box automatically fell away revealing a small, odd shaped chair. It had a twisted back, a bumpy seat and only three legs. At the foot of the chair were two books, one with the letter S engraved on it and the other engraved with the letter P. She loved reading books. At her sixth year of school, her reading level was excellent. Long words hadn't yet been fully mastered, but she did try.

'Miss Percival, you sit over there whilst I sit in the new chair and read the books. I hope the words are small and simple for me to understand,' she said. 'I wonder if the chair was to be a present from mum and dad. It's exciting, isn't it,' giggled Davidia.

She moved the chair to the window for more light with which to read. The sun didn't shine anywhere. The street was still covered in a grey mist, which blotted the warm rays from penetrating into the attic. Davidia picked up a warm scatter rug and then sat in the small chair. She leaned forward and picked up the book with the letter S. The pages suddenly opened automatically as if by magic. Her arms were instantly pinned to the chair's armrests and she couldn't use her hands. When the book's pages had finished turning, her arms were freed to use again. She leaned over to pick up book P and the same thing happened. Davidia was immobilised. Where was the robot controlling her movements? Once the second book had been read and returned to its original place, a cold, swirling wind tapped at the attic window. Dan had warned her not to open it. Davidia, being a curious and adventurous twelve year old, also thought that she saw a face in the mist which intrigued her, so she opened the window ever so slightly. The wind howled in anger. The window was suddenly wrenched open and Davidia flew through it, sucked into the darkness. It was pitch black. She had been swallowed, but by what? After what seemed to be an eternity, the howling wind scaled down to a blistering breeze and dumped Davidia with a solid thump onto the ground.

2. ROCK OF YOCKLAW

'Where am I? Am I hurt? Where's Miss Percival? Where's mummy and daddy? I should have listened to Dan,' wailed Davidia. She was in a strange land that she had never seen before. Her tears made the front of her dress all soggy. She suddenly felt alone. Her dress was soiled, her shoes were scuffed and her blonde hair was ruffled. It took a few minutes for her to survey her new surroundings.

The Valley of Preciousness spread before her eyes. It was a place of beauty, reminiscent of similar scenes depicted in prestigious oil paintings by well-known masters. It was a spellbinding view. At the beginning of the valley, a fabled stone known as the Rock of Yocklaw sat high on a hill standing as a sentinel guarding the Town of Importance based at its feet. Myths abounded in the valley and it was believed that the Rock of Yocklaw possessed an aura of protection, having existed for so long. It was said that it possessed special powers.

'It is so beautiful,' said Davidia. Her voice was lost on the breeze as there was no one else to talk to. For her years, Davidia was a confident, young girl and when confronted by a problem, she tried to understand and resolve it. Her parents always encouraged her to tell the truth, the whole truth and nothing but the truth, so there was no need for lies. Davidia didn't fully understand the impact of lies, but knew bad things could happen if you used them.

'That rock is tall,' she said pointing at the Rock of Yocklaw.

A crevice, or was it a crack, in its surface momentarily appeared into what she thought was a smile. She waved, but only the wind blew the tree canopy in response.

Davidia had no idea what to do next. This was her first experience of being totally alone. She walked around the Rock of Yocklaw, hoping to meet someone or something. The ground was covered in small stones. She aimlessly kicked at them as she walked.

'That's another goal for the girl's soccer team,' she yelled.

'Don't do that, it hurts,' said a tiny voice.

'Who said that?' asked a startled Davidia.

'I did. Look down at your feet,' a small voice continued.

Davidia could only see a mass of small stones all lying completely still. She raised her foot to kick at another stone, when she noticed a tiny hole appear in its surface.

'Did you say that?' asked Davidia.

'Yes I did. You must stop kicking us. We are not meant to move and if we do, bad things can happen.'

'But you are only stones,' she said. 'How can you talk? We throw stones at home. My brother, Dan, is a menace with them. He broke Mrs Zincloss' window, but we never told dad,' said Davidia divulging a secret, but it was the truth.

'Be careful. Do not disturb something you don't know about. You think I'm talking to you, but I'm not. We communicate by touch. When your foot touches me, we can understand each other. Take your foot off me.'

Davidia removed her foot, saw the hole in the stone's surface and heard nothing. As soon as she placed her foot on the stone again, they could communicate.

'At home we don't communicate by touch, but by using words.'

'What's a word?' asked the small stone.

'It's how people talk to each other by sound without touching,' replied Davidia.

'Oh. We don't use them here. There are no people here in the valley. Is that what you are, a people?'

'Yes. I am a people, a girl people, but by myself I am a person. A people are many of us persons together.'

'It's understanding feelings that we use. Do you know why you can understand me?' asked the small stone.

'No, I don't.'

'You have good feelings. If they were bad, then we couldn't continue communicating with each other.'

'Where am I?' asked Davidia. 'What is this place?'

'Stand on me a little harder, so I can communicate better. This is the Valley of Preciousness where light and sunshine is for everything. That over there is the Town of Importance where many life forms live.'

'That nice rock, what is it doing here?'

'We understand it is a relative of ours, but we don't know how close. It has been there a long time. Stay away from it. Strange noises come from within it and we don't know what makes it.'

'Does it have a name? Everything has a name.'

'It is known as the Rock of Yocklaw.'

'It's huge. Come with me and take a closer look.'

'I can't. It's forbidden for me to move. I'm a stone and this is where I stay.'

Before the small stone could offer an explanation, Davidia had removed her foot and communication ceased. The day was clear. She had no idea of the evils and myths that abounded in her new world. She went exploring around the base of the huge rock.

Suddenly and without warning, a grey, cold, thick, swirling mist blanketed the landscape, snuffing out any light.

'Who turned out the lights? It's not my bedtime yet,' she complained. 'At home I always read a bedtime story by myself when it got dark.' This was too early in the day. 'I don't have any books here. Brrr, its getting cold.' Davidia vigorously rubbed her arms. The cotton summer dress she wore retained very little warmth.

She shuddered and fell silently to the ground, a pillow of peace. Nothing stirred in the valley. It was ghostly silent. The moist mist had a deathly feel to it. It was The Evil Mist which had been creeping over many lands, growing stronger from its destruction of all life forms. It gorged on darkness and misery to everything. It had finally arrived in the Valley of Preciousness after years of previously failed attempts. The size of the evil demon that lived within the Evil Mist had grown progressively more powerful with each conquest. He was an unhappy demon who had in earlier times been ridiculed by his peers as unworthy of possessing a nasty personality. He was out to prove a point.

'I'll rule the world,' he boomed in anger. His sinister eyes scanned the ground for any movement of life. He vacuumed the surface with his gigantic mouth, detecting any living organism. 'I'll destroy every living thing. Nothing will ever survive in this valley again.' No one knew from where it had originated.

The mist had a long, wet tail and as it passed over the landscape – it applied it as a painter does a brush stroke, loose application with plenty of paint – however, in this case, it was wet dew, which stayed permanently on the ground. It never dried.

Davidia looked like an angel as she lay down on the cold, wet ground surrounded by dewdrops. She appeared to be at peace.

Inside the Rock of Yocklaw slept a strange creature of bulbous proportions, which existed for the protection of good. No life form knew of its existence, but there were rumours. It was awoken by the irritating, small mist puffs from the mist, as they attempted to invade the inside of the rock. Each mist puff was delivered by a mobile mist germ which had no eyes, but possessed a crooked mouth from which to expel a deadly mist puff. They were spat at any organism and once inside its body, it sent them to permanent sleep. The creature inside the rock had an army of internal germ squashers that roamed its system, possessing a special hunger for bad things. It had special glands that could fend off the evil mist puffs by converting them into clean air as it exhaled, whilst rolling along.

This was a life form called an Igloid. He was named Grunt, because that was the only sound he made when moving. He was the official guardian of the valley and lived permanently inside the Rock of Yocklaw. In times past, the ancient Igloodians had bestowed on one of their kind the role of guardian, the unintended consequence of banishment, so that the Valley of Preciousness would remain free for all time. Grunt was forever banned to be a guardian, but never knew what life form he truly was. His current body shape was the price of being a guardian. His ugliness had kept him hidden. However, the power of evil in the valley had been underestimated with the new invader taking up residence. That was not supposed to happen.

An Igloid had five legs with webbed feet, five sets of ears, special nasal filters growing through its many nasal passages, five eyes individually located at the extremities of its circumference for an all round view and thousands of skin pores, which opened and closed as he rolled along on his five legs. The skin pores acted as waste dispensers, which explained why he was constantly moist.

The Evil Mist had no effect on him; however, he alone couldn't remove it from the valley. It was indelibly written in his limited memory somewhere that a lie was the only way to rid the valley forever of this insidious invader. Grunt had no idea where to find such a lie, but he must somehow protect the valley. He couldn't tell the lie. It had to come from another life form.

Grunt was awoken by the small, annoying, pest-like mist puffs. How did they get in here? Doesn't an Igloid deserve his rest, he wondered. Damn annoying pests.

He peered through the rock wall down into the valley and saw a young life form lying there, motionless.

What a strange life form! It has a covering on it. What is it doing there?

He closely observed it for a while, until he realised that it had been put to sleep. The grey sky meant that evil had arrived in the valley. He believed that there was no chance of its revival; such was the devastating power of the Evil Mist. He resigned himself to recovering a lost cause. No one before to his knowledge had ever recovered from the sleep attack of the Evil Mist. It was an adversary of enormous cunning, danger, strength and desolation.

The life form looked so beautiful, helplessly lying there. Grunt knew that the safest place from the Evil Mist was inside the Rock of Yocklaw. He couldn't leave the life form there to decay, even though he thought that it was beyond saving. He made an unintelligible noise. Suddenly, a crack in the rock opened. He rolled out, scooped up the cute, young life form and took it into the labyrinth of caves under the rock. It was rather light.

'I'll have company for a time until I have to dispose of it,' he said to himself.

For the next few days, he looked at the young, pretty life form. A sadness grew within. There was no explanation as to why he felt this way. His skin pores began to emit minute water droplets in sympathy. He turned away to roll on his legs when he accidentally tripped over a loose stone. Perhaps it was a relative of the one that had spoken earlier to Davidia.

Damn those loose stone, he thought to himself. Grunt's only form of intelligent communication and understanding with human life forms was by touch, but he had the capacity for individual thought. With other living life forms, sound echoes between them were understood. His hearing was phenomenally acute.

The loose tripping stone sent him awkwardly stumbling sideways. The action of falling over released many water droplets from his rotund frame, which flew through the air and landed on the young girl. He watched in amazement as they were absorbed into her body. He sadly walked away wondering what to do.

'I will have to send her down the tunnel of eternity in the next few days.' The cave was darker than normal, with Grunt's upset attitude.

Suddenly, a strange noise echoed throughout the caves. Grunt thought that those pesky bats were squabbling again over the best roof hanging spots. Those annoying fliers were Grunt's only regular company. The sound grew louder. Grunt had never experienced the shrill sound of a child crying. It was fearful. A larynx in full flight was a deafening and scary sound, especially in an echoing cave system. He followed the sound and turning a corner, saw the twelve year old life form standing there, bellowing like a bull. Unsure of what it was, he cautiously approached.

Grunt thought that it made the weirdest, strangest noises. Even the high-pitched shriek of squabbling bats was more tolerable. It was every parent's bad dream – an uncontrollable, screaming child.

How did it wake up? thought Grunt. He was perplexed at the discovery that something had survived the sleep attack.

The moist water droplets that he had spilled on the young life form contained healing powers he was unaware of. The chemical reaction within the life form's body awoke her from a dark, heavy sleep. It also affected her brain and gave her the ability to communicate with Grunt, but by touch only. Neither of them had a common language.

Davidia sensed Grunt and screamed in fright. She shook with fear. Grunt was confused. He put a hand out to stop her shaking and touched her arm. She stopped crying. They both experienced the excitement of being able to communicate. When Grunt withdrew his hand, it was silent. He cautiously touched her arm again and their thought patterns intertwined. They understood each other. Slowly a trust built up between them and any fears soon subsided.

'What are you?' asked Davidia.

'I'm an Igloid. What are you?' asked Grunt.

'I'm a girl, a human people. My name is Davidia. Where am I? Where are my parents?'

'I don't know what a parent is,' replied Grunt. 'Perhaps I have them too.'

'Everything has parents, otherwise we wouldn't be here. Mine are called mum and dad. That's not their real names, but it's what we children call them. Do you have a name?' asked Davidia.

Grunt thought for a moment, 'I think it's Grunt. I have a memory from long ago and I think that it's my name.'

Davidia couldn't see in the dark, so she had no idea what Grunt looked like.

'It's too dark in here. Can I go outside?'

'No. It's too dangerous. The Evil Mist is still there. Nothing is safe with it around.' Grunt explained how the Evil Mist had tried to destroy her. 'He places everything he covers into a sound sleep. If someone isn't awoken within a few days, then they sleep forever. You are a lucky one to survive.'

'He doesn't sound very nice. Who is Mr Mist?'

'The Evil Mist appears when the earth's surface is disrupted or upset by nature. A demon known as Scatter lives inside the mist. Recently, when a gap in the ground opened, he escaped and wreaks havoc in revenge for being locked away. Over many years various protectors have trapped him underground, but he always manages to escape. He has a husky voice and blows icy cold winds with a deadly outcome. He slowly crawls across the landscape like a resentful life form, blanketing everything in a cold carpet of cool, water droplets. His face forms into a shadowy figure. The Rock of Yocklaw from its vantage point until now had barred his entrance into the Valley of Preciousness and to the Town of Importance. Alas, he has become so strong that it was impossible to bar his entrance this time. His wind content and strength is increasing and his menace towards all life forms is worsening. That's how he entered the valley and overcame you. I fear the valley and all in it are lost if we don't do something. You have been awoken by my water droplets and now you possess a power no one else has. It's the power to say NO. Only we can save the valley, the town and all life forms in it,' explained Grunt, hoping the young girl understood.

'How do I get out of here? It's pitch black. I can't see any-thing.'

'You cannot leave the rock or the valley until the Evil Mist is destroyed. Bright, sunny days and friendly winds cannot defeat it. It must be swallowed and then buried forever, deep inside the Rock of Yocklaw down a special tunnel called The Tunnel of Appraisal. I only know its name, but not where it ends.'

'But I'm only a young girl,' wailed Davidia.

'The Evil Mist is devilishly cunning. It hears through the winds and vibrations in the ground. His permanence on the landscape wilts all the vegetation under a seductive, sleepy spell. No life form eats the wilted vegetation and eventually only the rocks remain. The Rock of Yocklaw years ago, when life was happier, was blessed with a special command of the last prince of the region to protect all life form in the valley. It's believed he was a wizard of spellbinding proportions. I was once another life form, but I have no idea what type, nor do I know where I came from. I remember a terrible whirlwind from a land far away from here. It hurled me through the air. I woke up inside the rock, with my current physical appearance. Maybe the prince was a parent. That's how I got this protection gig. No one knows of my existence; however, it is rumoured that strange grunting sounds have emanated from within the rock from time to time. I had to reveal myself to you in order to protect you. I thought it was too late to save you. The town and rock have been protected for such a long time. However, it looks as though the Evil Mist has grown strong enough to defeat me,' said Grunt with a pained expression.

'What can I do?' asked Davidia, keen to join in a child's game.

'You must trap the Evil Mist with your special powers before it destroys the town and valley forever.'

'Do I have special powers? What are they?'

Before Grunt could answer, a low howl was heard. They ceased touch. Grunt rolled along the cave floor toward the surface. A special peering place from within the rock allowed his vision to penetrate the rock walls and see into the outside world without being seen. Two, huge, mist laden clouds floated through the air. Two large, dark, sullen eyes flitted gently from side to side. Scatter was scanning the landscape. The cold was unbearable. He was itching to wreak further havoc. He slowly drifted around the Rock of Yocklaw and his disinterest showed by a roll of the eyes as he headed further up the valley. His wispy, watery trail blotted out any light. Grunt shivered with the cold.

I'll defeat him somehow, thought Grunt. Those ice cubes of suffocation must be removed. Grunt rued the fact that he couldn't save the town or valley. It needed a special power. He returned to Davidia, who hadn't moved. They touched hands.

'Davidia, we need a plan.'

'I'm only twelve. What's a plan?'

'Innocence is the solution. The Evil Mist cannot handle a lie and there are very few life forms who know anything but the truth. You are young enough to know only the truth. Your mind hasn't yet been distorted or perverted to the ways of lies, which you learn as you grow up,' said Grunt, formulating an idea to defeat the Evil Mist. He suddenly wondered how he knew this. Maybe he had special powers too that he wasn't aware of.

'Does anyone else live in the caves besides you, Mr Grunt?' asked Davidia, unable to understand that the problem of escape and saving the town and valley rested squarely upon her shoulders alone.

'My lot in life is a solitary one. The bats are the only company I keep. There's a maniacal bat called Batbit who often sits with me each dark (night, in Davidia's world). He's in charge of Batforce. That's the group that all the bats belong to,' replied Grunt, warming to his young visitor. 'They live deep in the caves. Remember, the Evil Mist is very selfish and egotistical. This may assist in his undoing.'

'I don't understand all the words you say, but they must be good, considering you said them.'

'We have to be smarter than he is. The only way to catch him out is with a lie.'

'Is a lie the same as a fib? I don't know any lies.'

'A lie is when we say something to someone we know isn't true, or say something that is believable, but we know it not to be correct.'

'I don't know if I'm capable of not telling the truth. Mum and dad taught me to always tell the truth. They said that little fibs can grow into lies if you plant them early in someone's mind.'

'You must learn quickly, if you are to save the town and valley. I'll teach you what a lie is, but only one. Then the lie that you play on the Evil Mist must be one of your own. For example, that wall over there that you can't see, what colour is it?'

'It looks black to me, in the dark,' replied Davidia, who squinted to see what colour it actually was, but it still looked black to her.

'That is true. Now if I said it was yellow, then that's a lie.' Davidia nodded. 'The wall is still black, but when someone says it's yellow, they are lying. Now do you understand?'

'I think so, Mr Grunt,' said a confident twelve year old. 'I don't know if I can do it, but I'll try.' Touch ceased. Davidia sat down and thought of what lie she could tell the Evil Mist and how she could get it to him.

Suddenly, a rush of wind, accompanied by high pitched screeching, passed within centimetres of Davidia's hair. Was Dracula on the loose chasing a fresh meal? It was Batbit paying a visit. When he sensed any danger, he flew in to investigate it. Davidia didn't have the danger vibe. Batbit's two, tiny little feet dug into the underneath of Davidia's arm, causing her to yell in pain.

'It's only a pin prick,' said Batbit, also communicating with Davidia by touch now that he had a good foothold.

'Get off me, it hurts.'

Batbit let go of her armpit and flew onto her shoulder.

'May I introduce myself? I'm Batbit at your service. Our species aren't dingbats, but we are a special group called Batforce. We keep Mr Grunt company.'

'Where do you live?'

'Throughout the caves. It's a tough tussle, trying to find the best roof spots to hang about on. Do you hang from the roof?'

'I walk on two legs, flat on the ground.' Davidia stood up, still with the little intruder hanging on.

'I see. Are you sure they are in the right place? I haven't seen anything like them before.'

'You can see them in the dark? How?'

'I'm a bat. We sense them by sonic sound waves bouncing off them. Unusual shape too. There's that bulge halfway down. How unsightly.'

'It's a knee.'

'They're too lumpy for me. What are you and Mr Grunt up to?'

Davidia briefly explained the Evil Mist's visit and what had happened.

'That means dark flying will be off. I'll warn the group.' A loud shriek pierced the silence of the caves. 'Gotta go. Mrs

Batbit has a hysterical scream if I'm late to hang on the roof with her. You don't want to hear it in anger mode, its frightening.' Batbit flew off. Davidia was alone in the dark once again.

On the Rock of Yocklaw's summit was a hidden opening covered by a bush, which had turned green. The Evil Mist had tried to ensure it didn't survive by suffocating it. Life forms were somewhat protected by the rock. However, it still hid the secret opening. Grunt had shown Davidia the way there. The dull light danced on Grunt's circumference, sufficiently enough for Davidia to see what he was. She held her breath in disbelief. She must be in fantasyland to see such an odd looking creature. Her hand was held in one of Grunt's many. Somehow she felt safe.

'Remember, the Evil Mist has no peer in cunning,' reminded Grunt.

The summit gave the best vantage point in the valley. It was still shrouded by the Evil Mist. The magical powers that Grunt had given Davidia, would last only for a short period of time. Timing was important, if they were to succeed in defeating the Evil Mist. Davidia had climbed to the top of the bush and looked out. It was grey and bleak.

'Mr Mist. Are you there?' yelled Davidia, in her loudest voice.

Scatter, the Evil Mist's inner demon, felt a movement in his underbelly. A sound reverberated throughout his mistiness. 'That's impossible. Everything is asleep,' he angrily growled to himself. He decided that the moving irritant required permanent removal. His two, huge, doleful eyes searched for the annoying life form. 'How dare anything toy with me,' he continued rumbling. He whisked his eyes back through the mist, probing for the irritant. His furtive glances portrayed that he'd never been challenged like this before. It was a new experience. His anger mounted.

'I'll freeze you out of the valley,' he boomed in a low, growling, threatening manner.

Davidia had heard the unpleasant sound of an ugly burp full of particles of destruction. The cool, icy winds were felt by Davidia as they crazily rushed around her. Her skin became icy to touch. Her long, golden locks froze into shards of ice. Scatter felt the heat she generated. His eyes hovered over the ground trying to locate her. The mist puffs danced gleefully, having found her.

'There she is, there she is,' they called out.

Finally, Scatter honed in on her location.

'There you are,' he said, pleased with himself that he had snuffed out, or so he thought he had, the young girl. 'I'm all-powerful. Nothing can stand in my way and that goes for something as small as you.'

He flew around her, to ensure that there was no life movement. Pleased that he was victorious, he began to float away to pursue further destruction.

During this time, Grunt had remained concealed. His hand touched Davidia's foot and she magically burst into life again. Her iced body returned to life as her blood flowed through her veins. She once again became a fully functioning, screaming young girl. Her mouth opened with a huge yawn and out of its inner depths a voice boomed out quite inexplicably, 'Evil Mist, Evil Mist, I command you to leave this valley.' It echoed throughout the whole valley, being transmitted by the mist particles.

Suddenly, Scatter ceased floating abstractly. He focused on the sound of the voice within his wet covering. His anger erupted into dropping further droplets of suffocation over the landscape. He had heard of the Rock of Yocklaw, which protected the valley. There was no other explanation for the rhythmic sound that he had just heard.

'Where are you, you myth?' he grumbled to himself, with his agitated moisture particles angling for a fight. 'I can defeat anything.' His ego was insatiable. There was complete silence. The rhythmic rhyme echoed again. His water droplets were primed for a nasty show of force. He returned to the Rock of Yocklaw area and saw a small, living creature, miming words while standing perfectly still.

'Didn't I dispense with you a few moments ago?'

Scatter had never had a confrontation with a young human before; however, he treated every living thing as an enemy. His eyes glared hatred at Davidia. She smiled.

'Hello, Mr Mist,' she said politely. 'My name is Davidia.'

Scatter stared in astonishment. He wondered what this speaking creature was. He blew a puff of icy wind at her. Her clothes fluttered, her hair teased on the breeze, but she stood still and continued to smile as best she could. She didn't wilt under the icy blast. Her immobility was due to her preparedness for the question that would hopefully release the valley from its icy torment. She only had one shot at the lie, otherwise the valley and its inhabitants would be lost forever.

'What do you want?' he growled.

'The view from here is grey and there is no one else to speak to. My family are elsewhere.'

Scatter smiled to himself. The damage he had inflicted was a success and soon he would rule unhindered in an uninhabitable environment.

'Mr Mist, couldn't you leave the valley and holiday elsewhere?' asked Davidia retaining his attention.

'I like it here. It's cold, bleak, grey and always moist. It's perfect for a nasty character like me. I enjoy gloom because it matches my personality,' he replied.

'Wouldn't you like to be nicer?'

'Never. It's time you disappeared too and leave me to float and roam as I please.'

'Don't you have any friends?'

'I don't need them. I'm tiring of all this time wasting. Time to say goodbye.'

Scatter inched closer to the Rock of Yocklaw, preparing to strike at Davidia. Her antics of not succumbing to his almighty presence and superiority were wearing thin. He had havoc to wreak. Davidia was interrupting his progress. His impatience was on thin ice, as thin as the ice sheet that he had covered the landscape with. Davidia felt a tug at her foot. Grunt was gesturing that she climb out of the bush and into the rock for safety. Her slim frame and innocence suddenly had no fear.

'Mr Mist, do you like to explore underground as well as above? Mr Grunt and I live in a space we are sure you will enjoy,' encouraged Davidia.

Scatter remembered his previous internment underground, but that was by far a more formidable opponent than someone so small. His initial reaction to the question was fear and uncertainty; however, the size of his opposition charged his confidence. He believed that nothing could stop him. On land, he had a long wispy tail that followed him everywhere like a bad smell. Underground, only his head could travel safely. Scatter was too cunning to be trapped again.

Davidia suddenly disappeared into the bush; however, before she did, she waved, smiled and threw her yellow hair ribbon into the mist. Scatter found the colour attractive, which surprised him immensely, as grey and black were his usual favourite doom and gloom colours. He knew that he was too powerful to be destroyed, but didn't know that he could be. He thought that he was invincible. For a few minutes, he floated around aimlessly like a lost soul assessing his next move. His ego of nastiness grew like uncontrollable laughter at a good comedy festival. The opening of the Rock of Yocklaw was still visible. Suddenly, he plunged straight in, leaving his tail behind. He was now rudderless. His nasty mist puffs jumped up and down, annoyed that they couldn't participate in the hunt.

Scatter hunted Davidia, like a slimy snake down a rat hole. No child was going to beat him. He hadn't been without a tail before. It left his rear vulnerable. He felt lonely, which was no worse than what he had made many others feel. A tapping sound could be heard. He followed it. The caves felt unfriendly. Ego is not a dirty word and to munch on it everyday fed his self-confidence. Around a corner he abruptly halted. There sat Davidia and Grunt, throwing small pebbles onto the rocks toward the Tunnel of Appraisal. He had them cornered like a square.

'Hello, Mr Mist. This is Mr Grunt,' said Davidia smiling. They both stared confidently at him. Scatter rolled his eyes like pinballs; then suddenly they stopped moving and stared threateningly at them.

'This is goodbye,' he boomed. His voice echoed so loudly the bats from a few caves away shrieked with fright.

'What's the commotion?' said Batbit, who flew in to investigate the loud noise. As soon as he saw Scatter he flew madly down the caves to escape permanent damage.

Davidia and Grunt edged backwards. Scatter began to puff up his cheeks; however, without his tail in support, he exhaled a paltry amount of mist.

'That was pathetic,' interrupted Grunt. 'A big head like you can do much better.'

He teased Scatter, who puffed up again, his cheeks growing darker. This time, his puff was no better. His steely eyes dripped venom. He began to move closer.

'Stop,' said Davidia putting out her hand.

Scatter stopped dead in his tracks.

'That wall over there is yellow,' said Davidia, pointing to a sidewall. 'Mr Mist, I believe that wall is yellow. It is my favourite colour. My dress isn't yellow. Do you like it?' Her dress was yellow, however that was an additional lie of her own, which Grunt had told her earlier that she had to have one of her own, otherwise the Evil Mist couldn't be defeated.

Scatter knew that he had to answer. Inside the Rock of Yocklaw, in its mythical past, there was a code of mythical conduct that any question asked within its caves, had always to be answered by the truth. But to agree with a lie meant disaster and banishment. Before he could reply, Grunt spun on his legs like a spinning top on the wall in question. The friction he created gave the impression it was yellow. Grunt moved at lightening speed. Scatter couldn't see what generated the effect. It seemed to be true. The cave instantly lit up like a beacon, then faded into darkness.

'See, Mr Mist. That wall is yellow,' repeated Davidia.

Grunt again repeated his demonstration of friction antics. The wall did look yellow.

'Please answer me, Mr Mist. Then I can tell all my friends that I spoke to you. They would be most impressed.'

Scatter was tiring of the stand-off.

'I agree with you, Davidia,' replied Scatter, none too convinced that what he said was the truth. The shock answer of agreement to the lie caused Davidia to fall over flat on her back.

An extra leg began to grow from her stomach. She transformed into an Igloid like Grunt. It took only a few seconds. Davidia now had a mouth as large as a dinner plate. She opened it wide to see what it felt like. It created an enormous draught. The tonsil tango was about to happen. Scatter's eyes revealed surprise. The young girl had become a hideous creature like Grunt. Even with his nasty attitude, two of the same were too much to bear.

'Where am I going? What's happening?' Scatter complained as his head and eyes became elongated and distorted. He was being drawn into the abyss in Davidia's face. Her mouth operated as a huge, industrial vacuum cleaner. Scatter was being drawn closer and closer.

'Not the Rock of Yocklaw,' he screamed as Davidia completely inhaled him. Scatter ceased to exist.

Grunt immediately took Davidia by the hand and they ran down the Tunnel of Appraisal. Their many legs rotated like spinning wheels.

'Stop,' yelled Grunt. He thumped her on her back so hard, that she exhaled Scatter like a nine force gale into the Tunnel of Appraisal, gone forever.

'Did you have to hit me so hard?' whinged Davidia, breathless after having ejected all that wind. 'Why do I feel so strange?' She hadn't seen herself in Igloid form before.

'That's the last we'll see of that nasty demon,' said Grunt, pleased that they had tricked it. 'The valley and town are saved.'

'I can see in the dark,' said a surprised Davidia. 'How far into the tunnel are we?'

'We must leave immediately before The Tunnel of Appraisal takes us too.'

The two Igloids headed toward the central cave to safety. Davidia walked past a small alcove in the wall.

'What's that, over there?' she said, pointing with one of her many hands.

Grunt pretended he didn't notice the alcove. He walked past it. Davidia's sense of curiosity was pricked. She entered the alcove to find a shelf with a battered tin sitting there, covered by the dust of time.

'I wonder what this is.'

She picked up the tin, opened the lid and inside there were five trinkets, each made into a letter, all joined together on a chain. Her fingers carefully felt each of them. In her excitement to show Grunt, she whirled quickly around tripping on the floor. She put out her hands to brace for the fall, when she pushed against five jutting rocks each consisting of a cluster of five small stones. They gave way with her weight. She had unknowingly pressed the Ejector Stones of ancient times, placed there for the purposes of discovery when Grunt's duty of guardianship was to be terminated.

Everything went black and silent. Davidia felt she was flying. All occupants of the caves were tossed skywards into the unknown. What had she done?

3. VALLEY OF GRAGSLEW

'What did you do?' asked Grunt, as he tumbled along the ground like a bowling ball.

'I fell,' replied an indignant Davidia, who had regained her body shape into that of a young girl. The strangest thing of all was that she could now communicate with Grunt and all other life forms by thoughts alone, without touching. Her transformation in and out of being an Igloid had endowed her with this extraordinary ability.

'What's that you are holding?'

'I found it. It's mine.'

'May I see what it is?'

'Yes, but it's still mine.' Davidia's possessive power of "finder's keepers" was a child's game in learning about ownership.

'Do you know what it is?'

'It's a dirty old tin, see,' she said, offering it to Grunt.

He opened it. Inside, there were five small items attached together on a silver chain, tarnished from years of neglect.

'That's a necklace,' said Davidia. 'I want to wear it.'

Grunt's fingers caressed each item carefully. As he did, a strange feeling overcame him. Tears began to roll off his body. He shook uncontrollably and before long he was standing in a huge puddle.

'Mr Grunt, you are leaking water everywhere. Can't you turn off your tap?'

He didn't fully understand what had happened to him, but the feeling of family invaded his soul. It was a feeling he had never experienced before. What did it mean?

'Can I wear it, please, Mr Grunt?' pressed Davidia.

'No. Somehow I feel that this is mine from long ago. I can't explain it.'

Davidia pouted. Her angelic looks didn't win her the prize this time.

'Look, it spells your name. G is a grate, R is a rake, U is a …, I don't know that one, N is a nail and T is a talisman. My mum told me what a talisman is. She wanted to buy one for my next birthday. She might have it for me when I return home. Do you have birthdays, Mr Grunt?'

'There seems to be many differences in our worlds. I can't remember much about mine. I can only recall my life in the Rock of Yocklaw. Do you think there was anything before that?'

'We all start somewhere, Mr Grunt. I began when I was born. I suppose we all began somewhere.'

Grunt placed the necklace around his neck. He felt it belonged there. Unknown to him, it sent messages through time to a far away place, where his progress could be followed. His father had the necklace placed in the Rock of Yocklaw at the time of his banishment, in the hope that one day, if ever found, it would lead Grunt to discover who and what he really was. He had to trace his path and regain the memory that had been denied him. Homesickness would have hindered his task of being a guardian for good. He had now embarked upon a journey of no return, not understanding what it was about, or aware where it would lead. A blank canvas needed to be covered in positive brush strokes. His painting would be his memories.

A foreboding feeling ran through the Irrid camp. The loss of Scatter was harshly felt by the evil forces who wanted to conquer the five valleys.

'They will pay for this,' said the head Irrid. 'No place is safe from our evil. We will destroy the goodness in them.'

A small airborne missile dive-bombed them a few times. It was Batbit trying to attract their attention. His unmistakable screech finally succeeded.

'How did we end up here? What are we doing here? It's a dangerous land. I have flown around for a look and I don't like what I see. We might be in danger.'

'Davidia gave us the flight plan to allow the visit.'

'Next time try another flight path. This destination is going to be unhealthy. I feel it in my wings. Look, they are ready to fall off.'

Batbit was aerodynamically designed to fly so fast he was invisible in flight. Only his screeching indicated where he was. He was a conniving, clever, army general of Batforce, who had in their transfer into the new valley, been transformed elsewhere. His two extra large revolving eyes gave 360-degree vision at all times. Grunt was his only true friend and now Davidia was added to the list.

'Be careful,' warned Batbit, as he zoomed off to undertake further surveillance.

'I'm hungry,' complained Davidia. 'Where are the fast food outlets? Dad always took me there once a week for a treat.'

'I doubt if you will find one of those here, whatever they might be,' replied Grunt.

'I want something to eat.'

'Stop the demands. We have to work out what this odd place is.'

'There's a sign over there.'

It read, The Valley of Gragslew (also known as Halfwit Valley). Rules of entry. There are none.

'It's a silly name,' said Davidia.

'Silly or not, we have to discover where we are and what it means.'

'It means I go hungry.'

The landscape consisted of a patchwork of square shaped paddocks, all the same size. There was an enormous tree in one corner of each square. A small dividing fence half a metre high was the perimeter of every paddock. The fields were under cultivation. Crops of many different grass varieties proliferated. There didn't seem to be anyone working in the fields. It was a picture perfect, angelic countryside.

'This is beautiful,' said Davidia, feeling happier now that her hunger pangs were disappearing.

'Batbit said we should be careful. If he doesn't like it, then we should take notice.'

'What nonsense.'

'When we arrived did you see any life forms?' asked Grunt. Physically they were alone, but it didn't feel like they were. The many pores on his body bristled with uncertainty. His body censors were on high alert. He carried no weapons to defend himself, but an Igloid carried a peculiar form of defence; momentary invisibility and ability to communicate to land forms, such as the ground, trees and any life form.

'It might be uninhabited,' said Davidia, enjoying a playful run amongst the crops.

Suddenly, Davidia tripped over something hidden in the crops. She heard a hiss and saw the crops being flattened as something ran quickly toward a tree. Grunt turned just in time to see her fall over. He ran to her rescue.

'Are you okay?'

'It happens all the time when I play hide and seek. Did you see it?'

'See what? I only saw you fall over.'

'Something ran over to that tree. Let's take a look.'

They walked cautiously over to the tree, when suddenly from the trunk out ran three creatures hissing as they went, jumping over the fence and into the next tree.

'What were those things?' asked Davidia, never having seen such unusual shapes before. 'How rude to hiss, it's not good manners.'

Grunt stopped dead. He had no desire to chase them. It felt like trouble.

'Hisssslo,' said a strange voice nearby.

They turned to be confronted by a creature swaying like a palm tree in high wind. It circled the two of them from a safe distance. It was assessing their danger levels to it. A short time passed. It was like a stand-off in an old western, with no one daring to make that first fatal move.

'Hisssslo,' it repeated.

'Maybe it's saying hello,' said Davidia. 'Hisssslo to you too.'

The creature sneered. Its eyes kept a fixated stare at them. What was it thinking? Grunt approached it. The creature jumped backwards in fright, fearing an attack. Grunt stood still.

'Hisssslo to you,' said Grunt.

This settled the timid creature.

'Can you tell us where we are? What is this place?' asked Grunt, hoping that a chat would allay any fear of a fight. The creature understood.

'This is the Valley of Gragsssslew. We are called Grags. My name is Gragga. This is a stepping stone valley, the first of five in our world. I haven't visited any of the others yet, but I'm sure there are edibles there too. You look delicious. There are many meals in you. My fellow Grags love a good roast and so do I.' He began to salivate at the thought.

'Not this dark, Gragga, we are visiting. Perhaps tomorrow,' said the other half of Gragga.

'Who are you? Where did you come from?' asked Davidia stunned that a second creature was communicating from the same body frame. The second conversation was with Gragga's other half.

'I'm Gorgo, the dominant female side of the family. Gragga is all male and needs advice most times.'

'I do not,' he replied.

A Grag was a life form with two halves, one male and the other female. Only one side of them was visible at any one time. They could often be seen arguing animatedly amongst themselves with the unseen half. Each half tried to dominate the other. Phrases such as halfwit and half stupid became quite common. Conflict was ever present. On closer inspection, they had one large and one small eye, one long arm and one short arm, one hairy leg and one hairless leg. It didn't matter which half possessed these body parts, each Grag had a set of them. They wore protective shields to protect their soft, putty-like skin. A smile was as popular as the equator at the north pole, non-existent. To believe anything they said was a one-way trip to oblivion. They feasted on other life forms that entered their valley. They kept them in prisons specially built to house their food source. The Grags weren't great in number, but were devious and tricky with evil intent. They would sever a body part and keep the rest alive so that they always ate "fresh".

Gragga had never seen such ugly life forms as an Igloid and a human. They intrigued him. The excitement he felt at this new food source made him sway more erratically between his two halves, which began to argue with each other. Their gesticulations and noises were pure theatre.

'What are they doing?' asked Davidia.

'They are assessing whether to eat us or not,' replied Grunt, planning a quick exit.

'No way. I'm not edible,' said an indignant Davidia. 'That's pure nonsense. I'm not being eaten by those weirdos. Look how strange they are. A squashed snail or slug looks better than they do.'

Batbit screeched a loud warning. He felt that danger was nearby. The sound terrified the Grags, who skipped away to safety. In the distance they could see a group of Grags congregating together.

'It looks like half of them are missing,' said Davidia, not believing her eyesight for a moment. 'When they sway, only one half is visible. It's weird.'

'Be warned. They are up to mischief. I've found a cave over the hill which we can rest in,' said Batbit, not enjoying his new environment. 'Grunt, do your thing.'

Grunt grabbed Davidia and held her tight. He spun into invisibility, his main power, and flew into the cave that Batbit had located. It was thought to be uninhabited. The three friends sat down to reflect on their situation.

'There's nothing to eat,' whined Davidia.

'Do humans always complain about lack of food? Us Igloids go for weeks without a refill. What is it that you eat?' Davidia tried to explain it, but was wasting her time. In the valley there were only different forms of grass to eat, but they were highly nutritious. It would be a risky proposition sneaking into a paddock to obtain the grass. The Grags would be on the lookout for them.

'Batbit, it's up to you to fly in and grab the grass we need.'

'Me? Why is it always me? I'm the smallest and gets the most dangerous tasks.'

'Go this dark when there is no light.'

'When are we escaping from this valley?'

'I don't know how to,' said a forlorn Grunt.

'Well, I don't either,' said Davidia.

'Davidia, when we were flung out of the Tunnel of Appraisal, what exactly did you touch?' asked a pensive Grunt.

She thought for a moment.

'I think it was a group of five stones neatly placed together.'

'Mmm … , and nothing else?'

'No.'

Grunt took out his necklace, laid it on the cave floor and sat closely next to it. He began to rock back and forth. His body shut down. His arms, legs and any external parts withdrew internally and he sat there as a perfectly round object, a ball in fact.

'Is he imitating a circle? One of our neighbours at home almost had the same shape as Grunt, but it would have been very rude to say anything. Dad told us not to call other people names as it is impolite,' remarked Davidia. 'Now what happens with Mr Grunt going to sleep?'

Batbit and Davidia surveyed the countryside. There were no Grags in sight. It was late in the afternoon and the light was fading. Soon it would be dark. Batbit became quite excited at the prospect of hanging off a new cave rooftop and not having to squabble with Mrs Batbit for the best hanging space. He flexed his small claws. Yum. All was quiet.

'Boo,' said a voice.

'Boohoo?' replied Davidia. She knew her knock-knock games extremely well.

'Boo,' it repeated.

'Boohoo to you.'

'Boo,' it repeated again.

'Who's there? Don't you know any other word?'

'Me and yes.'

'That's extremely helpful. Where are you?'

'At your feet.'

Davidia looked down and scanned the cave floor for her new company. Nothing moved. In the dark it was almost impossible to see.

'You missed me,' it said.

'I can't see anything, there's nothing there.'

'Look at your feet.'

Davidia could see what she thought were her two feet; however, the toes seemed to be larger than she remembered. They wiggled. I didn't do that, thought Davidia. She looked again. Both feet were wiggling freely.

'Are those mine?' she said, thinking that a disease or an affliction had grown on her feet.

'No. They are mine. I don't get many visitors any more. Once I was a full body life form like you. Now my feet are all that is left. I hide in this cave because those Grags are fearful of tunnels. I hopped onto your feet to feel what it would be like to be attached to a real life form once again. Hope I didn't offend.' What a polite pair of feet, thought Davidia.

'Why is there so little of you left?'

'The rest of me has been eaten by the Grags. My feet were small enough to escape their prison by crawling underneath the steel grates. They eat the delicacies last. I'm fortunate to have this much left. There are others worse off than me. They have been completely consumed.'

'Does this happen to everything?'

'Sure does. I stumbled into the valley by mistake. One day I was out walking when a dark, grey mist passed over my valley. I couldn't see anything. I tried to find my way home, but became lost and ended up here. Now I can never go home. No one will recognise me.' The pair of toes wiggled with enthusiasm at having made contact with what it thought was a friendly life form.

Davidia realised that it must have been the Evil Mist that had visited that valley also.

'What type of life form were you before you were reduced in size?'

'I was a Jimp.'

'Do you know how we can escape from this valley? I don't want to be eaten and there's nothing here that I've seen that I would like to eat.'

'You have to discover that one out for yourself. Whatever happens, do not believe a word they tell you. They are devious. Remember, if they talk about location, location, location, it means prison. Once there, it's the end of the road. You will eventually end up in one of their awful dishes. They aren't very good chefs. Be careful. May I sit with you this dark?' Davidia nodded.

Batbit understood the gravity of their situation. It was clear they had no idea of how to escape. They were a hunted food source and all were hungry.

'I'll get grass for this dark only.' He flew silently out of the cave down into the valley. Each tree he flew past was alive with Grags. At one window he peered in. On the floor were a variety of small life forms performing tricks as if in a circus. They jumped and rolled about, being continuously prodded by the Grags with their bony fingers. When one life form jumped high enough, a Grag would roll underneath it and it landed straight into its mouth amidst great uproar. Batbit winced in sympathy and fright. He dived into the grass patch, collected dinner and sped like a speeding bullet back to the cave. He was shaking when he arrived.

'Dinner is served.'

'Is this it? I can't eat grass. In my world, only animals eat this,' said a disgusted Davidia.

'Use your imagination and pretend it's a food you like. There's nothing else in this valley to eat.'

Davidia slumped down, took a mouthful and surprisingly it was very tasty. It had to be as this is what the Grags used to feed their food supply; healthy, nutritional fodder.

The dark moved in, the air was still and silent. The pair of feet nestled near Davidia and she fell asleep. Grunt was still rolled up in a ball. The cave became their protector. The perils of tomorrow were yet to arrive.

Grunt sat silently. His yoga position of a bowling ball maintained a stationary position. Inside, in his trance-like state, his memories were researching his past existence. The necklace he wore transmitted visions of his past. It was a crowded world of jumbled scenes and unexplained emotions. Who were the life forms that kept recurring throughout his visions? A great battle had once taken place and a life form was banished without explanation. What was it that caused such disruption in his past and why? The necklace possessed a message. It was a set of instructions for Grunt to find his way home, but first he had to experience various trials and tribulations to earn the right to that pathway. Whatever the message, he had to locate the answers through his experiences. It was like reading a blank page of advice. Faith and belief would lead him safely through. In other words, he was on his own. There was no guidebook to assist.

The dark went quickly enough. Grunt awoke and regained his body extremities. All his bits poked out where they should be. Batbit had the most comfortable dark, hanging about without conflict from Mrs Batbit. Davidia woke up with her, 'I'm hungry' syndrome and Boo, the extra pair of feet, wiggled happily, having had a cave full of visitors. The leftover grass wasn't a terrific substitute for cereal; however, Davidia had really enjoyed a good chew last dark.

'We can't stay here all day,' she said. 'I want to visit the countryside. Those Grags seem harmless enough. They'll help us back to where we came from, for sure.'

'Do not trust them at all. I saw them eat some small life forms last dark,' said Batbit, who shuddered at the memory.

'Why didn't you save them then?' said Davidia, rubbing her stomach.

'I'm too small and they were too many.'

'I want to go for a walk. My dad always said exercise is good for the body and mind. Mum didn't do too much walking; she got puffed out on cigarettes.'

Before anyone could stop her, Davidia had walked out of the cave. The others were dumbfounded. Davidia had no reason not to trust anyone, she was only a young girl and the Grags had appeared to be so polite. The cave was on a small hill overlooking their town. There were no trees there, only a few different types of solid building structures made of stones.

As she approached the perimeter of the buildings, she noticed that a white line had been drawn on the ground around it. She stopped short of it. There seemed to be nothing living nearby.

She thought that it was strange to have a white line drawn so prominently around a few buildings. She wondered what it meant.

'Hisssslo,' said a voice extremely close to her ear.

She turned instantly to face Gorgo, the female side of Gragga. Her evil smile could fill a quarry. Those ice-cold eyes had a fire behind them. It was another word commencing with the letter "f" for food. Her rhythmic swaying became more pronounced. Davidia often got a glance of Gragga, but he wasn't being let in on this scene. The look on his face had been cloned from Gorgo.

'Hisssslo to you,' replied Davidia politely.

'Where are you going?' asked Gorgo, her eyes rolling wildly as if twirling on a roulette wheel.

'I was enjoying a walk. At home I went walking every weekend with my parents. We would go to the local coffee shop, sometimes for breakfast.'

'Continue then,' encouraged Gorgo.

'Why is that white line on the ground?' said Davidia pointing at it.

'It's a challenge for those who dare. We don't have any games, so we draw different types of lines. For example, there's the quick stroke around the body.'

Gorgo drew a circle around herself, but she hadn't explained that they were used on life forms before they were cut up. Davidia had to enter the white line area of her own free will, which meant in Grag terms, a willingness to become a future chef's delight. That meant only the top Grag could perform the necessary preparation tasks. Any other captured life form forcibly captured was available to any Grag.

'If I don't cross the white line, what will happen?' Curiosity was one of Davidia's traits, being so young.

'That's a surprise. Just one more step.'

Batbit came flying through the air, screeching a warning.

'Turn back, turn back, it's a trap.'

Davidia ignored his imploring pleas and took that final, fatal step.

Grags came rushing from everywhere, hissing violently. She was thrust to the ground and picked up like a toy. A procession of Grags whooped it up, swaying vigorously like a set of palm fronds in a tornado.

'Victory is mine,' said Gorgo, pleased at the result. 'After a few days of eating grass, she's all mine. You future, chubby little morsel, you.' What masqueraded as a smile almost made it across her face.

Davidia struggled in vain to escape. The cold, slimy hands of the Grags made her skin crawl in itches. Their thin, bony fingers pinpricked her when they grasped her.

Davidia was thrown into a prison cell. Three of the walls were made of solid stone.

There was one tiny window for light. The floor was dirt and the bed was made of grass. There was no chance of digging her way out. The fourth wall was a huge barred grate, securely locked with a padlock. A special key hung around the neck of the guard. Each guard was promised a tasty tidbit from every life form so that security was ensured. If any escapes were made, the responsible Grag was made into a Gragstew. Self-preservation was a great motivator for keeping all life forms securely incarcerated.

The prison had many cells neatly arranged side by side.

Strange noises were heard from each cell as a life form in some distress made its plea. No one was listening. The guards were cruel. They often taunted the occupant with the name of a food dish in which they would be the star attraction: eyeball soup, high thigh shanks, rack of chest ribs and a real favourite, offal delight. Each cell had a guard of its own who sat outside staring at their charges.

Davidia screamed at the top of her lungs, a piercing frightening scream. Her guard rushed over to her cell, showing signs of anger.

'Husssshlo,' it said.

'I won't husssshlo until I'm free,' Davidia yelled in response. 'Where are my friends?'

'In prison soon, too. Husssshlo, otherwise if the head Grag visits you, she mightn't use you as the main ingredient in her surprise dish.'

'I'm not going to be eaten. I'll sssspit at you.'

'What's sssspit at you?' asked the guard. This is the strangest creature it had yet encountered.

'Come closer and I'll show you.'

The guard came right up to the grate and placed its faces on the bars.

'Are you ready?'

Davidia sucked in her cheeks, rolled her tongue, coughed politely and then, with an almighty phut, spat out a large glob of mucus into one of its faces. It hit with such force that one of its heads rocked back. As quick as a flash it licked it in.

'That would make a delicious sauce,' it said. 'Are there seconds?'

Davidia sat down, disgusted that she didn't offend it. She began to sob quietly. The guard had never seen anyone cry before. It thought she was draining away.

'Sssstop that. You mustn't disappear.'

'Who else is in here?'

'A smorgasbord of life forms.'

'Can I meet any of them, please?'

'Only when you are in the same dish.'

Suddenly, a loud hissing noise was heard. It was Gorgo singing her success tune at capturing her prize dish, Davidia. All other Grags scattered like confetti at her approach. The grate to Davidia's cell was opened. It grated through the strain of never having been oiled. Gorgo offered Davidia her evening meal of nutritional grass cuttings. There were no testing facilities to verify its goodness content.

'Eat this. In cell five there is the perfect matching ingredient for me to share you with. Guard, close the grate,' she ordered. 'If she escapes I'll swallow you in small pieces.'

'Yes, Gorgo,' quivered the guard.

The cell door was shut with a bang. Darkness had descended. The dark hid the evil that pervaded the valley. It could never be erased unless …

The three cave dwellers were mortified that Davidia had been captured.

'She might end up like me,' said Boo, flexing what there was left of him.

'I warned her, but she is a stubborn young girl with a mind completely of her own. I wonder if she ever listened to those things she keeps calling parents,' said Batbit, upset that he couldn't save her.

'Nothing to do, but plan a rescue mission somehow,' said Grunt, missing his new likable friend. A few of his pores moistened with emotion. The cave felt a lonely place. An Igloid, a bat and a pair of spare feet sat in the dirt and discussed rescue tactics. Grunt had often saved life forms in the Valley of Preciousness, but had never encountered an adversary as slimy and cunning as a Grag.

'Can anything escape from the cells?' asked Grunt.

'Not at all,' replied Boo, remembering his time in there.

'Well then, how did you escape?'

Boo thought for a moment.

'I walked out under the grate. Had they not left my feet to eat last, I would have been wholly consumed. I'm afraid Davidia, being a prized catch, will feed the village when it is her turn to be dished up. They occasionally have a big fry up when an important life form is available. I don't think that they have ever eaten human before, so it's a celebration for all Grags. There's very little we can do,' explained Boo, realising that he had also nearly lost the arch in his feet. Nothing was functioning properly today.

'What if I was captured?' said Grunt. 'We can't do anything from here. If I was in the next cell, an opportunity may arise where we can escape before becoming an entrée, main, or dessert. I can still make myself invisible. Batbit can easily fly in and out of the cell window and through the door grates. They wouldn't be interested in you, Boo; after all the walking you have been doing, you would be as tough as old boots. Besides, you can walk under the grates unnoticed. The dust will camouflage your movements.'

The three oddities all agreed with Grunt's ideas. Nothing else appeared on the mental horizon to improvise an alternative course of action.

'It's settled then. I'll risk capture. Just a moment.'

Grunt sat by himself. He had no idea whether he had

any chance of success. Was he sacrificing himself, and could Davidia be saved? He believed it was worth the risk. He grasped the necklace he wore and kissed it tenderly. A strange feeling filled his heart. A message seemed to say, 'Son, that is a courageous decision.' Grunt wondered what a son was. Was he one of them? Who was the message from? Somehow, it elated him with confidence. He felt he wasn't alone anymore.

'Right. This is what we will do,' explained Grunt. Batbit, being the general of Batfoce, knew his time had come to lead. Boo wanted to kick backside because that was all he was capable of doing with his feet. All three stood at the cave entrance, perhaps seeing The Valley of Gragslew for the last time. None of them knew if they would live through the experience.

'Could you please scratch my feet?' asked Boo. 'They are terribly itchy.' Batbit gave him a foot massage instead. 'Thanks. I think its nerves.'

'Push.'

Grunt rolled himself into a huge ball. Batbit and Boo gave him an almighty push and he thundered down the hill toward the prison. Grags ran in fear. They were timid creatures and panicked easily. Some weren't quick enough to escape and were skittled. Mayhem set in.

'Did you see that?' one gasped. 'What a great dumpling soup that would make.'

'We could eat fresh for quite some time. It's so large.'

Recipe books were brought out by the inhabitants after having witnessed their largest potential meal roll down the hill. Houses hummed with frenetic activity. The Grags began to argue amongst themselves as to what parts each would get access to.

'It has plenty of legs, arms, and other protruding things to lop off and enjoy. A nice roast would set the tone of a good meal. Crispy ears and nasal nodules would be ever so tasty too.'

Grunt had certainly set off the salivating alarm bells. He stopped just short of the white line, just as Davidia had done. The whole valley had congregated around their quarry. They all wanted to see the creature.

'Hisssslo,' said Gragga, who had finally overcome his other half Gorgo to approach the bowling ball. 'Who's in there?'

'Hisssslo to you,' replied Grunt. His body parts were now all exposed.

'Continue on your journey. The young life form is waiting for you in the canteen.'

'Why is that white line drawn on the ground?' asked Grunt knowing any answer would be a lie.

'We tried to zigzag it across the road, but we were low on painting material so we made it a straight line instead. Go on, cross over it,' coaxed Gragga, experiencing wicked thoughts about food presentation; this goes with that, and so on.

Grunt anticipated his imminent capture. The whole Grag community had come to see another strange creature. It was a hell of a time for them. They had never before experienced such an intelligent food source.

'No one here has ever tasted one of your kind. It will be a pleasure to serve you,' continued Gragga.

Grunt sensed the unfriendly crowd feeling. He suddenly made an almighty noise. His skin pores pulsated wildly, his arms gyrated in circles and his legs kicked indiscreetly. An enormous passage of wind was expelled from his body in all directions. The Grags withdrew in fear.

'I'm sorry about that. Grass gives me indigestion and flatulence. Come on, put me in prison,' he goaded.

'But, you haven't crossed the white line.'

'I'm not going to either.'

Gragga had never met such an obstinate life form. It needed encouragement.

'The young life form which is in a cell will be publicly cooked today if you don't step across that white line now,' threatened Gragga.

The white line held no power. It was the Grag's perception that it did. Grunt had an idea that the Grags were insipid cowards and needed an excuse to justify an action, hence the white line. He decided to play their graggish, childish game. He stepped over the white line. A crowd of evil wishers pounced on him. He was so huge they continued rolling him into a prison cell right next to Davidia. The door was banged shut. His guard was promised a tasty leg if he didn't escape. Once again, it was thought impossible to escape from such well-fortified cells. Grunt sat down on the grass bed and sighed. The only thought he possessed was to save Davidia and himself from becoming a feast.

'Is that you, Grunt?' sensed Davidia.

Grunt crept up close to the wall and touched it with a few of his hands. He felt Davidia's presence. The stone cell walls were a formidable barrier. Their only exit that he could see would be out through the grate. For some unknown reason, their thoughts couldn't penetrate the stone walls. A blockage was in place. Grunt had to bide his time.

At the next light (day in Davidia's world), Grunt was released for his daily exercise. He passed Davidia's cell. Their thoughts flashed quick and fast. As he passed cell number two, a strange pain gripped him. He immediately fell to the floor. The cause was unexplainable. He rolled around like the dumpling many thought he should be. The guard became concerned.

'Hisssslo.' It prodded him carefully. Grunt groaned. Almost

as quickly as it happened, he was better again. As his eyes opened, he noticed a cluster of five stones protruding from the rear wall of cell two. He thought that was impossible. One of his hands held the necklace tightly. His fingers tingled. Was it an omen? Had he been warned or advised? He let go of the necklace. The rear wall of cell two was plain again. Had he imagined the cluster, because it was no longer there?

'Hisssslo, guard. Can you see that group of stones on the back wall of cell two?' asked Grunt, wanting affirmation that he either saw it, or his imagination had broken its leash. The guard looked closely.

'I believe you are mistaken, life form. There is only a flat wall,' the guard replied.

'I thought so. It must be in the grass that you have fed me.'

'There's nothing in the grass, just grass.'

Grunt strolled around the exercise yard. A sudden breeze blew. It was Batbit whizzing in circles unseen above Grunt. He whispered.

'A huge cauldron of water is being boiled along the valley. Hundreds of Grags are toiling, making ready for a festival of some sort. A huge platform is being built. I don't like the look of it.'

'I believe that Davidia and I are to be on the menu.' Grunt briefly alerted Batbit about the cluster he thought he'd seen. 'We have to be put in cell two somehow before we become the incredible edibles. Fly in and see if I am right.'

Batbit flew directly toward the prison cells. He couldn't resist the temptation of scratching a Grag on the way. He gave Grunt's guard a quick nick. The mark he left began to ooze a substance. The guard stood trembling. Its voice became shrill with fear. Its two halves yelled at each other. A battle was about to erupt.

'Look what you've done. I'll miss the feast because of you.'

'If I didn't have this job, you'd be nothing but an ungrateful half.'

'You're only half the person you should be. My half is safe. You have put us in jeopardy.'

Grunt watched the Grag self-destruct. Its body oozed a putty-like substance, which was its life force. Any breach in their putty-like skin meant doom. In a minute, all that was left was a pile of pink pudding. Another guard nearby noticed the event and stood fixated. When all activity had ceased, it and two others rushed over armed with food scrapers.

'We'll eat well this dark. What a bonus.'

In a flash only a stain was left on the ground. A new guard was appointed almost immediately.

'What are you staring at, chubby?' it said.

'You eat your own too.'

'Never waste a good feed. All the best bits of all life forms go to that Gragga and Gorgo. We get leftovers, but are allowed to eat our own as a treat, providing we don't cause their demise. We never miss an opportunity if it arises. You try and live on leftovers and see what I mean.'

Grunt had just seen a way to rid himself of a guard if he got close enough. He thought that if he scratched a guard, they would also drain away. He put his thought to the test. The guard came near him to move his lazy walking strides into a more active prisoner. Grunt swung at it with a stone from the ground and nicked it. After a while nothing happened. The cut self-healed. This led to the discovery that Batbit had something in his genes that caused seepage. Grunt filed that thought.

Batbit returned.

'There's nothing but a flat cell wall at the back in cell two.'

Grunt was confused. Why was it only him that could see it?

'Time's up. Move it, you lump of lard.'

Grunt was escorted past cell two again. He nervously glanced at the back wall. Sure enough, he could see the cluster of five as clearly as a reflection in a mirror.

Davidia had woken up. She saw Grunt pass by her cell door, but something made her remain quiet. The guards settled into their routine of bum-sitting and staring. The inhabitants of the cells accepted their fate of becoming an edible meal. Davidia and Grunt had no inclination to be eaten for the amusement of others. They would escape somehow.

Along the valley, the planning of a great feast was in full swing. All Grags had to contribute an idea for the best presented meal. Those secret, family recipes would once again be able to be used. The prize would be a fresh leg. There was nothing like a competition to bring out the nasty personalities.

'I don't believe that hair on that one's leg is all natural. I think it has had dyed grass stuck on,' said one half of a female Grag.

'That one's other half remains permanently unseen. I hear it has a case of grassflu which means it will eventually drop off and leave that one as a half alone,' said another.

'That one over there can only cook up a good story. The last meal it prepared with a life form, it bit it so hard its arm fell off. It hadn't properly cured it before cooking.' A group almost broke into a grin, usually an unseen pleasure in this valley of halves.

Gragga and Gorgo supervised the event closely. In two darks, they would celebrate the Feast of Glum, when all Grags could behave badly. They could spit, bitch, bite, kick and attack those that they disliked. It was an annual hate-fest of venting anger. A few casualties occurred, but that meant a food source for another. Nothing was wasted except a few inhabitants. It would be an ugly sight. The two halves could take a swipe at each other if they wanted. Chaos, that well planned mess many practiced, would rule the day.

The centrepiece would be a huge cauldron of boiling water above which a structure was built to hold Grunt and Davidia. As the frenzy of the insane day unfolded, they would be dipped regularly and publicly cooked, much to the delight of the mad crowd. The grunters in the crowd would wait for an opportunity to attack another. Evil permeated everywhere. Trust was non-existent. Harmony was unknown. "Hisssslo," their usual greeting, would be dumped with all other good manners. It would mean a big, fat zip.

The frantic activity meant that Batbit and Boo could almost move around unnoticed. Batbit flew air reconnaissance, while Boo did a land-based reconnoitre. He was tempted to foot someone up the behind just because he felt like it. He too could act ridiculously. A pair of spare feet hiding amongst the dust was hardly going to attract any attention.

'B to B,' signalled Batbit to Boo. 'Preparations are well under way. How's the view down there?'

'It's all uphill from down here. They are a mad, inconsiderate and selfish lot, always fighting with each other. We must warn Grunt and Davidia of their doom.'

The two friends carefully eluded the Grags and made their way back to the prison cells.

The sky suddenly went dark. All activity ceased. There was not a breath of wind or any sound. It had been suffocated.

'I won't tolerate failure. Sacrifice them to me so that I can revel in the agony and pleasure of their passing. No life form escapes from my valley. Be as nasty as you can. I know you won't let me down. May the best chef win and nasty personality prevail.'

A cool wind whistled around their ears. Then it was gone.

'Guard, who was that?' asked Davidia, who was now fully rested.

The guard seemed afraid to answer. 'That was Glum, the evil master. No one speaks of him. I must husssshlo; otherwise I might become a food source myself.' The guard turned away, preferring to stare at the wall than guard his quarry.

The small windows spaced in Grunt's and Davidia's cells were obviously shaped in size to be a tease only. They were placed too high for any view of the valley or interior of the prison yard. Batbit effortlessly zipped through the grates. He landed on one of Grunt's arms.

'The valley is frenetic with activity. The Grags are creating an unpleasant cook-a-thon with you and Davidia to be publicly roasted, which is the cooking style and not a hilarious fun dig at your personalities. The cooking pots are monstrous,' explained Batbit.

'Is there any way to escape from this fate?' Grunt asked himself. 'We can escape from the pot, but where to from there? We must flee this valley.' Suddenly, Grunt had a lonely, singular, orphan thought. 'Batbit, go to cell two and check again if there is a stone cluster on the back wall. Go. Be quick, whilst the guards are looking the other way.'

Batbit did as instructed. His morose attitude upon return affirmed he couldn't see them. Grunt sat deflated. He knew he could escape by spinning invisibly, but he needed an elsewhere to go to. Just then, Boo scampered into the cell beneath the grate.

'Can you climb walls?' asked Grunt.

'With both feet,' Boo assured him. He started jumping with excitement at being able to answer in the positive. He was a foot and toe achiever.

'Go to cell two unseen, climb over the back wall and tell me what you find. Go on, scoot.' Boo left a small dust trail as he scampered off on an important task. No one was guarding cell two. He quickly ran all over cell two and, halfway up the back wall, stubbed his toe on a protrusion. I didn't see that, he thought as he fell to the cell floor. He shook off his dustcoat and retraced his footsteps. Sure enough, he felt the protrusion again. There were five of them. As many toes as Davidia had on one foot.

'Did you discover anything?' asked Grunt.

'I certainly did,' replied Boo proudly. His feet were full of confidence.

'Spit it out. There's no need in keeping secrets here,' said Grunt starting to revolve in agitation.

'I can't do that; however, I felt a cluster of five lumps in the centre of the back wall. They cannot be seen, but only felt,' said Boo proudly.

'I knew it. Tomorrow, it's Cell Two for us,' said Grunt. His agitation ceased and his mood improved.

The cell doors were opened. It was feeding time. The term "zoo" hadn't yet entered their language, but that's what the prison cells were. The Grag guards tossed in an extra bunch of nutritional grass to each of them.

'Eat it all. At the next light, you and that other ugly life form that screams are going to provide fantastic entertainment and taste sensations no Grag has ever experienced before.' The guard almost choked with delight.

'I get the first bite.'

'No you don't, it's mine.'

Its two halves had a looming problem to solve – who gets to have the first bite.

Grunt gulped down his offering. His strength would be needed at next light.

Davidia sat alone. The other two were in Grunt's cell. Then, to cheer her up, Batbit flew in quietly and settled under her arm, whilst Boo was more content to sit on her feet.

'I don't want to be eaten,' wailed Davidia. 'Dad always told me to eat my greens, but I don't feel like grass for dinner.' She toyed playfully with the grass, thinking it might be her last meal. From somewhere within her, a voice chimed in, 'Be strong, oh Wisp of Wischink.' Startled, she dropped the grass. It made a nice mat. Her demeanour instantly altered. Forces began to circle around her head.

'It hurts,' she said out aloud. The strange voice continued, 'At next light, a strange event will occur. Grasp the moment. You are not alone. Sleep well this dark. Your journey is just beginning.' The voice faded away.

'Did you understand any of that?' she asked Batbit and Boo. Two negative answers resulted. All they saw was a young life form with slim hands, roughing up her long blonde hair. They didn't understand the odd scratching behaviour. They hadn't seen that before. Her bright, dazzling, azure blue eyes were full of an unexplained emotion. She had no idea what had just occurred inside her head. It was perplexing. Somehow, a feeling of strength beyond her years welled up in her young body. Had she fed her nightmare by eating so much grass? The night of the last supper would soon pass.

Grunt gripped the necklace tightly. His eyes closed. For a moment he was mentally transported to a far-away place. Life forms moved freely. He had never seen this type of life form before. A thought flashed through his mind, 'Follow your instincts.' It went blank. He felt as if another life force was present, but whose?

The Grags further up the valley had finally prepared the large water cauldrons for the cooking extravaganza to be held at next light. Gragga and Gorgo stood satisfied that their greatest cooking achievement was before them. Their sacrifice to Glum and their continuance of evil would be boiled in those two huge pots.

'You can have first taste,' said Gragga, realising that its other half was the stronger.

'How sweet of you, Gragga. Maybe we can enjoy it together,' it demurely replied.

'I want to taste that awful looking human life form first. She intrigues me.'

'What about that rounded unpleasant grunting life form? His size suggests deliciousness.'

Apparently, for one dark only prior to a great feast, all Grags ceased their infernal bickering. However, like all truces, once it was over, the never-ending conflicts continued. It felt like a carnival atmosphere. The sky was alight with flaming embers that delicately fluttered to the ground for a rest. The reflection of evil bounced off each Grag's eyes. Next light was eagerly awaited. That dark, the valley didn't sleep.

Davidia and Grunt sat silently, both wondering if their last meal had been consumed. The strange thoughts that they had both experienced had them both confused. Something was pushing their barrow, but what?

All the other life forms in the prison cells became restless. Many knew that the two main menu items would not feed the crowds and they knew their turn was coming. They would play bit parts and secondary roles in menu mayhem. No sauce that they were served with could be better than living. The dark was filled with tension and they couldn't eat fries with that. A weird feeling engulfed the impending edibles. It would be a lonely dark for all.

Next light crept slowly over the valley like a blanket of promises. The Grags had kept their bad attitudes at bay during the dark, but next light let loose their fanatically bad behaviour genes.

'You snivelling halfwit, that part of the leg is mine,' snarled half a Grag.

'If you weren't my other half, you'd be stewed,' replied the other half.

The day was off to a flier; snarlers everywhere. A crowd had gathered outside the prison gates to see the suffering life forms take their last walk and nominate what their fancy would be. Grunt and Davidia sat quietly. Their energy needed to be con-served.

'Guard, open the grates.' Grunt clasped his necklace. He felt five prongs on the "G" grate. I'm not alone, he thought.

Davidia took a deep sigh and closed her eyes. Her mind was

greeted with a gentle smile. She opened her eyes and realised that it was a vision meant only for her.

The grates were all opened and a myriad of life forms exited. Grunt glanced in at cell two and he felt a surge of emotion as he passed it. 'Remember us,' flashed into his head. He nodded, smiled and dripped moisture. They were to be paraded like skewered meat pieces out into the quadrangle first before being frog-marched, another food delicacy, to the valley centrepiece, the two huge pots. On the way, life forms were prodded, poked, hit, abused, insulted and leered at. Every nasty Grag was in attendance.

Grunt touched Davidia's hand. They melded as one in thought. Grunt transmitted to Davidia the moment of the escape plan and what he believed would save them. He couldn't explain the feeling. 'Cell two is the key.' Davidia nodded in agreement. She was so confident, she teased the Grags who were forbidden to touch her or Grunt.

'You look so skinny, nothing could live in there,' she said to one Grag.

'Bite me,' it said, sneering at her. It came so close that it was exactly what Davidia did. A quick chomp on a wrist and a scream of agony erupted. The Grag looked down and its putty like body began to leak its life source.

'Entrée is over here,' yelled a few other Grags, as they attacked the leaker. It was over in moments.

'Go on, do it again, I dare you,' teased another. Once a leak had sprung in their bodies, a Grag becomes a free meal for fellow Gragsters. Davidia smiled and waved her arm. The Grag ducked, fearing it was the next choice for devouring. The procession finally reached the village centre. Gragga and Gorgo stood out like unfashionable monuments on a pedestal. The agitated crowd swayed rhythmically.

Gragga and Gorgo became instantly visible in one

movement. It kept the crowd spellbound. This was the signal that the feast was officially opened.

'And you call us ugly,' commented Davidia, having seen a one-piece Grag. 'I've seen better looking cowpats.'

Gorgo sent a withering look of hate at her.

'You first,' she said, 'then that round thing can follow. Stand up on that plank.' Davidia was forcibly pushed to stand in front of the crowd on a wooden plank. Her soft, cotton dress gently moved in the breeze. Grunt stood next to her at a distance where they could touch by extending their arms. His skin pores ran wet with liquid.

Batbit and Boo had remained safely near the prison and kept an eye on cell two. Whilst everyone was at the fair, Batbit had managed to open cell two with the unattended keys. No guard stayed behind to protect an empty cell. They wouldn't miss the opportunity to be at the Feast of Glum. Batbit hoped they could escape before Grunt and Davidia were eaten. Boo and he made an unlikely pair shuffling around the prison cells alone.

Boom, boom. A loud thunderclap snapped into the atmosphere. Its deafening noise sent frozen barbs of fear along each Grag's spine. The intensity of sound had the Grags cowering in a subservient position. The bright light was instantly blanked out by the dark cape of fear, which was Glum.

'It's not bedtime again, is it?' asked Davidia.

'I fear it's trouble,' replied Grunt, aware that an evil force was nearby.

In the distance, a rolling black cloud tumbled over the landscape, growing larger as it neared the feast site. It had two large untrustworthy eyes filled with anger.

'Is this it?' it said, assessing the sacrifices to his wickedness.

'Yes, sir,' whimpered Gragga and Gorgo, fearful that Glum wanted their delicious prizes.

'What are they?' Glum asked.

'Something called a human – that's the girl life form – and the other one is just disgusting,' they offered as an explanation.

'Don't enjoy yourselves too much.'

Just then Davidia spoke.

'Excuse me Mr Glum, do you have any relatives?'

Glum's head shook in shock. He turned to freeze out the sound when he heard it continue. 'You look like Mr Mist. He was nasty too.'

'Are you challenging me?' countered Glum.

'My dad said if you can't say something nice about anyone, it's best not to say anything at all. Do you know what a smile is?'

Glum was becoming agitated at the "goody two-shoes" questions. He wanted to be evil, upset and hurt life forms. It was his mantra. Internally, his black clouds began to rumble.

'Don't spoil our feast,' pleaded Gragga.

'I'm not your feast,' said a defiant Davidia.

The Grags twittered amongst themselves. Of course she would be.

Glum was so upset that his authority had been challenged, he began to rain. Large torrents of water hit the ground in massive raindrops. The feast fires were drowned out and every Grag scattered for higher ground. The Feast of Glum became just that. Mud stuck to the Grags' feet as they tried to flee. It was obvious Glum was bursting a "foo foo" valve of utter desperation. His authority until now had been unchallengeable.

A young girl life form had created instant devastation by her impertinence and truthfulness. Grunt and Davidia stood motionless. They were left alone on the planks. The Grags had lost interest in them. Self-preservation was more important than perhaps a tasteless meal. Glum was writhing in pain. He wasn't finished yet. Massive winds began to howl and twist. Grunt sensed it was time to move. He grabbed Davidia by the hand and spun his invisibility talent. Poof! They were gone. No one noticed.

The prison was empty. All life forms had escaped in the floods. Glum became gloomier. Water rushed toward the prison with undue haste, as if it was trying to rid the land of an unwanted pest. The Valley of Gragslew was in an unprecedented dangerous flood. The nastiness of the inhabitants was about to be cleansed.

'Mr Grunt, there's water rushing in everywhere. Where's Boo?'

'Cell two. We have to get to cell two.'

They sloshed through the rising water, which was up to their knees. It was a struggle of wills. Strange life forms against an angry cloud who wept when upset.

'There it is,' yelled Davidia. 'Mum wouldn't be happy about ruining my dress like this.'

Batbit flew into the cell. Grunt had also made it. Davidia struggled with her dress. They couldn't find Boo. Perhaps his feet had become separated and he'd been washed away. The three huddled together. Grunt held onto the necklace around his neck. He felt the small grate in one hand. There on the rear wall, the ejector stones revealed themselves only to him.

'Hold on tightly together.'

Batbit's feet dug into Davidia's arm. Grunt felt as if a weight had been lifted off his feet. It had. He was floating. Suddenly, they heard frantic splashing. There for all to see was Boo bob-bing like a cork. Both feet were together.

'I bet you didn't know that I could water ski, did you?' he said. 'Are we to drown together? A nice touch, that.'

Grunt scooped up both feet in his other hands.

'Don't mess with the toenails.'

'Mr Grunt, what are you doing?' asked Davidia. They all felt doomed. Grunt outstretched an arm and pushed against the ejector stones.

'Mr Grunt, even you aren't strong enough to push that wall over.'

A whirring noise was the last audible sound they heard. Their minds went blank. They were in limbo land. The Valley of Gragslew was nothing more than a distant memory.

4. VALLEY OF RINTSLIP

'Wow! Did you see that?' exclaimed an excited valley member.

'It was faster than a flying rake,' said another.

'That flash was a warning from The Sinister. I told you it would be trouble when it visited. The council leaders ignored me. Now we'll all pay for it,' said a third member.

The Council of Jimps was in session, planning their next foray into valley management. The valley in which they lived was very fertile. Slaves were required to plough and harvest the fields, serve their owners and be treated as possessions for owners to treat as they wished. The smart Jimps treated their slaves well, but many others used them up, spat them out and a huge communal pit was the last resting place of dissatisfied and misused slaves. The only happy inhabitants of the valley were the Jimps.

'There seems to be a shortage of slaves. Have any new ones arrived in the valley recently?' asked a senior Jimp.

A sea of sideways nodding heads answered the question without a word. At the current loss rate of slaves, it was almost thought that the Jimps themselves would actually have to work. It was a situation of bad dreams no Jimp could face.

The Valley of Rintslip was the home of the Jimps, a race of strange-looking creatures whose most obvious attribute was to jump and kick their legs all day. They were constantly on the hop. It would be impossible for them to work in any coordinated fashion. Each Jimp had one long tooth facing outwards, honed like a curved blade, another set straight as a spike, both located on the upper jaw and a third serrated tooth attached to their bottom jaw for tearing at any edible item. Each foot had an extendable claw facing upwards, which only triggered when fighting. They were constantly in motion, sniffing the air, eating at a furious pace and dropping rounded reminders of the good meals consumed. At least their faces gave the appearance of smiling, even though underneath unpleasantness pervaded their very souls. An unhappy force lived within each of them.

'If any new slaves are found and captured, the council must be informed. Otherwise the Claw of Clusters will be enforced.'

The council members shrank in their seats so low that only their eyes were visible above the bench top.

'Not the Claw of Clusters! You cannot invoke that edict. It has been forbidden for eons,' replied a nervous member, once having been told of a family member who had experienced the shame it had brought.

'These are tough times. The prospect of work frightens me just as much as it does you, but strong decisions need to be taken and enforced.'

'What's the Claw of Clusters?' asked an innocent, youthful member. Another Jimp whispered what it meant. Suddenly, a loud burp burst forth and a plop, plop, plop on the floor was heard as three rounded balls of waste materialised. The innocent member was in shock.

'You mean I couldn't do that anymore?' The council nodded.

'Then, let's rake up some new slaves.'

A whooshing sound fizzed through the air at lightening speed as Grunt, Davidia, Batbit and Boo hurtled towards an unknown destination. A tall, solitary, tree used as a lookout over the valley stood in their way as they crash-landed into it. It was deserted at the time due to council business.

'This isn't the way to treat new arrivals, leaving us stranded in such a tall tree,' said Boo. He had no hands to assist in climbing down.

'My dad wouldn't let me climb trees at home. He always let Dan do it. Talk about favouritism. Where are we?' asked Davidia.

Grunt and Batbit sat quietly. They both had no idea where they were or why they were there. They were fortunate to have escaped the Grags and wondered what was in store for them here. The valley extended as far as the eye could see. Perhaps that was the end of the earth as they knew it. Odd shaped houses and odd shaped fields spread out before them. Something was puzzling them. The view seemed confusing.

'Boo, do you know what this place is?' asked Grunt.

'It's my home. I used to live here, well most of me did. It's called the Valley of Rintslip. I used to be a whole life form here. Just wait until you meet the rest of my family.' Grunt noticed that Boo's feet began to kick in a most peculiar manner.

'What's happening, Boo?'

'It's coming back to me. I'm re-orientating. I'd forgotten many things without my head. Now I feel it through the ground. I was once a real live Jimp and we jumped a lot.'

Fortunately for the others, Boo couldn't fully remember how badly some of the slaves were treated.

'Is it a friendly place?' asked Grunt, fearing that another unpleasant experience lay ahead.

'Yes, I think so. It's hard to remember being two feet without a body.'

'I'm hungry,' whined Davidia. 'What do they eat here?'

'Everything,' Boo paused, 'that they grow.'

Relief was felt all around.

'I'll fly down for a look, shall I?' commented Batbit, who wanted to stretch his wings. Like a falling stone, he dropped from the sky to skim over the land surface.

He noticed that in the fields, many different life forms were tossing rakes full of produce everywhere. Jimps were hopping around the edges yelling orders of, 'Faster, faster,' exhorting their slaves to maximum performance.

'I'll stretch your wings on racks if you don't move faster.'

'You can sleep in the poo shed if you can't improve.'

'No food for you this dark, you lazy, four-legged creature.'

A sea of threats and intimidations permeated every thought that Batbit understood. There was nothing positive said at all. The slaves were denigrated, stood over and bullied. Harmony was expunged from the slaves. Not one Jimp was seen to raise a rake. Batbit returned to the tree.

'We've done it again. Landed ourselves in trouble. That lot down there wouldn't win a friendship vote on a desert island. Call me untrusting, but there's going to be problems with that lot. When I was a small bat growing up in the caves, older bats took my hanging roof space and I was forced to cling to the roughest rocks. It's a repeat of the bullying.'

'Build a bridge and get over it. My dad told me to stand up for myself at school. A girl called Sally-Anne teased me for years with her in-group at school, until one day in the schoolyard she pushed me over. She and her friends laughed at me. I was very upset. Without thinking, I went and pulled her hair real hard. It hurt. After that, she didn't tease me anymore. I had made a difference. Dad was real proud of me.'

The others exchanged looks of support for Davidia's determination.

'It's a long way down. Where is everyone?'

It's true they were stranded like "shags on a rock;" however, the tree had numerous branches upon which to step safely whilst descending. Grunt broke many branches due to his ungainly shape and bulk. Davidia pretended she was her brother, Dan, discovering a new world. Boo skipped in hippity, hoppity fashion, excelling in tree-branch jumping. As a young Jimp, trees like this were a favourite challenge for him. At last, solid ground. Batbit flew many scouting forays, alerting them to any dangers that might exist. A sign by the roadside read, The Pool of Pududdles. An arrow pointed the way. Boo became quite excited.

'My family live near there,' he said.

'What is it?' asked Davidia, thinking somehow the word was misspelt. She thought it was referring to a puddle.

'A mystery,' replied Boo, his toes wiggling excessively. The arches in his feet had regained full formation and he was leaping everywhere in confusion.

'Where to, where to, oh toots of mine?' Boo began running like a pair of possessed feet wanting to make it first to the finishing line as if he was in a triathlon. The two jumping feet disappeared over the hill.

Grunt hadn't said much. He was thinking. It was often a painless exercise, but he was concerned over the lack of life forms in the countryside. Maybe they had siestas here. He absentmindedly toyed with his necklace.

'Ouch!' he exclaimed. He had pricked a hand on the small rake. 'Nothing is as it seems,' whispered something from somewhere into an ear. It was a warning, but Grunt ignored it. He didn't dream in the lights, especially since he was wide awake.

'Let's follow Boo's footprints to the Pool of Pududdles. At least we can meet his family,' said Davidia. She was hungry and wanted to eat something. Boo's family might have a hot cake, or a bun, or a pie for her.

Batbit had been scanning the landscape and returned excited.

'I sense food and plenty of friendly inhabitants up there near a freshwater pond. There was a family jumping about enjoying themselves.'

'Did it appear safe?'

'From the sky, yes, but from the ground, we'll have to find out.'

The three friends walked along the road toward the Pool of Pududdles. The small, odd shaped farming allotments were neatly kept. All food leaves grew in exactly the same way with identical height and colouring. It was as if a photograph had been placed over the ground. A picture-perfect, idyllic environment, or so it seemed.

'Look, there's Boo over there with his family,' pointed Davidia.

'He doesn't seem happy,' answered Grunt.

A group of Jimps were kicking at him, but without their extended claws. Grunt rushed over toward them. A space was made for the huge intruder.

'Are you okay, Boo?' he asked. 'They're kicking at you.'

'This is how we greet each other,' he replied. 'My family didn't recognise me, but they know my tricky foot moves which I was demonstrating to them.'

Grunt watched the jumping crowd who seemed to be on a perpetual trampoline. They jumped incessantly. Their protruding teeth were to be avoided. They snarled, grunted, farted, spat and wet the ground religiously. Any mess made was quickly cleaned up by the slave moppers. These life forms slunk in and around the toe jumpers and were careful not to be jumped on. They each carried a rake.

'This is Jiminy, Jodiny and Jempiny, my family,' said Boo proudly. 'My name isn't really Boo either, it's Jaminy.'

The Jimp family hopped around them wondering which one would make the best slave. The huge round one would exhaust easy, the flying food morsel couldn't be caught, but the other one would be ideal for leaf collection. The one utensil all slaves possessed was a rake. If it were ever left unattended they would be punished. The rake was the badge of a slave.

'Where's your rake?' asked Jiminy, the slimy father Jimp. He had a penchant for kicking his slaves and lately hadn't kicked any because they had died of exhaustion in the fields. The opportunity was now available for new ones with Grunt's and Davidia's arrival.

'We don't have a rake and besides what would we need one for anyway?' said Davidia, not keen to work or earn a blister or two on her delicate hands.

'Everyone in the valley has a rake.'

'Where's your rake, Mr Jimp?'

'Management doesn't need any, only slaves use them.'

'I'm not a slave, Mr Jimp, so I don't need one either.'

Jiminy began hopping erratically in anger – the impertinence of the young life form not willing to be a slave.

'Dad, Dad,' yelled young Jaminy, 'isn't there a test a life form must perform and fail before becoming a slave?' He didn't remember the bad parts of being a Jimp, or how they tricked and took advantage of life forms to become slaves. Jiminy wasn't happy that he had been reminded of the test. He thought it would be a waste of time. Anyway, no life form had ever passed the test before. Now that the test had been spoken about by a Jimp, it was mandatory to abide by it. Jiminy lashed out at Jaminy with claws extended to inflict the pain of disagreement. Jaminy missed the onslaught of attack.

'What is this test?' asked Grunt. He was used to adversity as a protector of good and wondered how best to appease the growing resentment and anger of Jiminy and family. They were desperate for new slaves; otherwise the catastrophe of work would fall on their shoulders. In Jimp society they would be ridiculed, abused and treated slightly better than slaves by their fellow Jimps. They would be unable to attend any social functions and eventually become a pariah in their own society. Competition for slaves was fierce. Work was a hated word which no one wanted to hear.

'Where do you live?' asked Davidia, feeling her rumbling stomach juices. 'Perhaps you can offer us a cup of tea?'

'What's tea? Never heard of it. Our house is over there,' answered Jodiny, the calming Jimp. She thought that if she could befriend the prospective new slaves, perhaps they might have a good working relationship. She began to lead them toward the house. Batbit had been flying overhead and noticed that Jodiny jumped every second stone on the footpath. Being a conniving, brilliant, bat commander, Batbit flew low behind her and let out a piercing screech. It was pure intuition. The noise interfered with her jumping antennae and Jodiny miscalculated the next stone and sank into a gooey, muddy substance. It was the Licorice Slick that bubbled just below what appeared to be a solid surface. Grunt remembered the voice that said, 'Nothing is as it seems.'

'She's sinking, please save her,' cried Davidia. Ruefully, Jiminy complied. His interest was in the slaves, not heroics for his family. Jodiny was dragged safely out. Jimps didn't possess the manners to say 'thank you;' however, Jodiny acknowledged her rescue with a wave of a foot.

'Tread carefully, Mr Grunt, we don't want to sink before we solve the puzzle, do we?'

'A puzzle. Is that a food source in your land?' said Grunt, unsure of what it was.

'It's a test. This land seems odd to me, like pieces not properly fitting in. At home mum used to play puzzle time with jigsaw puzzles. Dad always joked about being pulled apart and put back together again. Somehow Mr and Mrs Jimp don't seem to fit in. Maybe they are part of a puzzle too.'

They carefully traversed the ingeniously hidden sinking stones underfoot and crossed safely to the Jimp house. From the outside facing the roadway, it looked solid. However, behind the door lay another world.

'Go on, open the door, rounded life form,' cooed Jiminy to Grunt. 'Food and rest is almost yours. You only have to push the handle downwards.' One of the unknown tests for slaves to fail was that if they went or acted first on any occasion presented by a Jimp, it was instant failure and enslavement. Grunt and Davidia had no idea how treacherous a Jimp was. They were the magicians of the valley.

'Let me open it,' said Davidia as she hastily pushed forward. She grabbed the handle and instead of pulling downwards, she pushed upwards. The door wouldn't open.

'You stupid door. You aren't a talking door handle, are you?' she yelled. Jiminy felt he almost had a new slave in his grasp. Young Jaminy, alias Boo, who was ever so helpful, pushed Davidia sideways and jumped on the handle. The door instantly opened. Jiminy was passing wind with displeasure, grunting noisily and kicking at the wall. His control was leaking down his leg. Damn, another missed opportunity, he thought. Behind the door was a ramp leading downwards to an underground cavern. The interior was sparsely furnished with mats as the only ground cover. A dormitory was off to the side of the cooking room. A strong, thick, ceiling beam support fitted the length of the room. Huge hooks hung down from the beam.

'They look dangerous,' said Davidia, wondering what they were used for.

'This is where we sleep,' explained Jodiny, who was still grateful for being there at all. 'From these hooks we hang slings in which we sleep above the ground. Our legs are constantly active so we must hang high in order to sleep. It would be impossible to sleep on the ground.'

'We call them hammocks,' replied Davidia. 'Is there anything to eat?'

'Food sustenance must be earned. Tomorrow, you must cross the Pool of Pududdles. Then you will be rewarded. This dark you must stay here. Next light is a mystery.'

'I like solving puzzles.' Davidia's hunger was thwarted by the thrill of what tomorrow would bring.

Grunt had said very little. He was concerned over the warning by the voice in his head. He sat down and all his external parts withdrew into his body. The necklace jingled slightly. His body was nervous in the company of the Jimps. Davidia was a trusting soul whom he had to protect. Batbit had flown in quietly so as not to spook the Jimps and be impaled on one of their grotesque teeth. The Jimps hopped into their bed slings and their legs twitched all that dark.

Tomorrow would be the pool of reflections.

A vicious, nasty, storm was brewing within the council. Word had spread of the arrival of the new potential slaves.

'Why weren't we informed? It's council policy that any new slave is presented firstly to council, otherwise the Claw of Clusters will be invoked. Jiminy and family cannot claim them as a first right. Tomorrow, we will claim them and punishment will be swift,' said the head Jimp, as its fist thundered onto the table.

In the dark sky, an evil force sniffed the winds for foreign life forms. Somewhere from down in the valley there was a signal from the past emitting trailers of detection. For many years no such signal existed and no one expected it to be activated ever again. It signalled a threat. The Irrids had detected the feelings it evoked and wanted them erased forever. Grunt was safe underground for the moment and the source of the signal couldn't be located. The Sinister, another evil demon sent by the Irrids to conquer and control the Valley of Rintslip, patrolled the winds and airways. Its unhappy disposition welled up from being ignored as a serious force when it could only blow strong winds. Now it had tornado potential, a lethal activity it was dying to practice. The head Irrid kept a close watch on her nasty demons and unleashed them when under threat. The weak signals from the past had put a fear into her she hadn't felt since the time of the Great Split. Sinister would soon come into its own as a mad monster of wind theatrics and try to defeat any signal threats.

'We can't stay here,' said Grunt. 'There's trouble. I feel it in my pores. Look, they're becoming wet again. At first light, we must leave quietly and cross the Pool of Pududdles, hopefully to safety. I don't trust the Jimps, except for Jaminy, I mean Boo.'

Batbit agreed. Davidia was still half asleep. Danger lurked everywhere like a bad smell. Softly, softly, was the escape plan. Whatever the risk, it was worth the chance of freedom than to be enslaved. They didn't know where the Pool of Pududdles would lead, but felt that for their survival it was essential to take the risk. An inner force seemed to propel Grunt into action.

'Psst, are you awake, Davidia?' asked Grunt, as he prodded her on the arm.

'It's too early to get up. It's still dark,' she moaned. Fortunately they couldn't be heard or understood as they transferred thoughts to each other. The Jimp family were snoring loudly and wouldn't have heard any sounds anyway.

They are dreadfully noisy sleepers, thought Grunt. Had he known that in Davidia's world there were animals known as pigs that lived in a pig sty, he would have understood that their sounds were almost identical.

It was first light as they crept quietly like criminals trying to avoid detection, slowly, slowly, toward the front door. A loud snort was heard. They froze like icicles. Had they been discovered? Seconds went by which felt like minutes.

'Keep moving,' urged Grunt. 'I have no intention of being their slave.'

They made it safely to the front door. No one felt or heard them leave. The atmosphere that surrounded the three was filled with apprehension. It was decided that Jaminy, alias Boo, was to be left behind. It was obvious, even though he existed as only two feet and had been very helpful to them to date, his feet had regained the nasty Jimp jump trait. It was ugly foot bouncing. They felt that his past nastiness would eventually return in full to his feet and they might be on the end of a good kicking.

'It's early for breakfast,' said Davidia, realising that at home they never got up this early to eat. 'I'm hungry.' In the kitchen, there was a mound of loose food objects lying on top of the bench. Davidia grabbed at the nearest offering. It squelched in her hand. Goo oozed out of it. She was quick enough to lick it before gravity splattered it onto the floor making it inedible. Her face winced in a grimace as the terrible taste danced over her taste buds. Her hunger overrode the nasty taste and she swallowed it whole. Her body shook in fright. 'I'm not doing that again,' she promised herself. At least her stomach would no longer complain of being ignored.

Grunt ignored her comments. Batbit clung to Davidia's dress as the door opened. It was "so far, so good". They stepped out into the valley, which had an icy bite to it. Hopefully, they weren't followed by a series of nasty, gnashing teeth.

'Follow that sign to the Pool of Pududdles,' ordered Grunt. The plan was to approach the pool and try to cross it without failure. It was a puzzle test that a life form in Jimp belief was doomed to fail. This would allow the capture of new slaves to harass, kick, boss about and above all, work. A rake would be issued to each of them and they would be set to work forever as a slave until expiry in the fields. It wasn't going to be a pretty picture, if caught. No one had ever succeeded before to outwit and outsmart a cunning Jimp. A human, possibly the brightest animal known, plus the cleverness of Grunt, was about to be played out in a tantalising, teasing puzzle.

'There's the Pool of Pududdles,' shouted Davidia excitedly. 'It's beautiful. I'm going to paddle my feet in it.'

'Stop,' cried Grunt. 'They are dangerous and testing waters. All is not as it seems.'

Davidia stopped dead in her tracks as if struck by lightening. She hadn't heard any fear in Grunt's thoughts before and it stunned her. 'The Pools are filled with treachery. The clear pool may not be so clear once you are near it. Caution must be exercised at all times and remember that you have to outwit your opponent, a Jimp puzzle master. See the solution before you solve the problem.'

Unbeknown to the trio, no Jimp had ever crossed the Pool of Pududdles either. Were they to make the first ever successful crossing?

'It's a wet, water puzzle then,' replied Davidia. 'I like puzzles.'

The Pool of Pududdles was a warm, mud spring, which constantly spat bubbles under the watery surface. The exhaled air from those rounded, bubbly spurters gave the impression they were talking to you. 'Come on down, the water's fine.' In fact, they were actually spitting contempt at any life form that dared to cross. They were arrogant little mud holes. The grey muddy substance had often captured life forms by sending up the slimy reeds that inhabited the creek bed. The reeds tangled around legs, ankles and bodies and dragged the life forms down. Once caught, unhappiness became the emotion of a rake slave. The Jimps wallowed in their cleverness of the "pududdling" of every life form. The Pool of Pududdles wasn't very wide and solid ground was temptingly close on the other side. Once over there, it was thought that safety and escape had been achieved. Was this correct? Mmm. Achieve it first and see.

'I'm not crossing there,' said a stubborn and defiant Davidia. 'I'll get my dress dirtier. Where do we go shopping? I need a new dress. Mummy always took me for retail therapy when I wanted a new dress. Perhaps, Mr Grunt, you could take me.'

Grunt was focused on defeating the Pool and not listening to a whinging twelve year old. A series of small stepping-stones could be seen just below the water's surface. When a mud hole exhaled an air bubble, the ripple made them momentarily disappear. When the water stilled they reappeared and became a small reflective pool, with the stepping-stones clearly visible underneath. It beckoned standing upon. Batbit flew above the water's surface at skimming level. He noticed gaps between the small pools, which looked dark and murky. Any false step and it would be gurgle, gurgle, to the bottom of the pool. His early-warning radar detector system needed to be fully functional to warn of any stepping disaster.

'Me first,' said Grunt. Davidia pouted disappointment. He lent forward. His reflection danced off the small pool in delight. It arose to the same height as himself. They stared at each other. Grunt got the fright of his life. He had never seen such an ugly life form. Just then Batbit landed on his shoulder, 'Not that one, not that one, there's nothing underneath.'

'But I can see a life form, it's so ugly. What is it? It's got all those pieces protruding everywhere and covered in bubbly holes.'

Batbit whispered in his ear, 'It's you.'

'That's me!' he exclaimed amazed. He'd never seen himself before and couldn't believe it. 'That's me!' Davidia nodded in agreement. He now realised how others saw him.

'Unbelievable.' Grunt gazed in disbelief that the life form standing directly above a false stepping-stone was actually himself. Wow! No more sleepless darks for him. The stones seem to whisper, 'Step on me, step on me.' As Grunt put one foot forward the reflection instantly disappeared. In its place was a pool of a black, muddy, liquid substance, which led to demonic depths. He quickly withdrew his foot and because of his many legs, hadn't overbalanced and plopped into the pool. Suddenly, the pool returned to clear water again. It was tricky and confusing.

'Miss the reflection puddle,' encouraged Batbit. 'Davidia, you do the same.'

At times, telling a twelve year old a positive life action function would often be met with a contrasting viewpoint and result.

Grunt had done as instructed and his foot landed on a solid substance just below the water's surface.

'Safe,' he grumbled.

Davidia saw her reflection also rise from a clear pool. She admired how beautiful it was and lent over to touch it. The water began to bubble. A slimy, mud-covered reed slithered from the pool and passed over her wrist.

'Eek! Get off me,' she yelled. The reed began to circle her hand. It would be the end of her freedom if she couldn't be saved.

Grunt couldn't help her because there was no turning back in the Pool of Pududdles. It was only a one-way trip to the other side. He could only watch the dangerous situation unfold. Batbit had seen the disaster happening. Reeds weren't his favourite tasting food source; however, to have any chance of saving Davidia he had to forego his tastebud intolerance to reed chomping. He dived like a kingfisher at full tilt, mouth agape and latched onto the threatening reed with his razor sharp, short, spiky teeth. He shook it vigorously like a terrier. His teeth slit through the reed as quickly as a sharp machete through dense jungle growth. Noiselessly the reed released its grip and slid into the murky depths, leaving behind a mud, slime trail.

'That was horrible. It made my skin all goose bumpy. Thanks Batbit.'

Batbit did a loop of delight. Size didn't matter in this instance. In a confronting situation against a larger opponent, the deed achieved was more important than the size of the problem.

'Grunt, how was the aerodynamics? Pretty cool movements, eh,' gloated Batbit in his moment of glory.

'How do I get across? I'm frightened,' cried Davidia. She shook with fear like a tree leaf whose tenuous time as a deciduous leaf gently nudged by the breeze was about to end. She shut her eyes. A voice filtered in on the wind, 'The truth will see you through.' Her eyes opened, somewhat glazed, but she took that vital step. Her apparition didn't reappear and that first step proved positive. She stood on a solid surface. The small pools shimmered with enticement. Unwanted eyes from the deep waited for their prey. Any mistake would be their salvation.

The Sinister watched from afar the jigsaw puzzle being played out. He held any missing pieces and if failure was imminent, he would resolve it with tornado tenacity. There was a hierarchy of evil within the valley. The Sinister couldn't implement his tirade of anger unless the Jimps had first completely failed. He would then hose retribution on them as damaging as he could muster. Impatience wasn't the name of a flower for him. Any delay only fuelled his cantankerous behaviour. Tail swirls, water-spitting, wind-gushing at high speed and cloud-dumping were the favourite elements in his armoury of bad behaviour. His winds rumbled as he patrolled the skies. Occasionally, a lightening blast would erupt when he met another huffy wind source. He thought, when is it my turn?

'Step on the reflections that aren't you,' yelled Grunt, still reeling from the shock of seeing himself.

'I'll try,' she said, not feeling very confident. She gingerly stepped over another of her reflections and securely landed safely on the reflection of another life form.

'Ooh! What are those things swimming in the water?' asked Davidia, as long, black, dark, slinky, thin lines seemed to move everywhere like underwater spaghetti.

Batbit had guessed it was a Pududdle reed, the antagonist to halt any life form from crossing. It needed little encouragement to entrap any intruder. Nothing ever before had successfully outwitted the Pool of Pududdles by crossing safely.

To cross the pools, it required only ten safely-placed steps. However, they were not all in a straight line. Twists and turns had to be judged perfectly. Grunt twisted and rotated to find his next step, but all he saw was his own reflection. He couldn't move, stuck in the middle. Batbit hovered like a vacuum cleaner just above the watery surface. Then he skimmed over the pools like a flat, rotating stone bouncing all the way, when he noticed the change in his reflection. He knew he wasn't a picture perfect postcard, if anything, but he was aware of his own image. He hovered near Grunt.

'It's that one next,' he said, as he dipped his wing in recognition of where to step next. 'Hurry, my wings are tiring.'

The water felt thick with slime as it settled around Grunt's legs. Cautiously, he edged closer to the other side. Batbit's wings began to dip with tiredness. Davidia dutifully followed Grunt's stepping stone antics. With only one step to go Grunt slipped into the pool. A huge, air bubble bobbed on the surface where he had just been.

'Mr Grunt, Mr Grunt,' yelled Davidia in fright. 'Don't play games.' Her favourite friend had disappeared into the murky waters. She began to cry.

A huge clump of black reeds arose from the pool and dived into the air bubble. Suddenly, the turgid water erupted into a whirlpool. Droplets were tossed at random everywhere. It was Grunt spinning wildly to make anyone extremely giddy. He had to shake off the unsightly reeds from the mud-tinged water, which had attempted to trap him. Their sliminess was their downfall. They couldn't secure a strong enough grip. Grunt popped onto dry land. However, the reeds still had further business to attend to; Davidia. She was surrounded by swirling waters, which was quite a nice name really for a pet horse.

'Shut your eyes and jump,' called Grunt.

'I won't be able to see,' she protested. The alternative was unthinkable. A twelve year old working in the fields in servitude for life had no appeal. Her gentle, pink hands would harden over time into a calloused leathery pair, providing she lived long enough to experience the change. She shut her eyes. A voice in her head said, 'Don't be afraid.'

'That's not you, dad, is it?' she said to herself. It wasn't, but it was someone helpful anyway.

Overcoming her fear, she pretended she was a nasty Jimp and jumped. Surprisingly, she cleared the final pool and also landed on solid ground.

'I did it, I did it,' she yelled excitedly.

The three exhausted friends sat together recovering from their ordeal, when the mood of the valley quickly changed. A cool, chill wind began to blow. Its coldness sent shivers through their souls. The landscape seemed to freeze with fear. Foliage shrunk, rocks remained still, water hardened and the happiness in the sky fell to the ground with the force of a tornado. The Sinister was displaying its awesome power of failure by the Pool of Pududdles, the Jimps unbeaten, capturing hero unable to capture the life forms. Its displeasure was destruction. No sooner had the three friends escaped their watery fate, the Pool of Pududdles began to disappear, sucked up into a vortex in the sky. The eyes of the Sinister appeared menacingly above the opening. In an instant the Pool of Pududdles was empty. All that remained was a shallow creek bed as dry as a desert. Grunt, Davidia and Batbit looked on in amazement.

'It's gone,' said Davidia, 'Was it ever there?'

'This is a creepy place,' replied Grunt, wondering what had just happened. There were evil forces in existence he didn't comprehend. The Sinister couldn't see the life forms through his anger. He had settled the score with the Pool of Pududdles and now it could be every Jimp jumping for itself.

The intrepid trio thanked their lucky stars, or guardian of goodness, that they had made it safely through. Another challenge had been defeated. What next?

The enraged Jimp council were going to make an example out of Jiminy, who had the audacity to challenge their authority and try to capture the life forms himself without going through the proper protocol channel, the council. The council visited Jiminy early in the morning, but not early enough. Had Jiminy succeeded in enslaving the life forms, the council would have to abide by the rules; however, if a mistake was made, the council could veto Jiminy's control and he would be set to work himself. It was a risk every lazy Jimp would dare to take. Work was a fearful, four-lettered word. They jumped and snorted agitatedly at Jiminy's front door, keen to inflict damage on a fellow Jimp. Danger was only a retracted claw away. Rules were rules. The council stood for cruelty and control of its Jimp empire. They began to kick the front door. Scratch marks dug deep as claws were dragged over its surface. Their fighting claws were erect for a stoush with Jiminy.

'I'll kick him in the crackers,' offered one member.

'I want first swipe. I'll rip his fur out so it won't regrow,' said another.

'Get rid of him, so I can take his wife,' said a third. Bravado dripped like molasses when acting in a pack formation. Jominy, Jiminy's wife, was an attractive Jimp who could kick with the best of them. Her delicate scratching claws, jumping agility and fine fur was a Jimp turn-on. Jealousy played a part in their vigorous snorting and kicking habits.

Jiminy opened the front door unaware of the hostile reception committee waiting for him. As soon as he saw their state of agitation, his fighting claws rose to the challenge.

'Which of you dead beats wants the first swipe?' he asked. 'Go on, one chance is all you get.' Jiminy was a formidable opponent. Once he had to fight off a challenge for Jominy and that Jimp didn't jump too high for quite a long time. Some thought that it was the Claw of Clusters that had inflicted the serious damage, but no, it was just an accurate Jiminy kick.

'Where are they?' demanded the head Jimp. 'The life forms.'

'They aren't here. They have gone,' replied Jiminy, teeth also bared and waving his head to either bite or sink a pronged tooth into another.

'You let them escape?'

'We were asleep when they snuck out.'

'Where did they go?'

'To the Pool of Pududdles.'

'They won't get past those slimy reeds. Jiminy, you are ordered to capture the life forms and if you fail, the Claw of Clusters will be invoked and you know that means a very sore lifetime or worse.'

Jiminy took an extra high leap upon hearing those dreaded words.

'I'll do anything to avoid that.'

'Redemption for your misbehaviour can only be achieved by the capture and return of the life forms to the council. You knew that you should not have tried to usurp the council's control over all new life forms. You know the consequences of failure.'

The council jumpers slowly reduced their agitated jumping and snorting and left muttering amongst themselves about how they had fortunately avoided a physical showdown with jumping Jiminy.

Jiminy returned indoors and gathered his family to explain what they must do. He turned angrily and aimed a vicious, claws-erect, kick at Boo for bringing the life forms into their home. Fortunately, being only two feet, damage was avoided. Trouble with a capital T now existed for him. The Claw of Clusters was far worse than having to work for a living.

'The hunt is on. We must capture those life forms. If not, the choice available won't be our favourite playtime. It will be work, or the Claw of Clusters. Jaminy, those life forms are nothing but trouble. You must decide whether it's family or them, it's your choice.'

Jaminy, alias Boo, began to jump higher and exaggerate his tricky foot movements. Suddenly, his forgotten claws sprung to attention and he was now the feet again of a nasty, jumping Jimp.

'Let's kick backside,' he blurted out.

'It's decided. We're to stick together like glue and hunt down those troublesome life forms.'

The Jimps jumped excitedly at the prospect of a hunt. An ancient custom like this had almost been forgotten. They salivated at the opportunity. It was a chance to also prove how nasty they could be.

'To the Pool of Pududdles.'

Grunt grasped his necklace as he stood up. A sharp twinge of pain took a ride through one hand. The rake point on his necklace was razor sharp. As it pricked a finger, he became momentarily paralysed. He stood like a stone monument. Strange visions rumbled through his mind picturing for him a whirlwind of pathways to follow. A voice tried to tell him something. Just at the climactic point of delivery, it converted into a wispy mist. Nothing intelligible emanated; however, he saw a vision of a creek bed head into the distance then disappear. Was it an omen to follow?

'Mr Grunt, Mr Grunt, are you dizzy?' asked a concerned Davidia. She felt Grunt was about to topple over just like the great statues of the despots of the world when they were thrown out of office. 'You better sit down before you fall down. Dad always said grown-ups need rest during the day. Are you a grown-up in your world?'

Grunt had no answer.

'What do we do now? We're lost. There are no shops or malls here in which to meet friends. There's a lot of nothing but open countryside with nowhere to go. I don't like this place.' Davidia's bottom lip began to sag.

Grunt thought for a moment. This thought had extra company so it could be converted into a plan. His eyes scanned the terrain. He stood up. A couple of his legs began to gently thump the ground like beating a base drum in rhythm. The ground seemed to come alive with the thumping. Grunt had unknowingly triggered an ancient communication power all his ancestors possessed. The Thumpering. The ground acted as a communication highway once the special thump had been awakened.

'Is that music, Mr Grunt? It sounds like drums.'

Batbit sat quietly. His busybee wings needed recuperative time. The beating ground was very restful. He didn't have to fly anywhere.

Grunt stood legs apart with his feet firmly planted on the ground like a telephone pole and waited. Around his waist, a circle of skin pores wheezed in and out pulsating to the rhythmic thump. Grunt immediately stopped the thumping. Shortly, it all became quiet. Once again he scanned the countryside. The Pool of Pududdles had now become an empty creek bed, but it did extend along the valley. Were his visions guiding him where to go?

Far away on the other side of the ex Pool of Pududdles, the Jimp posse was jumping its way toward them. Jiminy had enlisted the assistance of Jergess, the head of the council's enforcement regime. He was a huge, awful, vicious brute at least half the size again of a normal Jimp. The Claw of Clusters was under his guardianship also. He delighted in the bad treatment of anything, fellow Jimps included. A good kicking was an aphrodisiac for fun. If Jiminy failed to capture Grunt and friends, then Jergess would invoke the Claw of Clusters well away from the village. Jiminy would never return and the myth status he enjoyed would be perpetuated and enhanced. In reality, the Claw of Clusters was a mythical cover for Jergess, the Jimp assassin. There was some serious jumping to do if they wanted to catch Grunt and Davidia. It seems that Batbit was too small to be good for anything except perhaps a tasty snack.

'That way,' said Grunt, pointing with a few hands. 'The underground whisper is that once the Pool of Pududdles has disappeared, there is only one chance of escape, which is given as a reward for removing such a nasty, devious, trapping device. The creek bed is a funnel of information. The ground tremor that my feet had created indicates that the way along the creek bed is the way to go. It's a sign.'

'It looks like a long way. My mum and dad sometimes took me for a walk in the forest. This should be fun.' Davidia slipped away, full of happy feelings now that she was no longer in conflict with her stomach.

Batbit was always on alert for danger. He knew capture could be imminent if they let their guard down. He took to the skies searching for any danger signs. There in the distance he could see a hopping party headed their way. It was the jumping Jimps. He let out an almighty warning screech.

'Those dopey Jimps are jumping our way. We must keep moving,' warned the flying tidbit.

'Let's move it.'

'I'll stall them,' said Batbit. 'I have a cunning plan.'

Batbit would need all his combative skills, guile and know-how to stall the Jimps who were much larger life forms than himself. He took off quicker than a wink. The Jimp chasers had grown into quite a number. The excitement of a hunt had conjured up their imagination, which was usually a blank page.

'What are we chasing?' chorused a few.

'Unemployment for Jiminy.' A roar of approval erupted. No

Jimp worked. It was the ideal reason for a pursuit. The group snorted and grunted more wildly as they jumped.

Batbit couldn't be seen in flight and he possessed a nasty pair of sharp teeth. He attacked from the rear, landed on a Jimp rump and bit hard. The following Jimp fleetingly saw him and kicked at him. He missed Batbit, but not the fellow Jimp. The same action was quickly repeated a few times. The Jimps stopped the jumping chase and began to kick each other in retaliation for what they thought was one of their own clan causing rump pain. Batbit was satisfied with his battle plan for delay. He last saw the furry jumpers arguing and kicking each other.

'That will keep them occupied for awhile.' He flew back to Grunt and Davidia who were walking along the creek bed. 'We are safe for a while. Those Jimps are otherwise occupied.'

'I'm tired,' said Davidia. Her legs were finding the pebbles difficult to walk over.

'We can stop for a short while. We don't know where this valley leads to, and besides, we must keep in front of those jumping Jimps.'

A short distance ahead, a small rocky outcrop jutted into the centre of the creek bed. It looked like it would provide a welcome resting place.

'Over there, we can sit on those rocks.' Davidia pointed to them. 'I miss my mum and dad. When can I go home?'

'Let's try and leave this place first,' said a disgruntled Grunt, who had never dealt before with a twelve year old human girl. There were many things he didn't understand about her.

'That spot is ideal,' said Davidia, making a dash for it. Just as she was leveraging her backside into position for a full resting place, a few rocks crumbled under her feet.

'You can't sit there, that place is taken.'

'Who said that?'

'I did. You can't sit there either, or there, it's all taken. There is no seating space for you to sit. This isn't a public resting amenity. I'm part of nature and I don't need your bum to tamper with my precarious situation.'

Davidia glanced around in the hope of seeing the speaker. She could have sworn the rocks spoke to her.

'But, we're tired and need to rest.'

'Find somewhere else.'

'Who are you?' asked Davidia.

'Don't ask any further questions otherwise I'll tell a lie.'

'You can't do that. Bad things happen when they are told.' Davidia was only armed with the truth; a lie was off her linguistic radar. 'I'm going to sit on you, whether you like it or not.'

The weight of her slight frame pressed down hard on the rocks. A few of the rocks crumbled and split.

'Now look what you have done. I am falling apart. I am crumbling. I cannot keep it together. At least I was safe under the water. Exposed to the elements I'll dry out and collapse. Something removed it off me.'

'Was the water from the Pool of Pududdles?'

'Yes. How did you know?'

'An evil wind took it.'

'That means that something has crossed the Pool of Pududdles for the first time. Did you cross it safely?'

'Yes.'

'Then it's your fault. You can't sit on me.'

'Yes, I can and I am, so there.'

In a matter of moments, Davidia felt a movement underneath her. The rocky outcrop was collapsing and crashing into the creek bed to form pebbles. She came crashing to the ground with the fragile rocks. It was suddenly gone, poof, like the wind.

'Now there's nowhere to sit,' she complained.

Grunt felt that they were running out of time. One look down the valley creek bed confirmed their temporary advantage. Water was once again filling the Pool of Pududdles and soon it would flow into the creek bed and sever their proposed escape route. Nothing seemed to make sense. 'All is not as it seems,' kept filtering through his mind. Grunt finally realised that tricks were constantly being played on them to fall into a trap. He also saw a series of splashes heading their way. The Pool of Pududdles held no fear for the Jimps when it was almost empty.

'Time to move,' he said.

They clambered over the pebbled creek bed, constantly heading upstream. Water in the valley often flowed uphill so they had to move quickly. After a short time, they came across a clump of very tall trees on the edge of the creek bed. They waved gently in the breeze that didn't exist. Batbit flew high above them to ensure that there were no traps set. He landed on the tallest. The view over the valley was fantastically beautiful, only spoilt by the nasty Jimps.

Adult Jimps were unable to climb trees. It had to do with loss of the youthful flexibility of their limbs. Their massive teeth were also a hindrance. They often speared branches at ground level and snapped them off. However, their determination was boundless. Their huge, blade tooth doubled as a saw to raze small bushes to the ground.

Batbit returned and landed on Grunt's shoulder.

'It seems safe. Climb that tallest tree over there. At least we would be safe for a while. If we stay at ground level, they will overtake us shortly and slavery would be our deliverance.'

They sprinted like athletes in a victory sprint. They climbed the tree in a thrice. Davidia felt that she was her brother Dan as she scaled each branch. Perched high in the branches, they felt safe. It wasn't long before the angry, snorting, jumping Jimps arrived and congregated around the base of the tree.

'They are as good as ours,' snarled Jergess. 'I get first kick at them; any objections?'

Jiminy felt he was saved.

'We can't climb trees. How will we get them down?'

Jergess had a bag full of tricks. He wasn't only an assassin based on his ugly looks. Experience had taught him many devious tricks to capture foe; however, such thoughts often didn't live in the mind of ordinary Jimps.

'We use our blade tooth. If it needs sharpening, select a pebble and run it the length, this way.' The Jimps were in awe. 'Once it's at perfect sharpness it will saw through the trunk; however, we have to cut it at this height. With each jump a thrust is made.' He demonstrated the art of tree-blade cutting. 'Work in tandem. It will take all dark to cut it down.' The group snorted with delight. 'Get started, I need some rest.'

'I haven't worked before,' moaned a new adult Jimp.

Jergess jumped menacingly forward. The Jimp thought he was going to be kicked into another valley.

'You stupid mass of fur, weren't you paying attention? For those of you who haven't experienced work, I will show you once more only.' He stuck out his huge blade, jumped at the tree and neatly sliced a narrow mark on the trunk. 'Now repeat that until it falls.'

The trio sat patiently on the treetop waiting their fate. Escape seemed hopeless. The only way was down. The Jimp lumberjacks began their task.

'Mr Grunt, what happens if we fall or the tree is cut down?' asked Davidia, wanting to be home safely tucked in bed at this very moment. 'It's a long way down.'

Grunt sighed with concern. He glanced over the land-scape. It was a desolate, living rockery, except for the Pool of Pududdles. His ideas bag had holes in it. They had all escaped through the perforations. Directly opposite them on the other side of the creek bed was the only rock formation that inter-rupted the flatness of the land.

Grunt felt his necklace as a comfort toucher. His hand tingled. With another hand, he gripped tightly onto a branch as all his other body extremities receded inwards, leaving him ball shaped. More weird feelings filled his emotional basket. A voice boomed inside his head, 'Be safe, my son,' then vanished.

'Don't fall, Mr Grunt,' said a worried Davidia, as rounded shapes usually rolled somewhere and from high in the tree-tops, it was only one way down.

Grunt was jerked back to reality as his large frame began to move precariously. He was greeted with the sound of jumping, squabbling Jimps.

'They are certainly working into a frenzy,' he said, as he glanced between his legs down the long trunk.

'What's that over there?' said Davidia, pointing to the rock formation. In the light, minute signals flashed across the val-ley as the sun's reflective rays struck at the right angle. The bright light acted as a warning device because they now took notice of it. 'It looks like a rock jewel. Maybe it's diamonds. My mum promised me one when I turned thirteen. She said the only thing brighter than a diamond was my dad. I didn't understand it.'

'Maybe that's it,' said Grunt. 'I have been having visions that the valley would lead us to safety. That configuration of rocks is in a cluster group.'

'What does that mean?'

'A group of items close together.' Grunt concentrated his

eyes on the rocks. Each vision was slowly merged into one frame. 'That group of rocks on the far right-hand side has the closest cluster group.' He wondered whether there were any ejector stones within the rocks and, if so, would they be revealed to him? 'We won't be here for much longer. When the tree begins to topple, be ready.'

'I don't want to fall,' wailed Davidia.

'I feel we will be safe. Hang onto my hand when it happens. Those Jimps will get a fright of their own. Batbit, fly down and see how they are progressing.'

Being a mischievous bat when least expected, he flew through the group shrieking loudly. One Jimp jumped in fright and got his blade stuck in the tree trunk. He hung like a limp piece of washing. Another jabbed a fellow Jimp, who in turn attacked him, scything his head with his sharp teeth. Panic set in for a moment.

'Stop,' yelled Jergess, feeling the pressure of having to manage such a stupid bunch of Jimps. 'Keep working.' The group settled.

An unfortunate Jimp had the misfortune to laugh at the wrong moment. Any sense of humour he may have possessed was smartly kicked out of him.

'By dark, they will have cut through. We cannot let Davidia fall into their clutches.'

They all hung onto the lush foliage. Dark descended. Darkness became a friend. Apprehension was high. Suddenly, a loud crackling sound grew. It echoed throughout the valley. The village Jimps heard what they believed would be the fatal sounds of capture. The tree began to tilt dangerously. Grunt took hold of Davidia's hand. The Jimps couldn't see them in the dark. The creaking, crackling sound grew stronger. The Jimps began jumping higher than before with the expectation of capturing the new slaves. Grunt used his spinning powers of invisibility and spun them out of trouble, safely landing amongst the rock formations. Finally the tree fell across the creek bed and splintered on the rocks. The Jimps jumped for joy. Winners all around. The Jimps ran wildly to where the new slaves would have landed, ready to claim the first prize as if it was a carnival spinning wheel. All they found was shattered tree ends, splintered branches and no life forms.

'Where are they?' bellowed Jergess, who blew up like a balloon in anger. 'Find them or I'll rip your fur from head to rump, then try and see if you can keep warm.' He certainly wasn't giving instructions on a course in good manners. 'Scatter, spread out, but catch them. If not, the consequences are not my responsibility.'

The Jimps fled and scattered like dandelion seeds in a serious wind. They searched in the dark in every crook and cranny where a life form could hide. That dark, the sound of scuffing feet, rock falls and yelling lasted until next light. All they came up with was a big fat zip; nothing. Convinced that the life forms had escaped, they reported back to Jergess, who was now pumped up in anger at failure.

'Impossible. They couldn't escape.'

'They have vanished. Not even a sniff of the wind could locate them.'

Jergess had no choice but to invoke the Claw of Clusters. He began an incantation of unintelligible sounds, hunched his body over as if in pain and spread his arms on the ground. His legs continued jumping as his body began to split open and double in size. His foot claws became two huge clamps. The hapless jumping Jiminy was nearby.

'The price of failure is yours. The Claw of Clusters has been implemented. Let this be a lesson to all of you. Never betray the council.'

Jergess stood tall. He was more frightening than before. He grabbed Jiminy on his rump with one almighty claw and squeezed hard. Jiminy let out a squeal of fear. He was banished. His jumping Jimp days were over. Jergess tossed him into the Pool of Pududdles to be swallowed by the murky, mud reeds; the fate he had in store for Grunt and Davidia. The last sight of Jiminy was gurgle, gurgle, gurgle, glob into the Pududdle mud.

Throughout the whole ordeal, Jaminy (Boo) had kept his distance. He didn't believe they had escaped, because he knew the ejector stones that returned him safely home might exist nearby. Jergess had regained his normal life shape and form. Jaminy approached him.

'They are still here, I feel it,' he said.

Jergess had no faith in a pair of talking feet and ignored his pleas.

'A storm is brewing. If I were you, I'd return home. The dark won't be a time to be enjoyed out in the open. Go home and kick butt.'

'Jiminy was my dad.'

'Rules are rules.' Jergess leapt away.

Jaminy knew that if he could find Grunt and Davidia, it would be compensation for the loss of his dad. He became the revengeful, nasty Jimp he had always been. Friends were a past passage in his life.

'Is it clear?' asked Davidia. Silence surrounded them. They had sought refuge under an overhanging cliff.

Batbit flew upwards, scanned the horizon and saw that there wasn't a Jimp in sight.

'It's all clear.'

Grunt and Davidia climbed out from their hiding place.

'Now what?' asked Davidia.

Grunt was seeking guidance from his necklace when a pair of small feet hopped onto his path. It was Boo.

'You didn't outsmart me,' he snarled. 'You'll pay for the loss of my dad.' Somehow, he had sent a location signal to the Jimp village and suddenly in the distance a massive crowd of uncontrollable jumping Jimps headed their way. The sight scared the life out of them. Behind them, a huge storm followed with the eyes of the Sinister above a mouth prepared to blow a tornado of destruction if they escaped again. The frightening scene had no end.

'You betrayed us,' said Grunt, upset that a friend had changed sides.

'I was never your friend, just a forgetful Jimp.'

The rock formation gave one final reflective glint. Davidia was struck by the beauty and intensity of its rays.

'Mr Grunt, follow me,' whispered Davidia. 'I saw something bright and it wasn't a Jimp. Over here.' She and Grunt moved sideways to a rock formation from where the brightness had emanated.

'You can't escape. It's my turn to kick butt,' yelled the bloody pest, Boo, who had turned into a formidable antagonist.

Their fate was staring down and bounding toward them. Grunt sat down, somewhat deflated. Was there a final gasp of hope that they wouldn't end up as a Jimp slave? He felt an unusual prodding formation dig into his body. Had he been nudged by an intruder? The bright light that Davidia had seen came from those very same rocks. It was from a close-knit cluster of five. He grabbed his necklace and caressed the sharp pointy rake. A gap in his brain opened and a positive thought from the past entered. 'Seize the moment, press ahead.' He instantly stood up. Were they the ejector stones from the past? He bent down pretending to fall over due to his large frame.

'You can't hide behind such a small rock,' mimicked Boo, who began to annoy Davidia. She picked up a solid twig that had fallen off the splintered tree.

'Do you know what baseball is, Boo?' she politely asked. She used the stick as a club and took a few practice swings.

'Never heard of it,' he replied.

'It's a secret ritual life forms play in my world as a final salute if captured by a foreign life form. Come closer. I'll show you.'

Dopey Boo did as advised. He had no reason to believe he was in harm's way. After all, this was his valley and the life forms had no chance of escape; the Jimps were closing in.

'Stand there. I'll show you how it works. My mum and dad took me to baseball each weekend and I was taught how to dispense a pitcher to the outer field.' Boo stood nearby and, suddenly, with an almighty swipe – he didn't see it coming – Davidia thwacked one foot so hard, it flew into the Pool of Pududdles. Her second swipe sent his second foot there as well. 'They were my first two home runs. Mum and dad will be pleased,' she said.

Grunt and Batbit were stunned with this intelligent girl life form. She was such an ideas girl.

'He won't be kicking my butt,' she said proudly. 'High fives all around, guys.'

A rumbling sound similar to thunder was coming closer. The ground was awash with the vibrations of the jumping Jimps. The Sinister closely observed the land form activity. He could only step in if ground failure was imminent. Today, he was confident the Jimps would succeed.

Grunt indicated that he had located the ejector stones, thanks to Davidia. He had one of his hands at the ready.

'Davidia, bend down like me.' She immediately obeyed. Batbit clung onto her dress. The showdown was set. In an instant the Jimps had them surrounded. They were heaving, puffing and showing signs of exhaustion, almost heart attack material.

'You cannot escape,' remarked a puffed head Jimp.

'We haven't enjoyed your hospitality, so we must leave,' said Grunt, still bending over.

'Seize them,' he ordered.

'Be careful.' Grunt pushed hard on the five cluster stones and remarkably they reacted. A huge hole in the ground opened up into which the Jimps stumbled. Grunt, Davidia and Batbit were once again hurled into the atmosphere.

The last thing they remembered was the Sinister being upset and howling with rage.

The Irrids felt the winds of change. So far, the signal from the past had succeeded in passing safely through two valleys. This wasn't over.

5. VALLEY OF UNDONKO

zzt, left, bzzt, right, bzzt, forward, bzzt backward, bzzt stand still, bzzt raise arms, bzzt move legs, bzzt stop.

Training school was in progress for the new range of drone robots fresh off the assembly line. They were being put through their electronic paces. Each robot had to be programmed to learn the electronic commands that would make it obey every instruction correctly. Faulty workmanship was banned and not tolerated. Any robot that malfunctioned was immediately stripped down and reassembled. There was no place for imperfection. These robots were commonly known as Blenders because they were gender-neutral.

In the Valley of Undonko, the master managers were the Minjans, a specialty robot that controlled all valley life from the Steel Tower of Minjocan. It was a mystery how the robots came into existence in the valley, but it was thought that a star galaxy in the universe had burst a seam and spewed out these mechanical space explorers. They had been in residence a very long time, based on the sophistication of their equipment and robot development.

As with all new technology, a few mishaps such as incorrect wiring occasionally occurred. These robotic misfits were called Untonks. If located, they were sent to the Circle of Hotto and thrown in to rust in a mechanical graveyard. The

Circle of Hotto was a hot spring, which accomplished metal breakdown extremely efficiently due to a special mineral element in it. Eventually, they would be reclaimed, recycled and reused to be a productive product once again, but this time in a proper robotic form.

To progress from Untonk to Blender was a Minjan master reconfiguration electronic achievement. Whilst the Untonks were on the loose, they often became very mischievous. Commands from the Steel Tower of Minjocan were often intercepted by an Untonk, who then relayed the message to a Blender with conflicting instructions. The Minjans hated the interference in their playground and if message tampering was discovered, then that Untonk was immediately dispensed with. However, one such Untonk called Unitse had inadvertently been incorrectly wired and was credentialed with artificial intelligence, where it could act completely independently. The Minjans knew a mistake was out there, but had no idea which one it was. It was the goal of Unitse to free all robots, give them artificial intelligence and enjoy a rust-free life bzzting everywhere.

The Minjans aimed for perfection. When another life form entered their valley, it was normally sent for breakdown and analysis. If it wasn't a metallic, metal, mechanical life form, then such a process was a disaster, because once pulled apart it was impossible to rebuild. Living life forms, if caught, were in mortal danger. Mechanical life forms could be reconfigured in many ways. They lived on electrical charges and powerful batteries in their system. To be plugged or unplugged; that is the survival question.

'I've got a headache from all this swirling and twirling,' complained Davidia as she hurtled through space.

'Those ejector stones have saved us again,' said Grunt, spinning like a top.

Batbit held on tightly with his tiny claws. He missed Mrs Batbit.

Like a materialising mirage, a landscape below them appeared. In an instant, the eagles had landed directly in an alleyway. They tumbled along the shiny, metal surface. Davidia enjoyed the slide, believing them to have arrived at a giant fun park. Finally, they halted at the end of an alley up against a wall.

'Anyone hurt?' asked Davidia. 'Miss Percival and I can bandage you, if needed.'

One of her favourite pastimes was role-playing with Miss Percival. Had she been here, she would have known what to do.

'All of me is here,' replied Grunt.

'Where's Batbit? Oh, there you are, under my armpit and hanging on. We're safe now.'

Batbit was slightly dazed. His small brain didn't cope too well with all the tumbling. It could have become misplaced.

'Where have we ended up this time?'

'It certainly is all one metallic grey colour,' said Grunt. He knew his colours from the Valley of Preciousness, where they had many. Here, there could possibly be only one, with slight variations. His hands rubbed the walls of the alley. They felt cold to touch and devoid of any warmth. Davidia did the same.

'It feels like one of dad's saw blades after he has cleaned them,' she said.

The trio walked slowly along the alley to the other end where it opened up into a wider version of what they were walking in.

A bzzt, bzzt, sound walked past, immediately followed by

another burst of bzzt, bzzt. They staggered backwards in surprise. A few of the Blender robots were out exercising their mechanical systems. They couldn't communicate what they were doing with other life forms. Orders from within their system, sent by the Minjans, directed their behaviour. A small camera on their helmets recorded all vision as they moved. Fortunately they hadn't been seen. They watched the slow-paced robots walk in a staggering fashion, without ever overbalancing. They were the perfect servant. The Minjans, in their historic travels, had seen various different sized life forms and had created their own range from small to large.

'It's a mobile mechano set. My brother Dan has one. He didn't let me play with it. Can we play with these?' asked Davidia. 'It would be so cool.'

Before anyone could reply, Davidia had walked in front of one. It bzzted to a stop.

'Hello, my name is Davidia, what's yours?' she said, ever so politely. Her mum and dad had taught her that good manners should always be used when first greeting a stranger.

The Blender stood still. It tilted its head forward with a small bzzt. The camera was refocused so that the Minjans could see what halted its movement. Imagine their surprise when a weird life form, none the like of which they had ever seen before, stood in front in a yellow, dishevelled dress.

'What are you staring at, metallic man?' asked Davidia, annoyed that there was no response.

Bzzt, bzzt was all that was said. The Blender raised its arm and grabbed her by her arm and began to lift her.

'You aren't going to bully me.' Davidia swung her other arm in a circle, latched onto a few loose wires and tugged real hard. The Blender suddenly stopped with a long bzzzzzt and released her. It stood motionless. The camera shut down.

The Minjans were furious that something had interfered with one of their perfect machines. Maybe it was a strange Untonk that had regenerated unbeknown to everyone. It had acted independently. They had to have it for analysis. They despatched a special collection group called the Recons that consisted of the specialist recyclers. They were specially formed from the better metallic materials because of the repossession tasks they had to undertake. Sole control of these better-produced robotic models was under the sole command of the Minjocans. Each Recon had a prod rod to immobilise all Blenders and Untonks. It emitted a small electrical charge, which shut down the robot's electrical circuit. To recharge, the robots had to be plugged in during the dark in the Aisles of Rest.

'They aren't much fun, Mr Grunt. Where shall we go? I know; find a fast food outlet; I'm sure there must be one here somewhere.'

They all looked around puzzled, wondering in what direction they should head. The streets had a similarity about them. The city design was that it was built in perfect squares, radiating out from the centre to large and larger squares. There were no shops, malls, parks, valleys, or rocks to climb, anywhere. All buildings were made of the same steel-like substance, which remained at a constant temperature. Describing it as strange didn't do it justice.

'Everything looks identical,' said Grunt. 'I've never seen anything like this before.'

Batbit stretched his wings and flew down a few streets for orientation. Because it was all the same, he lost his sense of direction and couldn't find Grunt and Davidia. The city was a lonely and foreboding place. This tiny little defenceless bat was now all alone. He began to shake with fear.

'There's not even a decent foothold to hang upside down on to. It's all so slippery.'

In the distance, he heard a bzzt, bzzt coming closer. He hid in a doorway, hoping the bzzter would ignore him. Today, his luck was at the bottom of the bucket. The bzzt he had heard stopped directly in front of him. A short bzzt and the camera had him in focus.

'It wasn't me, it was him,' he involuntarily yelled in fear, pointing his batwing in the direction of the pretend life form.

The robot bzzt, bzztd in response. It made no movement toward him at all. It stood there motionless. Batbit waited for the final blow or even worse, capture. When he opened his eyes, the robot had a quizzical look on his face. No robot that he was aware of could do that. He looked again. It had an arm extended toward him in greeting. Bzzt, bzzt, it encouraged. Batbit outstretched a wing in greeting. The robot's steely fingers grasped the batwing very gently. It bzztd a few times as it internally processed the greeting ritual. It determined that it was harmless. The robot moved toward the wall where a socket plug was located. There were many of these along the streets. It plugged in a finger and a small screen lit up on the street wall. It contained a message. Batbit fortunately could read, a skill not many bats possessed. He was a well-educated bat. In the caves back at The Rock of Yocklaw, a mimic taught him how to copy languages and recognise different shapes to mean different things. He was now analysing shape meanings. The screen said, 'I'm Unitse.' Batbit tried to plug in the end of one wing and received a small electric shock which threw him backwards. It felt as if he had received a rebuke for something naughty. Batbit used his high frequency voice as a responder. The robot bzztd and turned around, with one finger still plugged in. He analysed Batbit's shriek. On the screen it said, 'I'm Batbit.'

Unitse was the Untonk robot all Minjans were searching for and here was Batbit engaging in dialogue with a hunted object. The two newest best friends explained to each other who and what they were. That small screen did a lot of message flickering. Batbit was now aware that Unitse was a rogue robot the Minjan rulers wanted to capture and reprogram. However, the freedom that Unitse felt was so good that he wanted to retain it and promote it to his fellow robots. Having someone else to direct all your movements in life was a bit tiresome. It was time for robotic changes. Batbit was impressed that artificial intelligence had progressed to independence.

Unitse explained that he purposely followed many Minjan directions so the deception would not be discovered. He pretended to be a Blender. Batbit was impressed with Unitse's game of cat and mouse, if only he knew what it was.

Before Unitse unplugged himself, he signalled that he would lead Batbit back to his friends. 'Bzzt, bzzt, this way.' Unitse walked slowly at an absolute doddle of a pace. Batbit sat just above the camera so no one could frame him. In a few minutes after walking along identical streets they encountered a worried Grunt and Davidia.

'This is no time to play hide and seek,' scolded Davidia. She was worried that she had almost lost her smallest friend. Grunt didn't have an emotional card to play. He accepted whatever occurred. He didn't know what true emotion was at this stage, but feelings that ebbed and flowed throughout his body when he touched his necklace kept pressing him into unfamiliar territory. Perhaps it was emotional development.

A few other Blenders could be heard bzzting along the street. Unitse gave a final bzzt and walked off amongst his fellow drones. He waddled off as a drone mass representative with no other aim in life other than to be told what to do. He obviously hadn't heard of mothers-in-law. It was difficult to act like an obedient servant when he believed his powers had more to offer in a robotic life. His secret was safe with the trio of life forms who were in no way mechanical. If they were captured and attempted to be pulled apart for analysis, it would be their doom. The street felt strange and sullen.

'They could certainly brighten the place up with a dash of colour,' said Davidia. 'It feels so miserable here.'

Grunt agreed. The dark colours generated feelings of misery, low self-esteem and boring with a capital B. A robot had no emotional feelings, so it didn't matter what they did or how they acted. If real emotion could be introduced via their recharging system, it may improve their life style and bzzt, bzzt with more animation.

The drone that Davidia had disabled hung around like loose change unable to be spent. Davidia studied its structure.

'It's nicely built, much better than my brother, Dan's, mechanical set.' She pushed it with one hand. It responded with a low-charge bzzt as its battery system exhorted its last charge. It gave her a fright.

Grunt's skin pores began to moisten. His stress level was rising. In the distance he could hear via his group of ears a fast paced bzzt, bzzt and extra bzzts heading in their direction. It sounded like an electrical storm consumed in emitting aggressive lightening shards. The Recons were armed with their prod rods ready to poke and probe at anything they desired that needed a prod. Nothing had ever thwarted their armoury before. Grunt's watery condition worsened. Droplets pushed by gravity began to fall from his circumference. A small puddle developed. He thought he might be producing his own version of the Pool of Pududdles. A small rivulet ran down the centre of the shiny street. They stood mesmerised at the closing sounds of electrical activity. The Recons suddenly appeared from around the corner waving their prod rods as sticks of authority. They saw Grunt and Davidia standing there ready to greet them. They stopped.

'Bzzt, bbbzzt, bzzzt, bzt,' said one Recon to the other.

'Bbbzttt, bzzztt, bzt,' replied the other.

'Bzt, bzt, bzt?' asked the first one of them. The other nodded its head in the direction of Davidia.

'Bzzzt, bbzztt, bbbbbzt,' it replied.

It was agreed that the new life forms needed to be analysed; however, capture came first. They charged their prod rods with an electrical charge by placing them into a socket plug in the wall, and then fired them into the air to confirm their working capacity. It was time to charge and take control of the situation. They saw their non-functioning Blender stooped over in a ready-to-fall position. Unfortunately for them, they stood in the small water rivulet and slipped over on the steely street. Their charged prod rods fired in error and both Recons received a dose of electrical poisoning. Sparks flew like a fireworks display as their systems shut down. Metal, electricity and water were a lethal mix.

'Bzzzzzzt, bzzzzzt, bzzzzt, bzzzt, bzzt, bzt, bt, b ..., then silence. The prod rods hung limply by their side, all battered out with their charges fully expended. The Minjans in the Steel Tower of Minjocan were absolutely staggered that their finest recyclers had failed. The final image their cameras projected was of a chubby, round, bowling ball, washing itself with watery drips. Davidia watched with scant amusement.

'They haven't learnt to walk properly yet. The locals all

seem to stagger when they step anywhere. We didn't get to meet them,' she sighed. The Valley of Undonko was certainly boring entertainment for her. 'Where do we go from here? Any clues, Mr Grunt?'

His ideas book was floating in the clouds. They were also grey. Would his necklace guide them? He shook his body as a dog does when its fur is waterlogged. Batbit shrieked in anger as he was given a bat bath. Davidia smiled. At least it was a distraction from dullsville.

Grunt gingerly ran his necklace through some fingers. He wasn't sure what message it would transmit. Each time he had touched it, strange unknown feelings began to well up inside him. As a guardian of good, these feelings had been hidden from him for a long time. Faint memories of family slipped through with the hope of adorning his mental mantelpiece. Hope for what? He hadn't yet discovered the true message or meaning of the necklace. It acted as a guide rope on a danger- ous journey over the crevices of life. Once again he sat down and all his body extremities closed inwards to form his round bulbous shape. Before he could settle into a world of myths and moments, he felt a small hand shove him in his side. The world began to rotate as he found himself rolling along the street bouncing off the walls.

'Mr Grunt, Mr Grunt,' yelled Davidia, aghast that she had unintentionally set a monster marble tumbling along the street. She had placed her hand on Grunt to feel how wet he was when, whoosh, she set him in motion. Grunt rumbled along ending up at the end of the street and banging into one of the Blender houses. Its magnetised doors sprung open to reveal the liv- ing conditions under which they were placed. Each house was known as The Aisle of Rest, house number so and so.

Grunt was momentarily dazed. His legs and arms popped

out in octopus fashion, waving loosely as he regained his bear-
ings.

'Are you hurt, Mr Grunt?' asked a remorseful Davidia. 'I
didn't mean to do it.'

'It's a piece of apple pie. Delicious, but with not too crispy
a crust,' he replied.

'How do you know about apple pies? Does your world eat
them too?'

'Fast food is so quick that if you don't swallow quickly, it
will run away from you.'

'But you don't eat that. My world does.'

'Roses are red, violets are blue, friends are near and so are
you.'

'Mr Grunt you have had a nasty, bumpy roll.'

'Is it buttered or plain?'

'Batbit, I think Mr Grunt is not himself. He refers to things
in my world. How would he know that?'

Batbit just shrugged his tiny wings as he sat on Grunt who
couldn't roll any further.

The Irrids felt the tremor in Grunt's necklace. Its messaged
signal was enough to put them on high alert. Its strength was
gradually increasing in power. A closeness to their territory
was evolving and it wasn't appreciated. What were they afraid
of?

'Damn! Those brainless life forms have made it through
the Valley of Rintslip.'

A pair of almond shaped eyes dripped venom. Her demons
were failing her. She needed an extra clever, devious and manic
demon of such strength that nothing could withstand its power.

'I have a special treat for those in the Valley of Undonko. Unleash the Doof Doof beast. It will drive them insane. My ill winds haven't worked, but my next demon will destroy their minds in endless, high explosive sound.'

She allowed herself a few hums. With arms folded across her breast, she brooded. 'I dare them to reach here.'

A short time elapsed before Grunt regained his sanity marbles, which had fallen out of their small pouch. There was no message from the necklace. If there was one, it had been interrupted. Grunt peered through the doorway of the house. He checked the door for any traps.

'Maybe this will tell us something.'

'We haven't been invited in,' said Davidia. 'It's impolite to call unannounced.'

'After my bruising I couldn't care less,' said Grunt who showed a slight sign of aggressiveness.

They walked inside into a long hallway. Overhead, lighting shone brightly. All along the corridor were sensor cameras that tracked their every move. The Minjans were immediately alerted.

'They are in house 409. Go. Bring them to the Fatigue Management Factory. Professor Metal can learn about them there.'

Another larger group of Recons were sent to capture them. The previous lot were collected by mobile rust collectors and sent to The Circle of Hotto to rust and then be rejuvenated. No chances would be taken this time. With prod rods primed, success would be theirs.

The Aisle of Rest had on both sides of its corridor, various sized cubicles for different sized robots. These were the sleeping quarters of all Blenders. Each dark, they were securely placed in a fitted cubicle and plugged into a socket for their recharge. They were fed by an injection of soft electrical charges, which would then run their batteries and circuits for a full day. The supply came from a special electrical factory, which supplied the whole valley. Professor Metal was the overseer. He was a very important Minjan.

A switch was tossed and the doors of the Aisle of Rest automatically closed. They were trapped. Not one resident greeted them. They were all out exercising their mechanical prowess.

'What was that noise?' asked Davidia, as she heard the doors bang shut.

'The doors,' said Grunt. 'Soon we will have some unwelcome visitors.'

'They might be the welcoming committee to their city. So far, nothing has spoken to me. It seems rather lonely here.' Her lips began to droop.

'Stay together and we will remain safe.'

Batbit shook his wings.

'Are you scared, Batbit?' asked Davidia.

'Not at all. I was just exercising them. They get cramp, folded up all the time.'

In reality, Batbit had jumped at the loud clang of the closing door, but wanted to appear brave. There was nothing to do but wait. Batbit stuck a wing end into a socket. It didn't give him an electric shock this time. However, it turned on a small wall video screen. It showed the robots in various stages of construction development, from the beginning as a piece of metal and wires to the finished product. Grunt had been blessed with a photographic memory and he scanned the video screen in case it had a future use. He might become a metallurgist, which would be a very useful occupation in The Valley of Undonko.

The Aisle of Rest doors opened with such force that the hinges that held them firm suffered instant metal fatigue and fell off. The doors clattered noisily to the floor. At the entrance stood a dozen Recons all armed with their prod rods, which kept emitting small electrical impulses in case they were needed. They looked like a row of instant firelighters. The leader stepped forward. The others followed.

'Good morning,' said Davidia politely.

The leader felt an electrical vibration, but didn't know what it was. He plugged into a wall socket and the video screens were suddenly ablaze with communicative thoughts, such as with all communication that occurred between Davidia, Grunt and Batbit. Even though Davidia, as a human, had the ability to speak out aloud, which she did often and relentlessly, like all talkative twelve year olds; only her thoughts were transmitted to other life forms.

In a mechanical thought pattern that felt like it had emanated from two steel discs being clanged together, the screens transmitted the Recon thoughts controlled by the leader. Davidia's mind experienced the thoughts that had all been born in an echo chamber. Her head hurt. The leader was able to communicate via the screen's electrical impulses into the minds of the other life forms.

'Who are you and what are you doing here?'

'I'm Davidia, this is Mr Grunt and Batbit is hiding somewhere. We were looking for suitable accommodation. We're tired from our travels,' she replied.

'You must come with us.'

'And if we don't?' replied the stubborn young girl.

'You have no choice.'

Before Grunt and Davidia took another step, the leader poked them with his prod rod on his spare arm. It didn't work.

The electrical charge just fizzed out. They weren't mechanical so it had no effect on them

'That hurt,' said Davidia. 'How would you like it if I poked you hard?'

The leader was confused. A life form that answered back intrigued him. The fact that the prod rod was useless had the Minjans in a quandary. What are they? The Minjans had independent intelligence. They were directed from control to escort them to the Fatigue Management Factory to meet the professor. A guard of honour was formed around them.

'You must come with us.'

Realising that there was nowhere else to go, nothing to eat, no one to talk to, nowhere to sleep and nowhere to enjoy oneself, they reluctantly agreed. At least they wouldn't be prodded again. The leader disengaged his arm from the wall socket and followed his new brood of captives.

The walk was a slow, painful affair to the end of the corridor. It was like extracting teeth.

'Do you have any speed other than slow?' asked an impatient Davidia.

At the front entrance there was a cartage tray with small cubicles on the back.

'Climb into there,' said the leader, with almost the last of his charge.

In front of the tray were four robots, not with legs, but wheels.

'BBBBzzzzTTTT,' the leader instructed to them.

In an instant, the wheels spun automatically and the vehicle sped off to its pre-programmed destination. The road out of the city to Metalside, their version of countryside, was drab and lifeless. A metal world inhabited by nothing but machinery, left a lot to desire in décor living. Robots seemed to walk aimlessly everywhere. All electrical wiring was underground so at least that eyesore wasn't seen.

The ride was smooth and quick. They ended up at a fantastically monstrous factory that spread to the horizon. They alighted and were instantly greeted by an over-enthusiastic professor. His research into electrical and steel matter was legendary in the valley, but all life forms he normally dealt with were always cold. This was his first experience of warm, independent and assumed intelligent life forms that could act totally independently. What they ate was a major consideration. Davidia was more concerned with that aspect too.

The professor wondered how they got there. He put a hand toward Grunt, who felt the question through touch.

'We got caught in a wind shift and landed here. We're from Yocklaw,' he answered.

The professor had no idea where that was, nor did he care; however, an answer was the important thing because it proved the life form could communicate with him.

He motioned them to follow, but he had the capacity to move at walking pace.

'At least he isn't as slow as those other snails,' said Davidia, referring to the Blenders' and Recons' earlier walking efforts.

The interior of the factory was a mass of cables, wiring, sparks, machines, conveyor belts, mobile platforms and Blenders, all performing repetitive tasks.

'What is this place?' asked Davidia.

The professor took hold of one of Davidia's hands. A channel of thought leapt through them both.

'This is the Fatigue Management Centre for the valley. All life-giving power is generated from here. Without this working equipment, no life form can live in the valley.'

'My dad worked in a car factory once and it looked like this.' Davidia temptingly tried to touch an item.

Seemingly from nowhere, an electrical impulse zapped her hand. She jumped in surprise.

'Do not touch. It is protected from any interference,' explained the professor.

Davidia nursed her hand. A tiny, red scar marked the spot. It still held the heat. Miss Percival could fix it, if only she was here.

Grunt was as quiet as a church mouse. He absorbed what he saw and stored it in one of his numerous memory banks. He was as fascinated with the professor's work as he was with him.

'I have a space for me,' the professor advised. 'It is my planning space.' They entered a steel enclosed room, which had no furniture. A small alcove was indented into the wall. The professor explained that all Minjans plugged into special sockets and were fed a different electrical impulse mix. Each Minjan had its own separate steel room in which to be fed or recharged. This gave them greater flexibility and a different design format to all other robots. Davidia and Grunt were lulled into a false sense of security.

'Stay here for a moment; I have an electrical fault to attend to.'

The door was shut tight. From beneath the floor rose a flat slab. The ceiling opened to reveal clear light and a growing crowd standing around a rim above them. The walls fell away to reveal an equipment room full of weird gadgets, some which automatically crept closer. They were caught like rats in a trap and with no cheese. This was actually the inspection room, where any new life form was pulled apart and reassembled if possible. Danger, danger, flashed inside their heads.

All drone robots usually lay flat on the steel slab, whilst the professor and his team disassembled and then rebuilt them. However, Grunt and Davidia were islands of movement within their own right. The Minjans had never experienced this type of mobile, life form before. Grunt thought whispered in a low transmission pattern to Davidia to stand near the recharging alcove. He had confusion to install in the Minjans. The specialist equipment used to pull robots apart was in a fixed position, with extended robotic arms to do the gripping and ripping. Even though Grunt had many arms and legs he intended to keep them all. A long arm with pincer teeth suddenly darted at him. He rolled aside, using his rotund frame to good effect. The leg grapplers made for one of his uprights. He jumped over it. Two Blenders were sent in to subdue his activity. Due to their slowness, Grunt leant over and was able to deftly disconnect a few wires. The Blenders both bzzted to uselessness. The Minjans began to panic. A life form brighter than themselves was unacceptable, let alone believable.

Grunt suddenly picked up a Blender, laid it on the slab and proceeded to disassemble it, much to the amazement of everyone present. He tapped into the specialist equipment, which he used like an expert. Professor Metal had to take a fatigue pill himself. Such intelligence had never been experienced. After a period of time, Grunt laid all the robot parts around the room. He was meticulous in his task. There was no need to damage a perfectly good working product. He paraded around the room like a boxing winner, waving to his adoring fans, only this time his audience wanted to rip him apart. For once the Minjans had magnetised feet and couldn't move. They were metal and awe-struck. They had no instructions to issue.

The professor could only watch and admire the new life form's capability. Grunt sat down, grabbed his necklace and began to make an awful noise. It even scared himself.

Batbit dug his claws harder into Davidia's arm. 'That hurt.'

All Grunt's minute skin pores that leaked water were now bubbling like a hot spring with bubbles that burped. The Minjans wondered whether their world had been infected by idiocy, a condition they didn't understand. Grunt rolled around the floor acting like he was on a pain roller-bed of nails. The scenario almost halted the electrical production of the valley as the signals spread, referring to an uncontrollable, foreign matter. The whole stunt was pure theatre by Grunt. He might have been a thespian in a past life. He let go of the necklace and the lunatic performance stopped. His body was like a wet towel. Water sloshed on the floor. No one dared enter the room. His eyes noticed their concerns. Suddenly, he jumped up in the air to the ceiling as if he had been shot in the rear by a bullet or prodded by a spiky fork. The Minjans stumbled in shock.

'It's attacking us,' they signalled. Pandemonium, not the Russian musician, struck a chord with them all.

Grunt landed safely as he had many legs to choose from. He waved all his arms at once, looking like an octopus in high seas. He walked over to the plug-in alcove and placed one set of fingers in the socket. He lit up like an alien beacon. The video screen on the wall blinked into action. The message read, 'I will now reassemble the Blender.' The screen blanked. He returned to the slab and shut his eyes. He searched his memory compartments for the recorded video he had taken at the Aisle of Rest. Once located, he beamed it around his circumference and he could actually follow the process displayed on his stomach. Logically, he began the reassembling task. The Minjans thought that only a Minjan could possess this knowledge. Slowly the Blender began to take shape. Everything was put perfectly back in place for the Blender to be returned to the boring non-entity it was.

Grunt plugged it into the Minjan socket and it bzzt, bzzt, bzzted back into existence. To show there were no hard feelings, he also reattached the other Blender's disconnected wires. It too bzzt, bzzt, bzzted back into action. For a moment, a glimpse, Grunt could have sworn that both Blenders gave him a quizzical look, exactly like Unitse had to Batbit. Had he altered their life's course? The professor had to have a metal sedative, a.k.a. an increased electrical surge to cope with the miracle he had just witnessed.

'Mr Grunt, I didn't know you were a robot builder,' said an amazed Davidia.

'Neither did I; however, something had to be done.'

The door opened and in walked a pleased, but suspicious, Professor Metal. He had realised that Grunt's capability put him in conflict with his own construction and control programmes. He had decided to get rid of Grunt by inviting him out on an electrical inspection to the Circle of Hotto. There was only room for Minjans to rule in the Valley of Undonko, free from interfering strange life forms.

'By what are you called?' asked the professor, resting a hand on Grunt's arm.

'My name is Grunt.'

'I'm Professor Metal. I manage whatever you see. There is a special training ground further along the valley called the Circle of Hotto. Once a Blender has been reassembled, it's taken there for a final test before it becomes a working machine. They are completely under the control of us Minjans. One day, we hope to leave this valley and explore other valleys or worlds.'

'Are there any mistakes made when rewiring a Blender?' asked Grunt.

Professor Metal's steely eyes closed. His jaw jammed shut so hard that a small screw fell out and his jaw became unhinged.

'Wait here,' he ordered.

'Did you upset him, Mr Grunt? I don't like him much. He doesn't want to play with me. I think he's a bad robot. I'm coming with you to that circle thing,' said a determined Davidia. Seriousness was written all over her face like a front-page headline of a newspaper.

The professor returned with a shield of non-communication between them.

'This way,' the professor indicated.

A mobile transport waited for them. It also had robots in front to drive the vehicle. One drone Blender turned around and gave a quizzical look. Only Davidia noticed. Could it be that Unitse was with them, right under the Minjans' noses? She kept a careful eye for any indication that a 'friend' was with them. Batbit's role was that of passenger. Zip. They were gone.

The Circle of Hotto appeared at the base of a Minjan entertainment centre, which was dominated by a tall, steel tower. It seemed to pierce the sky. The Minjans came here to observe the throwing-in and the last sparks of the Blenders. A robot's life didn't allow too many pleasures. The hot springs rusted all types of metals, but had no effect on live life forms. Professor Metal arrived with his special guests, hoping they would provide an entertaining end to their existence. Steps led down into a series of pools of different depths. Blenders were passed through this series of pools on their way to becoming a rusty, junkyard robot. Grunt and Davidia thought it was a wash or swim time.

'This looks like my dad's spa at home. Dad and mum had it in their bedroom. I wasn't allowed to use it. They said it was too hot. This looks exactly like it.'

Grunt had no idea what a spa was, but the water he saw looked hot. Little wispy, steamy trails filed into the atmosphere playing follow the leader. Batbit disliked water and suddenly let go of Davidia's arm. He settled out of sight on a light railing where he wouldn't be noticed. Unintentionally, because of his positioning and camouflage, he might be the reason no harm would come to either Grunt or Davidia. He could operate as a backroom set of eyes.

'This is a most special place. From here we control all aspects of valley life. See that spire; it's the Steel Tower of Minjocan which dominates the entire valley. Entry is forbidden. Come, I'll show you the Circle of Hotto.'

Professor Metal led them to a series of pools in rooms filled with activity. A chain gang of Minjans were pushing uncooperative Blenders (Untonks) into the waters. As soon as the water touched metal, a small hissing sound, followed by a slight puff of mist, arose. The Untonks rapidly ceased moving as the acidic waters ate away at their structure. It was an unsightly scene. The robots sank beneath the waters. The last sight of them was a quizzical look on their faces. Was that Unitse?

'They don't look very happy,' said Davidia. 'They have all drowned.'

'There is a surprise for you in the next room. Come,' urged Professor Metal.

The doors slowly opened and there stood a huge Minjan with a flashing, red light in the middle of his forehead.

'This is our leader, Metroid.'

Grunt and Davidia refused to move. Metroid gestured with a giant finger, coaxing a forward movement from them. They didn't budge. Grunt sensed danger. Davidia too felt intimidated by his size. Metroid gestured again, this time with his hand. Still there was no movement. He took one step forward, when a flying tastebud flew through the door shrieking. Its sound impacted momentarily by switching off Metroid's flashing, red light. He almost toppled over. Minjans ran around confused by the strange sound that tingled their metal torsos.

'Has something escaped from the Room of Misery?' said Metroid, flashing properly again.

There was no answer.

'You there. I saw you disassemble, then reassemble a Blender. How could you know what to do? Are you a plant working for the Untonks? That is classified information. Are you a traitor? Answer me. Otherwise you will be flung into the Circle of Hotto.'

'What's the Room of Misery?' said a cautious Davidia, interrupting before Grunt could reply.

Metroid's red light stopped flashing and beamed a singular, bright-red light.

'What said that?'

'I did.'

Metroid saw this tiny, pint-sized life form with independent movement. He wondered how it worked.

'You need to be disassembled.'

'I do not,' Davidia replied defiantly.

'All new entrants into the valley are investigated this way. Throw her into the Circle of Hotto, immediately.'

Two Blenders picked up a squawking young girl and carried her to the edge of the first pool. They gently placed her on the steps.

'I don't have a bath with my clothes on,' she said.

One Blender shoved her violently. Davidia fell into the warm pool. She swam around like a fish, gulped a mouthful of water and spurted it out at the Blenders. It splashed on the cold, metal floor. A spot landed on the foot of Metroid and caused an instant burn. His anger vented with a wild arm-swing, which sent both Blenders flying into the same pool, gurgling into non-existence. Davidia continued to swim. Her clothes were being washed and she was enjoying herself.

'Mr Grunt. Come on in, the water's fine.' She spurted out another mouthful of water. It had a slight mineral taste. All robots kept a discreet distance.

Grunt had noted the difference in chemical reaction on the Blenders and Davidia. For the robots it was extermination. For Davidia it was a pleasure. The Circle of Hotto's waters were ineffective on Davidia. After a few minutes, Davidia sat on the steps that were in the pool. No one could touch her. The Minjans were frightened of the evil she possessed. Nothing had ever before survived the pools. Grunt saw an opportunity to barter for their freedom. He spun wildly and splashed into the pool also. He floated like a bubble and bobbed like a cork due to his size and body composition.

'What a pleasure! I haven't done this before. It's fun.'

'At home we call it swimming. Mum and dad took me to lessons when I was two years old. The water tastes a bit funny.' She looked over at the robots. 'Come on in, the water is warm. It's like my parents' spa.' Davidia and Grunt splashed around, spreading water everywhere. The Minjans were dumbstruck. Neither of them rusted, rotted or sunk to the bottom of the pool. These certainly were two very strange life forms. Grunt and Davidia certainly couldn't stay in the pool forever, so a method of compromise was sought.

'Is there any way that we can leave the valley?' asked Grunt, whilst safely in the pool.

'No one ever leaves the valley,' replied Metroid. 'We need to disassemble you and find out what special powers you have so that we might learn from them.'

'So there is no chance of letting us go?'

'None at all. Professor, get them out of there. Pull them

apart. Do your duty. If you fail, you get no renewable electrical charges for two lights and darks.' The Professor knew that missing out would mean that his system would be run down for quite a while.

A huge, robotic, overhead crane that was used for retrieving the rusted robot parts, swung out over the pool. Davidia swam in circles avoiding its pincers. Grunt couldn't swim, but float. He was an easier target. The pincers nabbed him. As he was hoisted upwards, he hung onto his necklace in case it fell off. He had a strange feeling. He hoped it was that he wouldn't fall. His mind went blank. A strange rhythm beat incessantly in his head. It felt like his many brain cells were about to explode. A voice whispered, 'Listen carefully.' A flashing vision of five pulsating objects moving as one, appeared then vanished. He shook his frame, only to find himself on the floor again surrounded by Minjans, not Blenders. Escape was impossible. Davidia was still swimming. Her arms were tiring. She decided that she was clean enough to leave the pool.

'Who has got my towel?'

The Minjans had no idea what a towel was or what she was. They surrounded her as she dripped water on the floor. No one dared touch her whilst wet, otherwise doom would be their next visitor. Soon, she was dry enough to approach.

'That was refreshing. Why don't you all go for a swim? Your skin could certainly do with a shine.'

The Minjans were truly intrigued in a communicating, independent life form. The last mobile transport back to the Fatigue Management Centre had already left. It meant a stay of one dark in the Minjans' quarters, which were dotted around the Steel Tower of Minjocan.

'You will stay with us for one dark and when we have the next light, you will both be examined by me,' said the professor.

'It's not a dental appointment, is it? Have you been speaking to mum and dad? I was supposed to have my teeth checked this week. I hope I don't miss my appointment.'

No robot had any right of reply and here the professor was being badgered by a talking book called Davidia. The trip to the Minjan plug-in socket quarters was via a series of corridors. Batbit was flying quietly above the group. He dived down and landed in Davidia's armpit. His sense of smell was acute, so he knew where he was. He was safe there where no one could see him.

'What's the rounded lump going to do to get us out of this mess?' he said.

'Shush,' said Davidia. 'He's thinking.'

'He won't hurt anything by doing that, will he?'

'I'm sure he has a clever plan. I want to go home.'

Bzzt, bzzt, bzzt could be heard following them. The Minjans paid no attention as Blenders worked everywhere. Bzzt, bzzt, bzzt came closer. A Blender walked past and gave them a quizzical look. Batbit, at that very moment, peered out from odour heaven and noticed that it was Unitse. He pushed out a wing in greeting. Unitse recognised his friend. At the end of a long corridor there was a T intersection. The Minjans were expected to turn left toward their quarters. Unitse, by this time, was in front of Grunt and brushed his arm as he drew level with him. An explosion of kaleidoscopic proportions erupted in his head. One hand grabbed the U in his necklace and a word zipped down the slide of memory and said, 'messenger.' Grunt turned to see Unitse walking quicker than all the other robots. He was to be a decoy and lead the Minjans away from Davidia and Grunt, who could then escape or at least try to. He got ahead of the small party. At the T intersection, he indicated via his camera that he was Unitse. The relay to the Steel

Tower of Minjocan was instant. A message was sent, 'Get him.' In the excitement of discovering the rogue Untonk, the Minjans forgot about Grunt and Davidia and now pursued Unitse.

'This way,' said Grunt, as the two of them ran down another long corridor. Everything seemed cloned. Once again the message, 'listen carefully,' hounded him.

'What's that noise?' said Davidia, as a weird, continuous thumping sound could be faintly heard. 'It's coming from down there,' she pointed.

'I'm more concerned that Unitse may need our assistance. What if they catch him and disassemble him? I had a feeling when he passed me that perhaps he's related,' said Grunt.

They all felt that Unitse was up to his "use by" date and the distraction he provided gave them time to consider their escape options. They didn't have any, but the help was valuable anyway. It was almost a case of the blind leading the blind. The musical sound that they had heard was similar to the noises made when electrical impulses erupted each time an electrical charge was turned on to feed the Minjans. Could this be the base of their power source and if so, could it be used to change anything? It was tepid thinking, but in a predicament, it's better to think a way out than pass it up.

A massive, steel door barred the entrance to the Room of Misery. Grunt pushed hard against it. A sound could be heard from the other side. The door was immovable. Once again, another flash entered Grunt's brains. It was an electronic sound. A vision of five pulsating objects also flashed past again.

'My head hurts,' he complained. 'There are things happening in there that I don't understand.'

'What things, Mr Grunt? Maybe, I can help.'

'Strange sounds and voices I've never heard before. They keep trying to tell me something.'

'Maybe your necklace is a window into other worlds. Each time you touch it, you go all silly and quiet. All your outside bits disappear into a ball. Touch it again. It might calm you or tell us what to do,' said Davidia, thoughtfully. 'We mightn't have much time if those dreadful Minjans come back. They have awful dress sense. I might be a small girl, but I already know how to dress well. Mum showed me on the internet how to bargain-shop.' All of this was beyond the simple life that Grunt had lived and shared as a guardian. Maybe his world was also odd for Davidia.

Grunt gave the U in his necklace a finger embrace. As sure as a pudding isn't a soufflé, Grunt's body began its contortionist actions. There was no perfect ten in his poetic movements. A flash of light escaped from his circumference and hit a wall socket. Sparks flew haphazardly in different directions. A large popping sound was made. A robot was dancing in a wall cavity. Well, at least it moved to give that impression. It possessed a quizzical look. A message flashed across the small alcove, 'Doof, Doof, beware, Doof, Doof.' In a blaze of blinding brightness, the light retreated into Grunt's circumference. He fell to the floor, smarting from the burn he felt.

'I'm a lightening bolt,' he said.

'See, Mr Grunt, something always happens when you touch the necklace,' said Davidia.

'It looked like Unitse,' screeched Batbit, who was having a quiet day with the word thoughts.

'Did you see anything, Mr Grunt?' asked Davidia inquisitively.

'I had a magical, floating, feeling. Everyone was nice, but I wasn't in this shape. I was different, I am different. I think I saw the real me. I didn't know if it was, but it felt like it. The feeling gave me strength beyond what I thought I could do. I'm empowered.'

'Wow! I must have one of them empowerments if it makes you feel so good, Mr Grunt.'

The Doors to the Room of Misery beckoned them. Grunt felt as if something was pushing him into becoming powerful. He puffed out his rounded body into a huge balloon. It was difficult to walk, but he placed two hands on the huge doors and suddenly they both spat fire. The space where he had placed his hands were now two huge holes. Somehow he had oxyacetylened the doors. He repeated the treatment and once again his hands blazed with fire. There was no explanation as to how he had gained this extraordinary power. The doors to the Room of Misery gave way. They walked into a massive room full of electrical impulses, which appeared to act nervously. Zap, zap, bzzt, bltts, ssstts were all mixed together. They stood gazing into a kaleidoscope of erratically behaving, light rays travelling around the room, as if following a lost leader.

'That was amazing, Mr Grunt. Are your hands sore?'

'No, believe it or not. I had a feeling I was being pushed.'

Unfortunately for Grunt, Davidia and Batbit, they had entered the Minjans most dangerous space, where the light rays accompanied by strong, electrical sounds sent anything in the room insane. Minds were blown away after musical tampering. Robots were disfigured and malfunctioned as their electronics were destroyed with insidious vibrations. Life forms such as themselves, who can act independently, are warm-blooded and survive on a different motoring system, should fail to stand the powerful sounds produced by electronics. Perforated eardrums, brain-cell destruction and choice of poor sounds should hasten their destruction – at least, that's what the Minjans thought.

In the Steel Tower of Minjocan, the Minjans had been tracking their every move. They sat smugly in their tin chairs, pressing buttons in safety, feeling victorious at having trapped the life forms. 'Increase the volume.'

They had failed to capture Unitse, who had once again blended into the mainstream of bland, clonic, Blender society. He would fool the Minjans for years to come waiting for his opportunity of control.

However, unbeknown to Grunt, Unitse was important in his journey as he had provided assistance in finding the exit from the Valley of Undonko. The robot life was not for Grunt. As with the passage of history, where the past is brought to the present, Grunt's father, Iglandus, had prepared well in advance for the hoped eventuality that one day Grunt would embark on a journey to discover himself. Support would materialise in many unusual ways and locations. It was time for the U in his necklace to be activated so his journey could continue.

The Irrids had been keeping a close watch on the progress of Grunt and company. They considered that the deafening sounds would crack his resolve and destroy his capability to continue. He represented a fearful signal that if it ended up in their lands, it could spell disaster – DISASTER, in higher case lettering. The evil mists in the first two valleys had disappeared as impotent messengers to halt Grunt's advancement.

'Let the Doof, Doof free to wreak havoc and devastation,' said the head Irrid, who was grossly unhappy. 'They will not succeed.'

The Minjans, who controlled the Steel Tower of Minjocan, suddenly had electrical interference. Were there beings in the universe stronger than them? There was an intruder in the force of their electrical sound waves. A huge attack in volume sent their sound signals in the Room of Misery off the Richter scale. No known living life form, as against a robotic one, stood any chance of survival.

The doof, doof, beat consisted of repetitive, loud sounds, not necessarily classed as connected together. It sent fear through the mind of anyone who heard it. Its doom, doom, beat weighed heavy on any listener to understand what it was they were listening to.

'What's that dreadful sound?' yelled Davidia at high pitch. No one responded.

'What is it?' It was impossible to communicate by sound. Davidia ran over to Grunt and took hold of a hand. He was confused and disturbed.

'It's awful, isn't it?' replied Grunt, having to cover his many ears.

Davidia was aware of music at home. She'd often snuck into her brother, Dan's, bedroom and turned on his CD player. It had also emitted brain-numbing sounds as she was currently hearing.

'We call it music at home, but I doubt if this is. It's boring. Doof, doof, doof. I can't understand it.'

Batbit shrunk in fear. It sounded far worse than his piercing screech.

The Minjans thought that they were onto a winner. They believed the sound was so powerful and dreadful that it was a sure-fire success to destroy them.

Suddenly, Davidia started to gyrate on her legs and sway from side to side. She began to hum and shake her head. The

Minjans were totally lost. Was she collapsing in her final moments? It certainly looked like it. However, she kept the routine going for quite some time. She pretended that she was in a musical video game and got lost in all the sound. The Room of Misery was rocking. Even Grunt moved round, but it was more from trying to recognise if any ejector stones were hidden in the room. He had the capacity to shut down any ear and deny the sound entry. Batbit's large ears were folded carefully to reduce the risk of damage. The three life forms continued to survive. The Minjans couldn't believe it.

'Increase the volume again.'

The light and sound rays behaved frantically like a bridesmaid elbowing her way to the front of the crowd trying to catch the bouquet. They criss-crossed each other as if duelling. It was becoming difficult to see clearly with all the coloured rays strobed across the room. The noise began to affect their judgement.

'Mr Guzzle,' stuttered Davidia, 'Can I have a break from this noise?'

The sound deliverers were pulsating wildly. They were placed all around the room at various heights. Grunt kept searching. He knew salvation was here somewhere. The noise stopped for a moment. Someone in Minjan management had accidentally hit the mute button. The sound deliverers continued unaffected except that they were silent.

'Can you see a group of five of anything?' asked Grunt.

Davidia and Batbit could see zilch. The light had affected their sight. At that moment, the door burst open and in walked Metroid who posed an ominous figure.

'Spray them,' he commanded.

A group of Minjans walked toward them armed with metro spray, which would render them incapable of movement. Batbit flew out of Davidia's armpit directly towards a wall. He flew at lightening pace around the room having no idea what he was doing, although it felt good to stretch his wings. It was a desperate flight as his friends only had moments of freedom and life left. Above the entrance door he noticed five pulsating sound deliverers.

'How many toes do I have? Not enough. How many toes does Grunt have? Too many. Davidia has, yes she has, five.' He flew past one of Grunt's ears and whispered a thought. 'There's a group of those sound things above the door, as many as Davidia has toes on one foot, just behind that big buffoon, Metroid. I'll distract him.'

The heroic little bat flew between Metroid's legs and scratched his inner thigh. The unusual sound stopped Metroid and his advancing metro sprayers in their tracks. Grunt in the meantime had taken hold of Davidia's hand. He knew it was time to unleash the power of Unitse, in the letter U of his necklace. He unscrewed the small container and spilt it on the floor. A yellow, rust-coloured liquid began to worm its way across the floor. A Minjan accidentally stepped in it and instantly changed colour. Its fine, steel colouring of morbid grey was now a bright, iridescent yellow. It reflected the brightest of light. The other Minjans' steel jaws dropped with a clang onto their chests. The Room of Misery began to change colour too. It became a brilliant yellow. The magic of Unitse was loose. Metroid stood stunned.

'Spray them immediately,' he ordered again.

The Minjans were too stunned to do anything except revel in their new appearance.

'They have all turned the colour of my dress,' said an excited Davidia.

Grunt knew that time was short. He spun into his

invisibility character and now stood behind Metroid at the front door.

'Mr Metroid, we apologise for the shortness of our stay, but it's time we left.'

'Destroy them,' he yelled ferociously.

The doof, doof sound suddenly recommenced worse than ever. It started to shake the Room of Misery to its foundations. From all the sound deliverers in sequence blasted an electronic enemy of Grunt's, which appeared as visions of thin, wispy, demonic forms searching for him. The brightness of the yellow room blurred their vision long enough for Grunt to place a hand on the five pulsating sound deliverers, which hadn't yet emitted their slayers of death.

'You can't steal them, Mr Grunt. The music might have been awful, but that doesn't mean you need to take the amplifiers,' said a twelve year old music expert.

'This is our means of escape,' replied Grunt. 'I feel it.'

'Look, everything is turning yellow. It's my favourite colour.'

Grunt pressed hard. The sound deliverers, which hid the secret ejector stones, gave way and once again a twirling journey began.

'Not more headaches,' wailed Davidia.

The Valley of Undonko disappeared under a bright, yellow haze.

An unhappy Irridia stood looking over her valley feeling as empty as a hole-riddled bucket. She breathed heavily with ice-cold breaths covering her thoughts. What is happening in her valley that worries her from the past? Her cold, unhappy eyes once held beauty and life. Now, a dark, bottomless depth seemed to have replaced any good. She brewed and stewed over the inability of her evil demons to destroy Grunt. Davidia would be collateral damage, which was of no interest to her. She vowed that Grunt must never make it back alive. He represented danger.

6. THE DARK ZONE

'I can't see. Who turned out the lights?' asked Davidia, as she, Grunt and tiny Batbit hurtled through the atmosphere in between valleys.

'There is no light in the dark zone,' replied Grunt, as the breeze wrapped its movements around him.

'How do we know where we are?'

'You must rely on the goodness of the ejector stones that have saved us and sent us on this journey.'

'Mum and dad always left a small lamp on for me at bedtime whenever it was this dark.'

'Your world seems a nice place.'

'My brother Dan is the favourite. He's older than me.'

'A favourite what?' asked Grunt. He never had a favourite anything because he didn't know what that was.

'He gets to stay up later than I do. That's all.'

It was impossible to see any expressions in the dark. Davidia's little eyes dropped some moisture. Maybe it was the wind causing the liquid loss.

'Is Batbit still with us?' asked Grunt. His best, little, cave-dwelling friend had been awfully quiet. Davidia felt under her arm.

'Who's prodding me this time? I was having a batnap. I'm over this flashing travel in the dark. I feel like a good feed of insects.'

None of them had eaten anything recently. Events had overtaken their hunger. It was relaxing travelling through the dark zone. There was nothing around them except endless darkness. Somewhere an opening would be found to squirt them through, back to "terra firma." In the meantime, patience was their companion.

The dark zone was the only safe path made available to them to travel between valleys. The ejector stones selected this route because usually there were no evil demons or sinister threats in the area. They were hoping that there weren't any mishaps during transmission.

Grunt had time to relax and reflect about the journey undertaken so far. He whistled through the atmosphere like a speeding comet. He wondered who and what was pushing his buttons. There seemed to be some sense of purpose for him to experience the difficulties he had faced to date. He had almost become a food source, had been enslaved and also pulled apart. Did his necklace hold the answers? Each time he had touched it, strange emotions and feelings filtered through him. Maybe his soul had been tapped.

'I'm going to touch the necklace,' said Grunt. 'Hold on.'

His hands fumbled in the dark, but grab it he did.

Almost instantly, a wave of serenity passed over him, making him feel secure as if he was inside a womb. A tightness gripped his body. He saw two sets of eyes lovingly wash over him. He was being adored. Was it his parents? It was a calmness he had never experienced before. Whoosh! It was gone quicker than a sneeze. A wispy mist appeared around him. Two evil eyes protruded like two large, unwanted, gaudy, baubles, hanging on a bracelet. 'Listen to your heart,' a whisper passed by. A vision of a ferocious fight erupted, with extraordinary looking characters swiping at each other. The scene faded out.

Who were they? His head was reeling with overload. A valley, none the like of which he had ever seen, momentarily hovered in his thoughts and then fell through one of his skin pores. It felt familiar, but why should it?

'Mr Grunt, wake up. You're scaring me. You have been sleep-talking in a very strange language.'

Grunt unconsciously let go of the necklace. His head stopped spinning and they were still in the dark zone. Where were they headed?

'I was head-dreaming. There are weird and wonderful things in our imagination. I saw things I didn't understand.'

'Well, if you were at home with your parents, you could ask them. Mine always explained to me the things I didn't under-stand. Mum would say to dad, "You explain it," and he would say the same thing. Eventually I was told.'

Davidia felt tired and whilst they were zooming to nowhere, she shut her eyes for a moment. Hisssslo flashed through her mind. Her body twitched nervously. A set of rolling dice tum-bled past. Each black dot was an eye. It opened in half and out popped a useless, plastic toy. Just before it shut like a clam, the sound of her brother's voice escaped with a 'hello.' She was missing her big brother. Her mind filled with a brightness that words couldn't do justice to. A massive book had opened before her and the light emanated from it. She peered closely

'Tell the truth and use words wisely,' it said.

'What are you?'

'I'm the Wisp of Wischink. Your journey is my journey. I am your guardian during your absence from home. Your mind is my refuge. I have been with you since you left home. I live in books and when you opened up those two books beginning with S and P, I was destined to be with you. You set me free to express myself through your mind in language. I assist with thoughts and good advice, I am a good reference source and I rest with your imagination. It's busy in here with that. It is important to be safe and above all, be truthful.'

'How will I know what the truth is?'

'I will be there on the end of your tongue helping you push out the correct words.'

The book closed and melded into the darkness. Davidia felt her tongue. There was no one there. At that moment, she woke up. It was still pitch black with nothing to do.

'I'm bored.'

'Perhaps, I can play with you,' whispered a long-winded sound that felt uncomfortable and fearful. Davidia could see the outline of two eyes and a sneering mouth. What was it? It was too close.

'I don't want to play with you. I want to play with Miss Percival. Do you know where she is?' asked Davidia.

The pair of eyes disappeared without a response.

All the time, Batbit was using his batscan techniques to contact Mrs Batbit through the atmosphere. He thought that she was probably at home gorging on those deliciously large, juicy insects that he used to share and not missing him for one moment. Batbit promised himself that if he made it home again he wouldn't squabble any more over the best roof-hanging spots. Mrs Batbit could choose first. He had almost had enough of his adventures.

A light appeared in the distance. It grew larger. Finally, they were expelled out at the end of it from a teapot style, pouring spout.

Where would they land?

7. VALLEY OF NITPICKLE

ump, bump, bump. Grunt and Davidia landed backside first on a flat, soulless landscape littered with thousands of various sized rocks. Most of them were covered in a squelchy, gooey, sticky, colourless slime. No wonder they didn't see the mess they landed in until it was too late.

'This is disgusting,' said Davidia, stuck fast in a slime trail.

'I can't move quickly or much at all. My legs have been attacked all at once,' complained Grunt as his large frame wiggled in defiance of immobility.

'It feels like the thick, treacle toffee that my nanna used to make. Every Sunday we attended church and Nan would make a special batch for Dan and me. One bite and my mouth was glued shut for an hour. It was ever so sticky. I think my parents enjoyed the toffee more than I did even though they didn't eat any. I always wondered why?'

'I hope you are hungry. You can eat your way out,' joked Grunt, who saw the humourous side of their predicament. He was beginning to loosen up.

'What is this stuff?' asked Davidia, as she squeezed it through her fingers. It ran slowly and clung for as long as possible before gravity gave it a final tug to release its grip.

Grunt closely sniffed the ground. The substance didn't react. At least it was inert and not a life form. It clung tightly to each rock surface as if it was afraid to leave. As far as the eye could see, reflections abounded from the rocks in a dazzling light display. The landscape was flat as a pancake, except for the minor undulations the rocks made. There wasn't one item taller than Davidia that they could see. There didn't appear to be any living life forms in the valley. It was hard to describe a valley that was a straight, flat line.

'Those ejector stones aren't so smart after all, are they? We've landed in an uninhabited, stone kingdom glued to the ground. Now what do we do?' Davidia was incensed. Sitting in a goo bath wasn't her understanding of fun. 'If we get this mess off us, how will it stay away?'

Grunt suddenly stood tall. The slime just slipped off him like peeling an orange. It literally fell away. He shook himself and the last offending, sticky mites were flung off to join the ground-based mess. Plop!

'That's better. My pores are cleansed. Those sticky little suckers took all the dirt from my pores. I feel like a new Igloid.' Grunt beamed with satisfaction.

'How did you do that, Mr Grunt?' asked a young girl, not believing her eyes.

'It's a secret?'

'You can tell me. There's no one else here. Sorry Batbit, except you.'

'It's all in the wrists, the wrists.'

Grunt leant over Davidia and rubbed the underside of his wrists over her clothing. A sweet, scented oil flowed from secret glands. As the oil touched the slime, it shivered in fright and it wobbled off Davidia's clothing, as fast as it was capable.

'That's amazing Mr Grunt. Thanks.'

'Just leave a tip for me.'

Grunt, being an ancient Igloid, possessed many fantastic

powers and capabilities that in his past world were the domain of the ruling class. He kept discovering his talents, especially when danger lurked. One day he would understand what it was he possessed.

'Oh! That feels good. I don't want to carry around all that extra weight. I can't do our feet, because it is in constant touch with the ground; however, walk this way and you won't notice the difficulties.'

Grunt then demonstrated walking in a cross-footed manner and, surprisingly, the slime left them alone. It preferred a larger area than a skinny foot.

'It reminds me of the trails that the slugs and snails at home leave as they slither across the ground. Where to now?'

Grunt stroked his chin because it was itchy. He noticed that not all the rocks were slimy. Some were left perfectly clean. The explanation wasn't obvious. Batbit was still shaken up by all the tumbling; however, he was wide awake and needed a stretch.

'Batbit, could you fly around and tell us if there is anything over the horizon?' asked Grunt, who wanted to move and not be slime-stuck. If they stood too long in the one spot their feet would become slime encased.

Batbit soared over the landscape. There were no juicy insects that he could see. In fact, nothing seemed to grow or live anywhere. It was rocks only, spread in all directions. Those clean, unslimed rocks required closer investigation. His curiosity overtook any safety precautions. He landed on one to rest his weary batwings. Whilst he was preening and stretching them, the rock moved slightly. It unsettled him. He waited. It moved again.

'Is anything there?' he cautiously asked. He had his batwings tuned for a quick take-off.

Before he could elevate, the rock surface changed into a carpet of needle spikes, similar to miniature, thin, slender cannons. They jabbed into his feet. In fright, he flew off just in time as hundreds of pointed nails were ejected at him. A few hit his body to inflict a pinprick of pain, but no serious damage. He watched as the spikes receded back into the flat, rock surface. Dotted amongst the goo trails, he noted that there were many other clear rock surfaces. He thought that at least something lived in the valley.

Davidia and Grunt were walking carefully towards somewhere, when Batbit did a flying, multi-loop landing onto Davidia's hair. It was long and a very easy place to land. Grunt was too round and slippery. Land incorrectly at one's own peril and one could probably end up in goo land.

'I saw something move,' Batbit excitedly explained. 'A clear, flat rock spat some spiky things at me. Whatever it is lives under those clear rocks. Tread carefully. You don't want spikes in your feet.'

'You didn't imagine it, did you?' asked Grunt. 'You haven't had any bat juice lately, have you?'

'Check one out for yourself.'

'What did they look like?' asked Davidia.

'From the air, like a flat rock.'

'I wonder what this place is,' said Grunt, realising that whatever it was, it didn't have a happy feeling about it.

The three friends stared in all directions, wondering which way to go.

Slurp, slurp. A mini vacuum cleaner was hoovering the landscape under the protection of their rock-like backs. Lichen grew in abundance and was the only food source in the valley. The inhabitants that fed on this plant form were known as Noots. They were rectangular in shape and carpet thin. Each had four upters (legs) with one on each corner. They had one rotator on a front and back upter. They also had two extra pop-up rotators (eyes) on their backs. Their defence mechanism was the hundreds of nail cannons on their backs, which were fired to ward off any danger. The strength of the nail fired and the damage inflicted depended on the strength of the danger faced. Their utterer (mouth) was on the underside, which continually extracted the lichen. They settled in one spot and fed until it was time to move. From their rear, a slime ejector squirted out a substance after they had finished eating. It had a two-fold purpose, one as a waste dispenser, and the other as fertiliser for the encouragement of growth of more lichen. The valley was a huge slime farm with the lichen well protected under a clear, flimsy covering. The slime wasn't a deliberate hindrance, but a clever farming technique. The Noots easily slid over the surface on their gliding little upters. When on the move en masse, the landscape resembled an enormous, mobile carpet. Other life forms weren't a food source, but because of their height, did blot the landscape's uniformity. The Noots intended keeping their valley as flat as possible for ease of movement. They weren't uphill climbers; however, a life form lying on its side or back was sufficient height for them to traverse. They protected their land flatness fiercely. Any intruder in the valley became the base ingredient for building that small undulation. The Noots could then test their minimalistic, climbing skills.

The head of the Noots was too busy feeding to notice any ground tremors caused by moving life forms. The land was a communication highway, which signalled intruders by vibrations registered through the slime mass.

The head Noot, Noosy, thought that it would be nice to experience some excitement in her humdrum existence. All there was to do was eat and squirt. Noot life was as simple as it could get. She returned to improving her hoovering technique to extract the stubborn lichen. Even it didn't want to join in being a food source this time.

Suddenly, her undercarriage shook. Her utterer ceased sucking. She unfolded herself at full stretch. Her rectangle was the largest of all, containing the most sensitive feeling powers. Her pop-up rotators scanned the horizon. Nothing. She thought that it could have been a false alarm. Once again she shook. Something was definitely shaking the slime carpet, which sent any movements it experienced to its leader. This could be the most exciting occurrence in the valley since the last life form was entombed in a slime ball. It had been many darks and lights since the last encounter with foreign life form matter. Perhaps it was time for another challenge and entombment.

'Agh! This stuff is a nuisance to walk through,' said Davidia, struggling to walk cross-legged. 'My shoes will be ruined. Look at the soles. They are encased with slippery goo. My mum didn't buy these for instant obsolescence. I need a new pair.'

'Are your feet off the ground?' asked Grunt.

'Yes.'

'That's all that is important. Under the slimy veneer, there are sharp stones that will cut your feet to shreds. Your ruined shoes are protecting you. Besides, there's not a shop or boot-maker in sight.'

'I want to sit down. I'm tired.'

Davidia saw a clear rock at seating height and headed for it.

'Don't sit there, it's dangerous,' shrieked Batbit, after his previous encounter and recognising the rock might be a wary item.

'Fuddletwit,' replied Davidia.

The clear rock dipped slightly with Davidia's weight. Underneath, a Noot was sucking the life out of a lichen haven.

'Now what? I can't even finish a good feed without being used as a rest spot,' it said.

It popped up its rotators to see Davidia sitting there twiddling her fingers. I wonder what that was. The Noot couldn't be bothered to send up its defensive nettles. The life form wasn't interfering with its eating function. To be on the safe side, the Noot decided to signal its leader by tugging at the slime mass in a precise manner. Tug one, two, three, and then a twanging flick by its front upters sent a shaking message shimmering off into the distance. Noosy was a clever and calculating rectangle, whose responsibility was to ensure that her colony ate well and enjoyed numerous climbing activities. The message was received loud and clear.

'Foreign heavyweight life form becoming a nuisance. Need assistance to dispense with it.'

She thought that the audacity of something annoying a fellow Noot was unacceptable. The one thing that Noots detested most was being annoyed. Their calm and simple lifestyle didn't require unnecessary interference, even though Davidia wasn't an interference. Perception was more important than fact.

'I'll give her a scare,' the Noot said to itself. It tried to raise all of its nettles, fully charged; however, Davidia had sat on most of them. That didn't work. 'I'll move.' That was another wasted motion as she was too heavy. As a last resort, it decided to flatten itself. That worked. Davidia thumped to the ground in a crumpled heap, landing squarely in a slime pat. The goo tried to stick to her clothing and ran down her legs. Grunt's oil held the offending mess at bay. It couldn't obtain a good, clinging hold.

'That was unfair. Who let the air out of the rock?' complained Davidia, nursing a new bruise.

No one looked positive. Two shaking heads meant that it wasn't them. She stood up and bent over to pick up the Noot.

'Keep your pick-me-up things off me,' said a squeaky voice. It sounded as if someone was strangling its vocal chords. The Noots communicated through ground vibrations with other life forms, by sending small tremors which ran up the leg of any recipient and converted into an understandable thought. Once contact had been established with a new communicating life form, all future thoughts ran down legs, upters and any other ground contact points. The Noots had the choice to receive or deflect any unwanted thoughts.

'Where did that come from?'

'Down here on the ground.'

'Where? I can't see anything.'

The Noot raised all its nettles for a firing and let them loose. Bam, wham, bash! Many landed on Davidia. Small pinpricks were felt on her arms and legs, leaving behind tiny, red welts.

'Ouch! They must have mosquitos here too.'

'Do you want more or have you had enough?'

'If I knew where you were, I could answer you.'

'I'm on the ground. You sat on me.'

Davidia's clear rock seat had stretched into an odd looking rectangle. It stood as flat as was possible. Its little upters seemed out of place situated at each corner.

'Where's your mouth?'

'My what?'

'Your mouth, where you eat through and speak from.'

'Oh! You mean this slit in my undercarriage. Go on, turn me over.'

Davidia gently and with trepidation saw a gap in the rectangle's underside. It moved.

'This is my utterer. I speak and eat from it.'

'How do you see? I have eyes; only two, though. What do you have?' She pointed at her face.

'I have four rotators. I can see in a complete circle with them.'

'Why are you so flat?'

'It's easier to move around without any weight and besides lichen doesn't hold a great deal of nutritional value to fatten us up. When we are made, it's to a specific size, so we have to manage with what we are given. Special sizes are for the leaders.'

'What are those things called, that you stand on?'

'Upters, so we keep off the ground. We walk on them. Put me down and I'll show you.'

Davidia did as requested and instantly she saw four little upters furiously take the rectangle off into the distance. For good measure, it squirted a fresh load of slime at her feet. It was meant as waste product and not as fertiliser.

'Ungrateful little carpet piece,' she muttered.

'Not all of us are naughty,' said another Noot nearby who had come out of hiding. 'There are some of us here with special markings that you need to be aware of.'

'Why? We're just visiting.'

'You are in a forbidden valley that is ruled by an underground force. If it rises, there is no escape. You have seen how flat the land is. There is nowhere to hide.'

'Who are you?'

'A not-naughty Noot. Beware of the Noots with two black dots above their back upters. They have special powers most of us don't. It's rumoured that an underground force has scarred them into service for being really naughty. To redeem themselves, any new life form in the valley must be caught and be made into a building block to climb over. Then they get four dots and belong to the ruling Nooters, which is a special class of angry Noots. They are very dangerous.'

'Why should we believe you?'

'Look at my shown side and you will understand.'

There on the Noot's shown side were four dots. Davidia fell over in surprise.

'This messing up of my clothes is getting to me.'

'I warn you, the valley is riddled with fear. That is one reason why we keep our unshown sides to the ground and continuously eat. It is impossible to know which Noots are ready to earn their dots.'

'But, if you already have four dots, you must be an angry Nooter.'

'They aren't real, but are excellent camouflage, providing I don't have to act as a four dotter. Note that I have three black and one empty one. That's how you will know me when we meet again.'

'Is there a place we can eat? I'm starving.'

The Noot just shook its rectangle. There was nowhere.

Irridia sensed the strength of competition was nearing. Her breast sensors tingled with delight at the thought of a physical encounter. The signal from the past grew in strength with each new transmission. She knew that if it entered the Valley of

Triplock, a powerful eruption for all life forces would explode. The Irrid army would fight against whoever it was that was coming. She had no idea what form the combatant would take. Being a mother, her intuition was that it would be nasty.

Her demonic failures in each valley had her concerned that her evil wasn't bad enough to succeed. If she couldn't subdue the carrier of the signal so far, perhaps Nitpickle would provide salvation for her and prove once and for all the power of her nastiness. A half smile leaked across her face. Today wasn't a good day for leaks. Memories were destined to interfere with her bad judgements.

Her favourite demon that delighted in unpleasantness and loved a dirty task, lived underground. It was Dustbag, a dirt-filled force that followed the dirt seams to the surface. Its vision permeated clearly through the ground. It followed and stalked its prey from underground. No wonder it was so dangerous – nothing knew it was being watched.

'Dustbag, it's time you enhanced your reputation.'

'How many dots have you got, Nootster?'

'Two. The same as many of you.'

'The word is that you are next in line for an extra two dots.'

'Is someone whispering about me? What do I have to do to earn them?'

'Something diabolical that no Noot has ever achieved singularly on their own, by themselves, without anyone else.'

Nootster couldn't imagine what that would be. Most Noots were friendly and non-confrontational, except when that Dustbag started blowing dirt everywhere – then it was every carpet piece for themselves: rotators became blinded, dust rested on their shown side weighing them down so badly their upters collapsed and they couldn't move; the lichen harvest was ruined for many darks and lights; the already thin carpet pieces became almost transparent through lack of eating; and the valley became a virtual wasteland for a time. Dustbag delighted in the chaos and havoc it caused. Underground entertainment was limited, so when Irridia sent a message to do something, it was greatly received. For maximum destruction it had to be above ground where its vulnerability increased.

'Capture Dustbag, in a slime ball, then we are free of the evil in the valley.'

'If Dustbag isn't here, doesn't that mean that the angry Nooters would take over instead?'

'You clever little carpet piece, that's the plan. Unless you capture Dustbag, you will never be an angry Nooter.'

'What about the leader, Noosy? Shouldn't she be aware of the plan?'

'I don't take orders from that overfluffed rectangle. I've earned my four dots and intend to keep them. Are you with us or against us?'

Nootster was in a quandary. He neither had the power, intelligence or capacity to intern the dangerous Dustbag. When he was made from the leftover carpet pieces, it wasn't infused with much in the way of good brains. He was easily led, trimmed and frayed. He had to appear brighter than his shape, so with the bravado of a new carpet piece fool, he accepted the plan, knowing failure with a huge F would occur.

The valley was in the grip of deceit and danger. How could he formulate a plan involving Noosy, without the angry Nooters knowing? Betrayal meant that he would be trimmed into a square shape and be the butt joke of all the rectangular shapes.

'It's a deal.' Nootster shook an upter, gave a small squirt of goo and glided off into the unknown.

'Remember, we are relying on you.'

'I'm too small to make a huge slime ball by myself. I don't know how I'm going to do it.' Poor Nootster, he had a problem larger than himself to solve. His gliding took him far away from the angry Nooters. 'I don't really want to be bad, but it's my destiny.' Nooter's stages of importance were determined by carpet piece hierarchy. His rotators drooped slightly. A small goo drop fell to the ground. 'That's new,' he said aloud.

Noosy had been alerted to the intruders in the valley and began to make her way there to decide their fate. She had a faithful bodyguard of Shenoots that were large, female carpet pieces, cut from the finest of carpets. Their power was in their shown side, where extra slightly larger nettles held dangerously sharp nails. These could penetrate a hard surface. Davidia's and Grunt's outer layers would offer them no protection.

'Girls, sector rockininny has intruders. Form and file. Forget feeding your utterers. Let's glide.'

The Shenoots joined together in one large carpet formation. The ground gave the impression that it was moving.

'Your sides need trimming,' said one Shenoot to another. 'They feel rather rough up against my neatly trimmed edges.'

'Your upters look like they have bent slightly. Have you been squirting enough to stay thin?' Another asked, 'Are you overeating?'

'Girls, concentrate on locating the intruders. The first to find them has the distinction of the first firing.' Noosy knew that they all relished a challenge.

The girls giggled with excitement. It wasn't quite a slumber party, but it was more of a carpet get-together. They all hoped that they would be the first to fire.

A large, dark, cloud of rotating dust particles formed on the horizon. In its midst, well camouflaged, the naked eye couldn't identify Dustbag. He was travelling with his dirt-particle irritants, ready to pile them out on the landscape and ruin everyone's day. He had been underground for quite a long time and had been released by the Irrids. The dirt particles he now had as carrying companions were the heaviest and dirtiest he would have the pleasure of blowing anywhere.

'It's been a while since I have been this filthy,' said a huge particle, pleased to have been released from underground and showing its potential for recycling.

'Drop me off there,' another particle suggested.

'It's too flat, try a mound,' said another.

Each time they spoke from their open gappers, minute particles escaped as fine dust, floating aimlessly within the cloud. Dustbag was scanning the landscape for a good dump spot when he noticed two tall silhouettes. He coughed in surprise.

'Steady there,' chorused a few dust particles. It wasn't yet time to be scattered over the land. A suitable site hadn't been located.

Davidia and Grunt could see the fast approaching dust cloud. It blackened the sky.

'We need to stand perfectly still,' said Grunt, 'and shut our eyes, ears and any space where dust might enter our bodies.'

'I can't shut mine,' said Davidia, because she couldn't. Humans weren't built to have opening and closing orifices.

Batbit could hide under an armpit. Grunt could completely shut himself down into an inoffensive ball, but Davidia was stuck with exposed gaps – even placing her fingers as best as possible couldn't manage it. She began to cry. A pear-shaped teardrop spilled at her feet. She followed its downward trajectory as if in a trance. It shattered on the slime blanket covering the ground. A small gap was made in the goo. Suddenly, Davidia recognised that the goo was easily shaped and acted like soft plasticine. In haste, she bent down and felt the sticky mass.

'I'm not going to like this,' she said kneading it with her fingers.

Her tiny fingers stuffed a small amount in her ears. The goo settled quietly and made the perfect earplugs. Next was the nose. Fortunately, the composition of the goo allowed for filtered airflow without admitting any matter at all. Her voice did sound rather funny when she spoke. For a final slap and slather, a handful was plastered over her face for eye and mouth protection. She could see clearly. All was in readiness for the statue stance. Surprisingly, the goo liked its new carrier and stayed where it had been placed.

Dustbag drew near. The two silhouettes didn't flinch. He encircled them.

'Let me get at them,' said an impatient particle. 'I haven't landed on anything that tall before.'

'What are "them?"' asked a crumbling dust hazard.

Dustbag hovered above Grunt and Davidia. What unusually shaped creatures they were. Most of what he dusted was flat and his dust was spreadable. If he dumped now to cover them properly, he would have to use up all his dust in the one spot. He needed reserves. In a whiff, he was gone. A few dust particles that were left behind whinged unendingly about their poor job performance. Dustbag had taken most of them back to add to a refill.

'It's gone,' said Grunt. 'It will come back no doubt. There was something evilly familiar about that mass. My nerves were twitching anxiously. I held my necklace tight when it was near. A clear vision appeared full of crosses and circles, with the crosses moving over each circle; then it vanished. It was a wipeout of life forms. That mass reminded me of …' His voice trailed off to rest with his other vocal enacters.

'Mmmph,' replied Davidia as she scraped off the sticky goo. 'There, that's much better. You aren't squashed are you, Batbit?'

Batbit crawled out looking like a crumpled piece of paper. He stretched his wings to check any damage. They were all intact. He flapped them a few times and was soon airborne.

'What a relief! Armpits aren't my preferred hang-out. It becomes rather odious in there tucked up into a small space.' He zoomed and dived, checking his flying technique was functioning properly. 'I've still got that whizz factor that Mrs Batbit chased me for.'

He flew far enough away to still retain sight of the silhouettes of his two friends. Were his eyes playing tricks on him? A large, clean, grey area of ground seemed to be moving effortlessly in a precise formation towards them.

'I don't believe it. The ground can't possibly be moving. Rocks sit and erode; they don't get up and go.'

He flew down to investigate and carefully landed on the shown side of the Shenoots. His light weight saved him. If the Shenoots had discovered he was having a free ride they would have raised their nettles and sprayed him with nails. It would be skewered bat meat on the menu had they eaten life forms. Even so, he would be embalmed in a spit ball and used as climbing practice. He wasn't yet ready to become an amusement climbing piece. He listened intently as they transmitted their thoughts.

'What's the plan when we get there?'

'Check the danger level of the life forms and capture them. They cannot stay in the valley. They might find our special stone clump and steal it.'

'Where would they go? Nothing lives in the valley except us Noots. We can't convert them into one of us, can we?'

'They would be very poor carpet quality and possess inferior breeding. Only the great Nitters of Nootsland know that answer. Are you prepared to get a needle up your squirter and be unpicked? I doubt it. It's easier to spitball them and they can stay forever.'

'What are you looking for, Shenna?' asked one jealous Shenoot. She had always envied Shenna's finer carpet lines and weave pattern.

'I'm looking for an idea to assist Noosy. You haven't seen any, have you? I don't know what they look like, but they often visit.'

'The last time I saw one, it was so far in the distance my rotators couldn't see it clearly enough to know what it was. They are extremely elusive, almost as slippery as our slime.' The Shenoots laughed so much their carpet formation bounced up and down. Batbit landed with a thump on their shown side. Simultaneously, many rotators popped up.

'Agh!' they screamed as if choreographed.

Batbit escaped with his torso intact. A field of nails shot up at him. The Shenoots' firers worked perfectly, except Batbit was too quick for them.

'What was that black thing on our shown side?' asked Noosy, who had been concentrating on leading the charge and planning the capture.

'Wasn't it a flying rock?'

'It was an ugly dust particle.'

'Did you notice its skinny upters and its utterer were full of sharp, white, protruding points? It couldn't be accepted into our social circle.'

'Girls, be alert. That thing was a foreign life form, none the like of which I have ever seen before. It was rather scary looking. Perhaps when we find it, we can give it the Shenoot makeover. Be wary of anything not Noot.'

Noosy had once before met oddball foreign life forms. They were nothing but trouble. Her position as Noot leader depended on her ability to lead and protect all who live in the Valley of Nitpickle. She was determined to capture the strange life forms and remove any threat to their existence. However, she had never encountered the villain, Dustbag, before. She was only a very small carpet piece when he had last sprayed the valley with a dust storm. She had no memory of that event. Life under her rule had been quiet and healthy. That was all about to change.

'Grunt, there's trouble heading towards us. A large carpet group are planning to capture Davidia and you and use you as climbing equipment,' said an excited Batbit.

'I love games,' said Davidia.

'This will be a game where you can't play.'

'That's not fair. At home I was allowed to climb on the jumping equipment, stairs and slides. Mum and dad always let me play.'

'Grunt, this is serious. They also said something about a special clump of stones, but not where they are located.'

'We must avoid being caught and trick them into showing

us where the special clump of stones are. There must be a strong reason why one set of stones are so special, whereas others are not. From which direction are they coming?'

Batbit indicated that it was somewhere from over there, wherever that was.

Nootster was following his own trail of disaster. It was a lonely trek. He knew he was doomed to be laughed at forever by the angry Nooters.

'How big a slime ball do I need?' he said to himself. The trail of squirts he left behind were practice for a large slime ball. It didn't matter how much lichen he hoovered up or squirted out, it was insufficient to capture anything of significance. His rotators looked sad, his upters bent with the weariness of his impossible task, and his utterer was uttererless. His emotions of despair almost brought him to self-destruction by thinking of unpicking his weaved fabric and reducing himself into a ball of carpet material. The Nitters of Nootsland would collect him in his unwound state and refurbish him into another carpet piece, but it wouldn't be known as Nootster.

The best quality and quantity squirters of slime were the Shenoots. If only he could enlist their help, he would succeed. What would they think of him when he exposed the two black dots on his shown side? They would immediately recognise that he belonged to those no-good, angry Nooters who should be rewoven. It was a risk worth taking. Perhaps he could change. Maybe he won't be unpicked.

Nootster meandered aimlessly across the landscape, unsure of where he was headed. Out of nowhere, a huge billowing dust cloud headed his way. Dustbag was returning to find a new dirt seam to enlist and enlarge his group of pestering dust particles. If he was to dump properly over those silhouettes and nearby countryside, he needed a powerful new supply of dust.

'Now where did I remember meeting that unsavoury dirt seam? What was its name again? Mudmuddle something. It's in this area somewhere.'

Nootster lay flat on the ground and popped up his rotators. Dustbag wasn't interested in one solitary Noot. He had larger life forms to dirt up.

'There it is.'

A seam of blackish-coloured dirt exposed on the surface was exactly what Dustbag wanted. The Seam of Mudmuddle beckoned him. This was the joining of two dark characters. The air was thick with thousands of particles exercising their open gappers and creating a blinding dust blanket.

'Stay here,' ordered Dustbag. 'Wait for my return.'

Whoosh, he disappeared into the earth as if searching for its middle. The Mudmuddle seam opened wide and down he went. Negotiations had to take place before the Seam of Mudmuddle would join his destructive journey.

'We get to ride at the front of the dust cloud.'

'Agreed.'

'The first dumping is ours so we land on the ground as the lead dirt particles.'

'Agreed.'

'Keep those second-rate dirt particles from opening their open gappers whilst in transit. It's too dusty travelling with them.'

'Agreed, anything else?'

'Allow us to begin another seam as we are absorbed into the ground.'

'Anything you want. I need your help to dump and cover

two massive silhouettes, the like of which I have never seen before. I want your largest, dirtiest and most unpleasant particles to do us both proud.'

Negotiations were over. The seam began to break down into different-sized particles. The Seam of Mudmuddle, for all its bad characteristics, had a plan and purpose for the different particle sizes so that when they were dumped, it was to be in sequence. The heavier particles were to be dropped to form the base and the lighter particles to form the top. The seam prided itself on how close its particles stayed together.

'Ready?'

Dustbag returned to the surface to find most of his dust particles resting on the ground. They were tired from floating. Arguments had been occurring since Dustbag had gone underground.

'I've got more dust in one particle than you have in your open gapper at any time.'

'My dust is the finest choking film on any surface.'

'You call that dirty? Look down my open gapper. It's the best quality dust.'

'What's crumble clod doing with us? You'll fall apart in flight.'

They had tired because of all the arguments.

'Do we have to travel again? I was enjoying my rest.'

'Today, you are to travel with some brothers from the Seam of Mudmuddle. They are helping us to become a dirty, flying, dump force. You will all get to show your nasty, suffocating side. Any takers?'

The army of dust particles stirred. The blanket of dust arose. Nootster was glad to get rid of them off his shown side, so he could continue his journey. He now knew what to follow. Suddenly, a howling sound blew out of the ground. The Seam of Mudmuddle particles were spoiling for action. It had been a while since they had last acted angrily and it was a good feeling. Whoosh, the ground opened and a dark, sinewy film of dirty, dust particles arose and circled in formation with Dustbag. The army of irritants were ready.

'This is too hard, Mr Grunt. My legs are tired from crisscrossing all the time. Can't we rest?' moaned Davidia. After all, she was only a young girl who hadn't done any weights or endurance training. Her fitness levels were very raw.

'We cannot stop. The slime might grow too powerful for us to avoid.'

'I thought this was going to be fun. Now I'm lost, hungry and with nowhere to go. I want to go home,' sulked Davidia. It felt like playtime was over for her.

'Keep alert Batbit. The silence is deafening. Listen; put your ear to the ground. There might be a vibe or something to hear. I'll make a clear patch for you.'

The slime goo resisted movement. Grunt had to hold it up as a covering whilst Batbit placed a large ear to the ground. His hearing antenna picked up a scraping sound.

'Something is slithering along the surface. Its soft sound indicates that it is light. It could be that carpet blanket I saw before. The strength of the vibrations means that they are near.'

Grunt replaced the slime covering. He watched it ooze back into place as it resettled.

'What was that?' asked Noosy. She had detected the relayering of the slime cover. 'Something is tampering with our hard work. I felt a slight tremor. Our slime is under threat. Be ready girls, we may have to act.'

Nootster had felt the same movement as Noosy. He had no idea what it was. He became more convinced that he had to approach Noosy and the Shenoots to achieve his goal. His aimless wanderings now had a new direction. It was Noosy or perish. The slime coverings were a message highway and the quickest mode of message transport. Nootster stopped, stood as tall as he could on his four upters and gave the slime covering a-one, a-two, a-three and a special upter twang. The message scampered across the covering like a bolt from the blue.

'Out of my way. Important message for delivery,' it seemed to say as it ran straight into Noosy's back upters. Her group halted immediately. The messenger shortly came under siege by a team of angry upters.

'I had those cleaned only at first light. Now look what you've done, they're marked,' scowled Noosy. The Shenoots all nodded in agreement. 'What are you pestering me for?' she asked.

'Important message, important message,' it repeated.

Noosy stood on the messenger with one of her rotator seeing upters. The message was then transmitted through her other upter. It said, 'Angry noot, Nootster, needs Noosy's help.'

'Me help an angry Noot? Not likely!'

The message kept transmitting, 'Have to capture Dustbag.'

The mention of that evil name meant Nootster had Noosy's attention.

'Girls, lets hear what the angry Noot has to say.' Noosy sent back a message with a-one, a-two and a double-legged twang by her rear upters. It was a stern message. 'No tricks, otherwise it's reweaving for you. Meet us in short light.' The message sped off for its last delivery. Once a messenger has returned, they dissolve into the slime covering. Nootster anxiously waited. Shortly, he had his answer. 'Yes,' he yelled at the ground. He slid quickly toward Noosy and the Shenoots. The name sounded like that of a new, fresh, punk band. Before long he had reached Noosy.

'You don't look such a bad carpet piece,' said Noosy, noticing that he only had two black dots.

'His weave could be improved,' said a Shenoot.

'Are there any more fine rectangles like you?' flirted another Shenoot.

'Girls, girls.' The group quietened. 'Who are you and what do you want? Any false moves and it's a nail shower for you.'

Nootster explained his predicament. Capture Dustbag or forever become a laughing-stock carpet square. Noosy was aware that the angry Nooters wanted to run things in the valley. By removing the most dangerous obstacle, Dustbag, their chances would improve. However, they didn't possess the capacity to do it. Nootster was on a fool's errand. It was their way of getting rid of him from their group because deep down he was a good, not naughty, angry carpet piece.

'If we do help you, you realise that you will lose those two black dots.'

Nootster's shown side sagged in agreement. His whole rectangle gave a little shimmy shake. He knew that the good in him was greater than the bad.

'You can slide with me,' said a wanna-be-friendly Shenoot.

'Want to share some lichen sucking with me?' said another.

'Do you want to clean my upters?' a third chimed in.

Apparently, a male Noot, naughty, angry or not, was a prized encounter. The flirty Shenoots lost no time in putting their best upters forward. Perhaps they might find the time to make a few small carpet squares.

'Girls, stop the fussing. We have those dangerous life forms to rid from the valley.'

'I've heard that you have the best goo squirters of everyone,' said Nootster flattering Noosy, who let a small squirt go in surprise.

'Reform and slide.'

The group regained momentum and headed for Grunt and Davidia. The intruding life forms needed to be expunged from the valley or otherwise slime-balled and entombed for future climbing pieces and practice. Whichever result occurred, it would be a success for Noosy and the Shenoots. However, the only dampener could be that dust storm Dustbag, who had his own agenda, far worse than Noosy's. His plan was annihilation of the life forms on behalf of the evil Irrids. Grunt was becoming an increasing danger to his past, without knowing.

The showdown was nearing. Noosy and the Shenoots were nearby. Above, hovering like a humming bird was Dustbag, carrying his litany of destructive deliverers. Grunt and Davidia were wondering how they would escape from the valley. Out of sight, a special, not-naughty Noot kept two close rotator eyes glued on the impending event.

'Where are those silhouettes? I'm ready to dust them down. Are you ready particles?' asked a puffed-up Dustbag.

He was full blown with the irritable particles who were vying for the best dump vantage points. It was suffocating time. He blew up a dark storm. Light disappeared from the sky. He zoomed in low over the landscape poised to pounce.

Underneath, a large section of the ground moved. It caught his eyes just as he was about to spew and cough out his freeloading particle passengers. They had their open gappers gnashing for a delivery. He aborted the dumping and retook his position in the sky.

'You weak, lily-livered storm cloud. Couldn't you let us out?' asked an agitated particle.

'I was ready to jump, but now we are too high,' said another.

'Next time, be the nasty dust cloud you are. It's embarrassing explaining to young dirt particles about the time we didn't dump.'

Dissent was rife. The angry dust particles were all peeved off at Dustbag's inaction. What a wuss of a storm cloud. Dustbag told them to shut their open gappers and exercise patience. Their time would come.

'The ground down there was moving. It's been a long while since I've seen that.'

'It's those do-gooders, Noosy and the Shenoots. What brings them here?'

'Those two huge silhouettes, I bet,' said Dustbag.

'It's time they got dusted too,' remarked a primed dust particle.

Dustbag hung loose in the atmosphere, planning his next approach.

⁂

'Who's showering us with fine dust?' said Noosy, who felt a layer build up on her shown side. It permeated into her fine weave and was a terrible irritant. She shook her rectangle furiously to rid herself of an unwanted pest.

A few of the Shenoots popped up their rotators and noticed

it was heavenly gloom. The sky was dark and foreboding. An airborne intruder was howling like a spoilt brat. It was a misbehaving dust storm up there looking for a place to land.

'Not on my landscape,' commented a defiant Noosy. She remembered a story told by daddy Noot from times long gone about the fierce dust storm that almost destroyed the valley. This wasn't going to happen again on her watch. 'Keep your rotators on him.'

'Stop! There they are,' said Noosy, having located the cause of slime stress. There stood two huge silhouettes, which were both much taller than they were, towering over the valley. What a pair of whoppers. Noosy wondered if she could communicate with them. She tried a special slime twang with her front upters. A messenger was sent wobbling along the slime highway.

'Look! The slime has the jelly wobbles,' remarked Davidia. She placed her hand on the wobbling slime and touched it. 'Ugh! It feels creepy.' A thought ran up her arm, feeling a tingle as it did so. It had escaped from the goo.

It said, 'What are you?' Davidia stood frozen like an icicle.

'Mr Grunt, it spoke to me.'

'What spoke to you?' he asked.

'The slime did. Didn't you see it run up my arm?'

Grunt shook his head. They both wondered who or what had sent it? Grunt turned around to see a large group of rectangles closely together. Their nettles were raised for a firing. Many rotators appeared above them scanning the landscape like periscopes.

'That patch over there looks like it's alive,' said Grunt. 'Let me tickle the slime.' It quivered at his touch and once again jelly wobbled to the Shenoots. 'Incoming message,' it said. 'My name is Grunt. We are lost, but we're peaceful.'

'You can't pull that slimy old trick on me,' said Noosy. 'Girls, be ready for a firing. They don't look peaceful to me. Have you seen that round thing with all those bits hanging off? It's enough to turn me off lichen sucking.'

The Shenoots tightened their formation and under Noosy's orders sent a thousand nettles at Grunt and Davidia. The air was strobed with a sea of darts covering the landscape like thin, pencil-drawn lines. Grunt recognised the danger and folded into a ball for protection. Davidia shut her eyes in fear. A voice said, 'Stand firm, no harm will come to you.' Batbit was secure in his favourite armpit. The nettle shower rained down on them. They all bounced harmlessly off Grunt. His thick exterior provided complete protection. Davidia waited. As soon as a nail touched her, it melted away. Nothing penetrated her soft skin. Noosy and the Shenoots had their rotators up doing three hundred and sixties. They couldn't believe their rotators. Davidia heard another voice, 'The truth never puts you in harm's way.' She opened her eyes.

'What happened?'

'I think we have scared those things over there,' replied Grunt. 'I'm sending them another message.' Grunt gave the slime another tickle message. Once again it jelly-wobbled to Noosy. 'Incoming message,' it said, 'We're visitors, but we're peaceful.'

'It's a con,' said Noosy, not believing the ineffectiveness of their most powerful weapons. 'We'll, lay a slime carpet, the thickest we have ever made, to capture them. Girls, hoover up the lichen like never before and prepare your squirters for a massive ejection.'

'What's the plan?' asked a curious Shenoot.

'Under cover of our shown sides, once the thick slime carpet has been laid, we'll convince them to follow us and walk into the trap. The thick slime will entrap them. We'll open our carpet formation like a swing door, then jump on them, push them over and using our special squirter mixer, the special occasion one, overslime them. Once caught there can be no escape.'

The Shenoots worked furiously. They built a slime carpet almost to the height of their upters under camouflage and out of sight of prying eyes or dust storms.

'Fantastic job, girls,' complimented Noosy. They were all exhausted.

Nootster worried about his problem of capturing Dustbag. Somehow, he had to use the thick slime carpet to entrap him. Dustbag wouldn't have seen it being built from the sky. Nootster had a dilemma. How could he redirect the capture of Grunt and Davidia to Dustbag? The not-so-naughty Noot stayed on the sidelines ensuring it wasn't in the path of any conflict.

'Come on, Dustbag. How long do we have to do dizzy-time floating up here? Can't we drop on the two silhouettes?' whined an agitated dirt particle.

'It's time we did what we were collected for, drop, stymie, suffocate and leave a dirty mess on those two things down there,' commented another dirty pest.

'My open gapper is tired of coughing fine, pretend dust particles. I want to spew out the real, angry, nasty particles that I carry around.'

Dustbag was annoyed at such disharmony within his

dusty cloud ranks. The Seam of Mudmuddle's members were the main dust particle agitators. He was waiting for the right moment to attack. From where he roamed, the ground was now still. The two silhouettes were stationary. It was time to drop. He wiggled and thrashed his fine tail as the trigger for the approach. He built up a horrific noise and mobilised his wind within. The particles were expressing unbridled enthusiasm for a drop. The sky turned gruesome grey. At ground level, Noosy heard the threatening indicators of a dust storm. It petrified her and the Shenoots. The not-so-naughty Noot darted in amongst the group. The approach startled them.

'Dustbag is more of a threat than those two things over there. I have communicated with them. Don't be misled.'

'Why should we believe you? You have three black dots on your shown side,' said a suspicious Noosy.

'They aren't real. I use them as protection from being attacked by the angry Nooters. I'll shake one off.' The not-so-naughty Noot quickly rolled over on to her shown side, wriggled and regained her proper stance. 'See, one dot has gone.' Nootster noted that it had very fine upters.

'What about the two silhouettes?'

Before any further communication could develop, a huge, hissing wind sounding like a malfunctioning distress siren filled the flat valley with darkness. The only visible items on the landscape were Grunt and Davidia and that was where Dustbag was headed. He didn't notice Noosy and the Shenoots move their position, carrying and protecting the thick, slime carpet. The not-so-naughty Noot scampered back to Grunt and Davidia and relayed an impromptu plan.

'Crawl under the carpet of slime. Noosy will allow it. As Dustbag approaches to bury you under his dust, lift up the slime carpet by the front two corners and Dustbag will fly straight into it. He will stick in the goo.'

Ingenious. Noosy and the Shenoots were almost upon them. Dustbag was a full-blown, wind tyrant expressing dissent and anger as he howled. He swooped from the heavens and flew at lightening speed above the ground toward his victims. The nasty dust particles began fighting with each other as he closed in.

'I cough first,' said one of many open gappers.

'It's me, it's me,' chorused a team of them.

'It's party time,' said the Seam of Mudmuddle's members.

'Mr Grunt, it's awfully dark,' said Davidia. 'I don't like the lights turned out this dark.'

'They aren't lights. I feel trouble in the air. The valley is under threat.'

'From what, a dust storm?'

'It's something more fearful than that. There's a darker side to what is happening. I can't explain it. Someone is pushing that storm's buttons. I don't know why,' explained Grunt.

'Who would want to scare us?'

'Not us,' said a chorus of carpet pieces. Noosy and the Shenoots had stopped at Grunt's feet. A wobbly jelly messenger ran up his leg and its message affirmed what the not-so-naughty Noot had told him. Grunt and Davidia had just enough time to crawl under the thick, slime carpet. Underneath, it was non-stick due to the special occasion squirter that first sprayed slime on the ground, before it was overlaid with the thick, sticky, goo from the normal squirters. The thick carpet of slime was dense enough to stop anything from passing through it.

'This is like hide and seek. My brother Dan used to hide from me all the time. Mostly, he hid under the bed where he read his magazines that he wouldn't let me read. They were probably on cars or something like that.'

Grunt was truly amazed with all the different things that Davidia spoke about from her world.

'Lay flat. When we are told, we have to grab a corner of this carpet and stand up straight, real quickly.'

'It's not heavy is it?'

'It doesn't feel like it.'

They could see through the sticky goo to the Shenoots' underside. Their leg rotators kept them under close surveillance. All was quiet except for the beating of their pounding hearts.

Dustbag was almost at the point of impact when Grunt and Davidia disappeared from sight. He was at full throttle headed toward them and couldn't change his course, which was directly over Noosy and the Shenoots. Swirling winds made it almost impossible to see. The Shenoots' rotators tracked Dustbag. When he was almost on top of them, Noosy gave the signal to fling their formation wide open into two halves. Grunt and Davidia gripped a corner each of the thick, slime carpet and blindly stood tall, holding it up as a wall. Thump, bang, glug, squish, a trap had been sprung. Dustbag had flown into the slime trap that had originally been set for Grunt and Davidia. Abusive dust particles struggled to open their open gappers and dump their dangerous, dust-riddled cargo. Grunt and Davidia fell backwards with the impact. Noosy and her Shenoots wrapped the other corners quickly around Dustbag.

His trail of dust particles fell harmlessly to the ground as his eyes seethed with anger. He had been glugged by the Noots. Grunt and Davidia could see a dangerous demon stuck fast in a massive slime ball. Their fate had been spared.

Nootster knew his future was secure; however, he preferred the flirtatious Shenoots to his angry Nooters even though he had succeeded in his request. He had made up his mind up to join them. Happy carpet pieces made the best producers of new carpet squares.

The not-so-naughty Noot decided to follow Noosy and her group, because it believed that trouble was still in store for Grunt and Davidia. There was no given explanation as to why a not-so-naughty Noot looked out for their welfare.

'Great work, girls. This is one dust storm that won't bother us again. We'll entomb him with all the other trophies at Noothill. Bring those two things with us and we'll decide later on how to deal with them.'

Grunt felt the communication via the slime at his feet. His necklace also began to jangle. A hand touched it and an electrical charge zapped him. He received a tiny shock. He went to take it off his neck, when he felt an inner thought rampage through his body. 'Danger, all is not as it seems.' It swirled like a whirlpool with no stopping. The void into which it was spinning was endless. Had he been warned, but against what? The Shenoots had rolled Dustbag neatly into a massive slime ball and were rolling him along as a dung beetle does performing its duty, moving its food objects in the same manner. Grunt and Davidia followed a non-slimed trail the Shenoots had made from their special occasion squirters. It was now far easier to walk. They had no idea where they were headed, but followed in the hope that they may find a means of escaping from the valley. The ejector stones, if they existed, needed to be located.

As a matter of habit Grunt toyed with his necklace. A pointy object stuck fast into a finger.

'Ouch,' he exclaimed. A small drop of blood seeped out of the unfortunate, wounded finger. The seepage formed a few large globules, which refused to fall off. Gravity was tugging and teasing them to drop. It wasn't the right moment. Grunt had walked close by to Noosy who was busy lichen-sucking a trail as they went. Inexplicably, his hand shook vigorously. The wound had unleashed an excruciating pain, which ran up his arm. 'Stay away, I don't want to know you,' Grunt's mind was yelling. His hand flicked the blood high into the air. The droplets gently fell, plip, plop, onto Noosy's shown side. They slowly spread over it, layering it with a thin, transparent, blood field. Much to Grunt's amazement a vision appeared. It showed a small clump of five, large, slime-free stones, stacked one above the other. They were perfectly clean. As quickly as a good thought deserts it originator, the vision vanished. His hand recoiled from holding the N in his necklace. Pain was the message it had sent, plus an indication of possible escape. Were those clear stones the ejector stones he sought? His mood became upbeat. 'I might enjoy this walk.'

As the light faded they arrived at Noothill. Dustbag was rolled through the main gate, which had a sign above it, "Climbing Practice Only," and pushed in. He was rolled into position and that is where he would stay forever. Noothill was filled with slime-balled, valley intruders. They all looked fresh, having been perfectly preserved in a slime ball. The small, round hills that they made were used by all Noots for climbing practice and a vantage point to see further than the upters of a Noot in front of them. It was their main form of entertainment.

'I don't like this place,' said Davidia. 'My mum has glass ornaments that look exactly like they do. They just sit on a mantelpiece and do nothing except collect dust and stare all day long without moving. It must be pretty boring.'

'There isn't much activity. Perhaps their diet is low on protein,' replied Grunt wondering how he knew that comment. 'Where's Batbit?'

Davidia felt under her armpit and pulled out one crumpled bat.

'Am I in nirvana?' he asked. He was disorientated, having been tossed about like the contents of a salt and pepper shaker.

'It's okay Batbit. We're with friends now. Noosy and the Shenoots. They saved us from an evil wind. It has all happened around you, hasn't it?'

Little Batbit gradually regained all his senses. His first view of Noothill reminded him of ants trapped in tree sap. The stones in the landscape reminded him of parts of the Valley of Preciousness where he was once happy. He sighed for its comforts. He thought that Mrs Batbit was probably pining for him.

'This is a terrible place. Flatness everywhere. I still don't feel comfortable. Something is itching at me and it's not an annoying insect.'

Grunt also wondered what their fate would be. He approached Noosy. Her nettles instantly arched up. Grunt twanged the slime with a message. Noosy flashed her rotators and upters in anger. 'Who dares to interrupt my lichen sucking?'

Grunt's message got through.

'You must stay one dark with us and at early light a decision will be made.' Noosy kept on sucking.

Darkness arrived, hiding a myriad of evil thoughts. Later that dark, Noosy slipped away from the group. Only Batbit could follow and see in the dark with his echo sounder. Noosy travelled up and down a few undulations. Before long she stopped. A rounded shape appeared. Batbit noticed that Noosy climbed upwards, stopped and then draped her rectangle over something. Her four upters hung loosely, one from each corner of her rectangle in complete peace. He imprinted on his tiny brain the path she had taken. At light he would relay the path to Grunt and Davidia. He thought that it meant something important. The trio slept on the ground. Surprisingly, the slime made a good bed. There would be no danger this dark. The not-so-naughty Noot kept one rotator half open in case any problems arose.

At next light, Batbit explained what he had seen the previous dark. Noosy and the Snoozers. That was a reference to the stones she lay upon. She still hadn't returned to the Shenoots, who by now were waking and looking for their leader.

'Not again,' said a worried Shenoot. 'She stays away at dark on those smooth things. No one knows why? It could be dangerous out there. Those angry Nooters have been known to unthread us when we haven't paid attention to our safety.'

There was rumbling in the patch, or was it a quilt?

'Can we leave now, Mr Grunt? There's nothing to do here, except listen to the dreadful sound those carpets make when slurping up that green stuff,' said Davidia. She had already tired of the place. There weren't any playmates here for her.

'There's nowhere for us to go. Look around. A nothing view everywhere. Flat, flat, and flat. Inside the Rock of Yocklaw, at least there were insects to be amused by. Where's Noosy? Batbit said she slept over there somewhere.'

The Shenoots all had their undersides in vacuuming mode. Their rotators and nettles were inactive. It was the ideal time to escape. Batbit flew into the air and motioned with a wing in the direction that they should take. They weren't noticed, or so they thought, which surprised them.

Unbeknown to them, the Shenoot's upter rotators had kept them in view. It was a fool's errand to think of escape. Quietly, they headed for Noosy. Behind, at a discreet distance, a sea of Shenoots also quietly followed. They were so agitated their squirters released anger goo, a substance so powerful one step in it and they became immobilised. Two steps and it was over. The Shenoots were annoyed because their hospitality had been compromised by Davidia and Grunt who walked away and headed uninvited towards Noosy's special place.

'That didn't take long,' said Noosy, messaging them. 'Welcome to my special place.'

'There's nothing here except rocks. What's so special about them? At home, I keep a few pet rocks in a fishpond. They're not special at all,' said Davidia.

Noosy showed her aggressive side. She squirted a ball of goo at Davidia that almost pushed her over.

'That hurt.'

The Shenoots had surrounded Noosy's special place squirting angrily as they encircled it. There was no escape. The goo was far too thick and sticky for even Grunt and his invisible, spinning windmill speciality. Davidia was a young girl who always told the truth. Now it couldn't help her. Batbit flew overhead wondering where this would all lead to. It was a stalemate. Suddenly, the Shenoots joined sides by wrapping their upters together and forming a canopy over them, squirting as they went. They were building a giant, slime ball tomb. The Shenoots were performing as if part of a circus act, balancing precariously on each other as the tomb grew.

'Mr Grunt, we're in trouble. I don't want a slime house to play in.'

'It's not a playpen, Davidia. They intend to keep us trapped in here forever,' replied a calculating Grunt. He then remembered the vision that he had seen on Noosy's shown side and he somehow felt it was close at hand. Batbit flew down and landed on Grunt's surface.

'Batbit, try and remove Noosy off those large stones for a few moments. I wonder what's under her.'

Batbit had often flown dark sorties to feed both Mrs Batbit and himself. This felt like it was to be an urgent flight. There was tension in the air. Noosy was standing on all four upters giving instructions. There wasn't much room underneath her, but that is where Batbit intended flying. He honed in on Noosy like a dart from the heavens. With a pounding heart, he aimed for Noosy's underside. Down he went. Halfway through underneath her, he let out his trademark screech. The released vibrations startled Noosy and she slipped off the rocks in shock. Her stumble revealed five, large, clear stones, upon which she had been standing. It was her favourite sleeping space. The slime cave was almost complete. Batbit headed for Davidia who placed him under her armpit. Nothing came easily.

'That was the vision,' Grunt told Davidia. 'Walk quickly over to them and climb up,' ordered Grunt.

'I'm not in the mood to play.'

'Do as you are told. Don't be so stubborn. It might be our only way out.'

'Alright then, but I'm not happy.'

Noosy recovered quickly from her fall and when she saw Grunt and Davidia climbing toward her special sleeping space, she turned her rear toward them and fired anger goo directly at them. Before it could cause them any harm, the not-so-naughty Noot fired a goo goo missile, which knocked it off course. This allowed enough time for Grunt and Davidia to stand safely on top.

'Now what, Mr Grunt? Everyone can see us.'

The slime cave was almost complete. The Noots could easily pass through it, but it was deadly for anything else. Time was running out, just like for the not-so-naughty Noot who had made good her escape.

At times of pressure, Grunt grasped his necklace. It always seemed to hold the answers. The N's sharp point pricked another finger. This time no blood flowed. His body swayed uncertainly on the stones, threatening to topple off. Memories flooded into his mind like an overflowing sluice gate, holding back the waters of the world. These were the memories of his past ready to be spilt. 'Son, son,' a fading voice called. 'Who's there?' Grunt awoke, realising that he was jumping up and down on the stones like an excited child.

'Davidia, do you want to jump? Copy me, it's fun.'

Grunt was acting like a twelve year old and Davidia couldn't resist the temptation to act like the child she was. They both jumped together. Their combined weight, more on Grunt's side than Davidia's, set off an underground alarm bell. Hot ashes sprung to the surface, forcing the ejector stones to explode and send the happy jumpers forcibly upwards. Whoosh, the sky went dark. The hidden ejector stones springboarded them to elsewhere, safely from permanent entombment and becoming a climbing toy.

The last vision of Noosy and the Shenoots that they saw was the collapse of the goo cave on top of them.

It was goo bye.

***

Cold, dark and dangerous days lay ahead. Irridia, the head Irrid, shivered with hate at the failure once again of one of her most dangerous and feared demons. She might have to deal with the perceived threat herself. Signals of fear were growing stronger. A blip from the past would soon haunt her. Retribution was near. Whatever the outcome, she was confident that pain and the evil side of existence would win. Her army of evil was a force to be reckoned with. That dark she consoled herself in the Cave of Murm. Brrr!

8. IRRIDON

'What a dump this place is,' said Davidia, as her surrounds suggested unpleasantness.

'Don't criticise everything new,' replied Grunt, as he had inner feelings of good, but didn't know why he should feel this way.

'Why not? At home I could say anything I liked. Mum and dad often said if I didn't have anything nice to say then don't say anything at all. I'm not home now. This place frightens me.'

The land was covered in a grey, dense mist. Visibility was limited to one hundred metres in all directions. The ground felt constantly moist. Gnarled trees fought for a taller existence, only to be denied warm, sunny rays. The cloud cover was stifling for a good time or a quick flora growth rate. Any life form movements in the distance could be seen as darting shadows that quietly disappeared when approached. The fun in the Valley of Irridon had been suffocated out of all life forms. The only enjoyment was practising evil and misery, which flourished everywhere. Niceness didn't exist. Harshness, bad manners and deathly stares abounded. The inhabitants freely shared their nasty side, the worse the better. The strength of evil grew as their worsening, nasty skills were honed. The valley was home to a mentally unhealthy growing group of Irrids whose mantra in life was conquer, destroy and be miserable. Even in their moment of increasing gains of land and power, satisfaction escaped them.

The trees seemed to live in fear of growth. The ground was under constant wet stress. Rocks were thickly covered with a green mat of weeds. River waters weren't clear, suggesting unhealthy flows. Life forms darted like stooped old men running away with a stolen loaf of stale bread tucked under one arm, trying to avoid capture.

Grunt and Davidia had landed in the badlands of Irridon by mistake. The necklace had them headed for the Valley of Triplock, which would now have to be entered via a detour through Irridon, its neighbouring valley.

'Come on out, Batbit,' said Davidia.

Batbit opened his eyes wide enough to stretch his small face. He took one look and shook his tiny head.

'It looks bleak, bleak, bleak. Who chose to land here? Are we on course with that necklace of yours?' he asked Grunt.

Grunt really hadn't considered whether his necklace was a navigation system for them to follow. Perhaps it was.

'I'm not sure. Each time we have a problem it helps to solve it. Maybe it's a jingling message band.'

'So far, in each valley we've been through, it has aided us with good advice. I doubt if it meant us to be here. Did you upset it at all?' Batbit was acting as the devil's advocate. The necklace could be leading them into a trap. It appeared obvious to him that they were in the wrong place at the wrong time. Nothing felt good here.

'My batwings are nervous.'

'Fly about and see if anything is recognisable,' advised Grunt. He and Davidia were ground based and couldn't perform that task.

'I hope I don't get lost or caught.'

Batbit flew upwards. His sonar was on full alert. He had to fly low because of poor visibility. His sonar kept bouncing off weird and wonderful objects, some stationary and some moving. He went crazy with confusion. He wondered what this place was. Trees wiggled. Water froze then unfroze, as if teasing a pair of dipping toes. The land changed colour, but only in shades of grey. Life forms wandered about on strained nerve ends. His ears picked up the noise of agitated voices. He was fearful of any encounter. Where were Grunt and Davidia? Had they been swallowed? The misty conditions misdirected and interfered with his sonar. He flew in circles for a while and took refuge in the fork of a struggling tree.

'Be careful. Your sharp, spiky feet, hurt,' said a wiggling tree branch.

Batbit almost fell out of the fork with shock.

'I religiously have my nails manicured by Mrs Batbit. They aren't that sharp, are they?'

'Just don't press too hard.'

'Who are you?'

'A Wiggler. My branches move continuously. It's a technique developed to keep my sap moving, otherwise I would freeze still.'

'Where am I? What is this place?'

'If I tell you, nothing must know from where the leaking source came. I don't want to be limbless.'

Batbit nodded. If he wasn't unbalanced just yet, he was well on the way.

'I promise and cross all my toes.'

'A dangerous, evil force lives here in the Valley of Irridon. It grows like a poisonous fungus. It lurks everywhere. I could be part of it too.'

'How will I know what's dangerous?'

'You won't.'

'Why are you telling me?'

'I want to grow. Being stunted and not reaching my full blooming potential is tedious. I'm tired of being small. I want to be tall. One day the sun will be allowed to visit. Beware of the Irrids.'

'The what?'

'You'll know. This chat is sapping my energy.'

The wiggling tree branch went silent. Batbit sat alone. Was the mist staring at him? Brrr, he shook. His highly tuned ears heard the sound of voices. He thought that it must be Davidia and Grunt. He flew in the direction of the sound. To his surprise, it was a group of local inhabitants honing their fighting skills.

'Lop off an arm,' yelled one participant.

'You can do better than that. Take out a leg,' yelled another.

'This is how it's done,' commanded a large life form.

Batbit watched the war game practice with keen interest. Strange looking weapons, which appeared to be alive, were swished, thrust, jabbed, stabbed and whirled with relish. The wielders of death and disfiguration were life forms Batbit had never seen before. They were as tall as Grunt, wore half masks, covering either one side of their head or horizontally across the head. Coloured eyes sparkled with each game thrust. The torso was stooped slightly as if self-esteem had been drained from them. The command life form stood perpendicular. It was an imposing figure. The other life forms cowered in its presence. Their outer covering was wrinkled like a corrugated road. One foot was huge with three toes, whilst the other was small with six toes. They lacked the fluidity of streamlined movement. They ran occasionally, suddenly stopped as if stunned, then walked sideways for a few steps, turned around and darted behind any solid or living structure. Their weapons were gripped tightly in razor-sharp claws, which could dis-embowel an adversary with one well-placed strike. Gruesome games were afoot. Their only weakness occurred when meeting a new challenging life form. That moment of indecision was time enough for an opponent to strike first or take an advan-tage. Emotion would be their undoing, not losing a contested battle. They were an unloved, fighting machine, which did the bidding of the leader, whoever it was.

'Are you hiding?' asked a small weed that Batbit stood next to. It was the same height as Batbit.

'I'm resting,' he replied.

'I think you are hiding. I would.'

'From what?' Batbit had to learn about those shadow-danc-ing life forms.

'Those dancers that you have seen.'

'Are they a dance troupe preparing for a show?'

'Life form capturers actually. There are many more than before.'

'What are they? They are strange life forms.'

'No stranger than whatever you are,' said the weed.

'How do you know all of this?'

'I see it every day. The moisture sits on my blades and I weary of carrying it. It falls off when I am stood on by those dancers. I have often been trimmed by a slashing blade. They strike at everything. It takes ages to regrow.'

'If they capture me, what would be my fate?'

'Amusement by torture, then destroyed. It's said that the Irrids have no feelings.'

'Do any other life forms live here besides the Irrids?'

'Possibly, but they don't last long. You won't last long here, either. They can smell your body odours.'

'Even without passing wind?'

The ground rumbled with foot traffic movement. The weed went limp. Batbit flew once again into a tree, just in time to see a snarling group of blade-wielding slashers rush to the exact spot where he had been hiding. Their flared nostrils were sniffing the ground vigorously.

'There's an intruder. Let's gut him.' An insidious laughter echoed throughout the stunted trees as they hunted in earnest for Batbit.

Time stood still. Batbit waited fearfully, hoping he wouldn't be discovered. The Irrids scampered off in another direction. It wasn't safe to be alone. Batbit experienced the feelings of being lost. Where were Grunt and Davidia? He thought that he hadn't travelled too far away to lose all contact. All the flying had made him thirsty. He saw a trickle of water lead to a pond. He flew down and landed at the water's edge.

'What are you doing?' asked a water droplet.

Batbit scanned his surroundings to check that no attacks of anything were nearby.

'I'm going to have a drink,' replied Batbit. 'Flying is thirsty work.'

'Go somewhere else. It's not safe here.'

'Whose speaking to me? I can't see you.'

'Look into the water.'

There was a pool of water droplets bubbling to the surface. They each took it in turn upon bursting on the surface to warn Batbit. His reflection gave cause to some amusement.

'Why shouldn't I drink here?'

'The water is impure. It has been poisoned. We have been trying to clean ourselves, but so far it has been hopeless.'

'Why don't you trickle elsewhere or be absorbed by the soil?'

'We are landlocked and the soil is impervious. Recycling is our only relief.'

'Do the Irrids drink here?'

At the mere mention of the name, the water began to freeze over. In moments, an ice slick confronted Batbit. He thought that this was bordering on ridiculous. A dank, damp landscape that freezes had him tossed. Where to now? he thought. He couldn't ice-skate or take a drink.

'There it is,' yelled a blood-thirsty, screaming group of Irrids who had sniffed out Batbit. Savage, menacing thrusts were aimed at him. He screeched in fright as he took flight. The Irrids stopped dead in their tracks upon hearing the scream. They looked at each other confused.

'What did that?' asked the leader.

Silence meant that no one knew.

'There may be another evil in the valley. It is only big enough for one, us. Nothing will stand in our way, understood?'

The snorting, snivelling group all nodded assent.

✳ ✳

'Batbit has been gone a while,' said Grunt, worried that his friend may have encountered trouble.

'It must be difficult to see in this mist. Perhaps he flew into something,' said Davidia, toying with her long tresses.

'There's something familiar about this valley,' said Grunt, wondering what it was.

The ground sent feeble tremors through the soles of his feet. They tingled. It was a living thing providing knowledge of where he was, but he couldn't make any sense of it. There was a language connection with an ancient tongue that he couldn't translate.

'Davidia, I may have been here before, a long time ago. My body is acting strangely. My sense of smell has improved and I agree that Batbit should spend less time in your armpit.' A smile fanned out over his face. 'There is a sense of belonging here, strange as it may seem.'

'Maybe you played here as a small Igloid? My mum never let me play in our neighbour's house, which was believed to be haunted. Maybe you have a haunted place here?'

Grunt thought for a moment. He dismissed the notion. It was too fanciful to believe that he had been in such a dreadful place when young. He thought that if he had, he certainly would have remembered it. The curse of goodness that he had to uphold dismissed his memories to a forgotten pile of thoughts. Now a few of the rascals could be making a comeback. The unknown might provide a scare from his past.

'Now what do we do?' asked Davidia, feeling quite sad that Batbit may have encountered trouble.

'I have a feeling,' replied Grunt, who was thinking so heavily his brains almost fell out of his body. 'We need to move quickly.'

'We can't see anything much and this mist is so cool, my bones are stiffening.'

'We don't need sight in the ordinary sense, but we do need to see. Follow me.'

They didn't know where Batbit was, so they headed off into the direction where they had last seen him fly.

'He could be injured. Miss Percival would save him.'

'He's safe for the moment, but we might not be. There's strange shadowy movements occurring in my mind and I think they come from here. Can you hear any running water?'

'Water doesn't run anywhere, it flows,' said Davidia, commenting on a well-known and accepted saying.

'Listen.'

They stopped still. Only the sounds of the forest could be heard.

'You can't stop here,' said a miniature tree fern.

'Who said that?' asked Grunt.

'I did. Down here, in the ground.'

There, at their feet was a group of miniature tree ferns with drooping fronds. Moisture had fastened itself to the small fronds weighing them down.

'Have you seen a small bat fly past here?' asked Grunt.

'What's a bat?'

'A small flying animal or life form.'

'A life form, or we think it was, flew past here. In the mist it could be anything. Shadows are everywhere. It's hard to tell what anything is anymore.'

'Why is the valley so wet, misty and dull?'

The tree fronds seemed to sag further.

'An evil force lives in the valley. It's dark all the time. No warmth exists anywhere. We look forward to the day the sun returns to the valley. Nothing grows much. All of the forest waits to decay and compost. There are no other challenges like producing green leaves, tall trunks and homes for small life forms. It's lonely here. We all miss the past.'

'How did it happen?'

'The Irrids moved in. Be careful. They are deadly dangerous.'

'Why are you telling me this?'

'You are a life form with feelings. The Irrids don't have any. We can tell.'

Grunt held the necklace in one hand. It was emitting small pulses of energy. Each time the word Irrid was mentioned the impulses stammered. A meaning was being sent to him. He thought that it must be a warning of some sort. A short, sharp, pain ran through his fingers.

'Is there a river or creek near here?'

'There used to be a flowing river on the other side of those trees. It doesn't flow well any more. We think it's ill.'

Before any further communication could take place, a rush of wind whistled through the fronds. Grunt watched as the miniature tree fronds fell to the ground. The infertile soil had finally exhausted their ability to survive. Their stumps looked like hives on the ground. Davidia had been very quiet. She had walked slowly toward the trees.

'Get away from us. You feel like trouble,' said some leaf litter.

'Is someone there? Do you need any help?' asked Davidia. She had no idea what she was talking to. It seemed that the vegetation loved a chat because nothing new happened to liven up their usual routine.

'Don't walk on us. It's hard enough to lie flat.'

Davidia bent over to pick up the leaf litter and like any child was going to toss it around in play.

'Don't touch us,' yelled a tightly knit clump.

Davidia jumped in surprise.

'Mum and dad always said that when you talk to anyone, it should be face to face unless you do it by telephone. So, who am I talking to?'

'Us. You almost picked us up. We're too tired to move. We've been here so long. If anything touches us, we'll disintegrate and lose our physical shape.'

'Oh. I shan't touch you then, but where are you? It's so dark here.'

'We're leaf litter.'

Davidia realised that she had almost stood on them.

'Why are you so unhappy? I only wanted to play.'

'Our nutritional levels are very low. We have enough difficulty composting for the good health of the trees, that if you threw us anywhere we couldn't get back to assist them to survive. It's so wet and uncomfortable down here.'

'Can I help?'

'No. Go quickly. The ground is trembling in fear. The Irrids are nearby.'

The forest floor went quiet.

A snorting, snivelling sound headed her way. Grunt heard it also. Danger, danger, flashed through his body. The necklace began to glow.

'Mr Grunt, your necklace is almost as bright as my dress. It's signalling something.'

Grunt felt a pain. His mind unravelled a nasty vision and all his eyes opened wide, as if stunned by flash bulbs.

'Davidia, give me your hand,' demanded Grunt in a state of high excitement. Danger had unleashed a curious defence mechanism he didn't know he possessed. As soon as he took hold of Davidia's hand, they both instantly flew upwards and over the trees, landing on a frozen river.

'How did you do that?' asked Davidia. 'It was cool.'

'I'm not sure, but this strange land has an unusual effect on me. Did you hear that?'

'Hear what?'

'The sound of breathing from a life form.'

'I can't hear anything. Is your imagination turned on?'

'It's coming from over there, across the frozen river.'

They both carefully avoided slipping on the ice and made it safely across.

'Up in that tree, I hear it.'

It was too dark for Davidia to see anything except shadows.

'Shush.'

They both listened. Grunt had higher sensitive hearing capabilities. He also had more ears. Sure enough, small puffs of moisture were emitted into the atmosphere in short, nervous, irregular bursts. It was Batbit in hiding. His fear had immobilised him.

'There aren't any other life forms around, so it must be Batbit.'

'Batbit,' yelled Davidia in her high-pitched, female voice. Her vibrations resonated in the trees.

Batbit shook with fear. He had been discovered. Where were his friends? The cold had numbed his reaction to anything. Was it real? Was he doomed to freeze to death? His tiny head struggled for a view. The sight of a huge, grotesque, rotund, bowling ball was the best antidote to slipping away. He groaned when he saw Grunt.

'Up here,' he moaned.

'Batbit, is that you?'

'Yes,' he struggled to reply. His warm blood was turning to ice just like the river below had.

'He's over here.'

Grunt located Batbit, suffering from dehydration and slight hypothermia.

'They were fierce and strange. They tried to sniff me out,' said Batbit, rambling somewhat.

'Who did?'

'The Irrids. I saw them practicing arm lopping and leg severing. They were vicious. I fought them by myself. They are bigger than the trees. Are there any insects here, I'm hungry?' Batbit was mentally disorientated and his focus was splattered like random graffiti.

'Davidia, place him in his favourite armpit where he will be warm. We missed you, our little friend.' Grunt carefully picked up the fragile ice cube – he felt like one – and passed him to Davidia.

'Miss Percival and I will look after you.'

The dull landscape seemed to trigger everyone's imagination.

'Did you feel the movement in the airwaves? There's an unpleasantness about to infest our valley. We must defy the threat and not succumb to its evil. I fear that it all may be lost. The Irrids' power trebles each series of darks and lights and before long they will be powerful enough to challenge us. It will be a time of deep regret. Our valley of happiness may disappear forever. We must defend it as best we can. How will we be able to save our valley?'

King Iglandus was the wise ruler of the Valley of Triplock, the valley next to the evil Valley of Irridon. He knew dark forces were planning against his rule. Evil seemed to grow more quickly than good. Under his rule, Triplock had flourished. After many darks and lights, he was now an ancient ruler, past his best "use by" date for a physical clash. He had grown so old and without further reproduction of his life form, had no one to pass his mantel onto.

Many eons ago, he had a new life form called Ignatus, the apple, pear and every other fruit of his eyes, but after a bitter emotional dispute with his wife, Ignatus' mother, Ignatus was kidnapped. He was hideously transformed and banished, never to return, but Iglandus held special powers and he somehow transported with the banished Ignatus a means of communicating with the past and a passage back home. However, these days, he had given up any hope of ever seeing the return of the banished one. He looked over the valley from his hilltop home and reflected how beautiful and peaceful it was.

His army of defenders were highly skilled. Any defence of their homeland would be at great sacrifice. His mood saddened as he thought of what could have been.

'Where would that river flow, if it was unfrozen?' Grunt asked himself. He was planning something, but was confused about what it was. His body was growing stronger without enlarging and his mind became filled with visions he had never experienced before. He began tapping on its surface with one leg.

'Stop that. It might shake me loose.'

Grunt immediately stopped.

'I don't see anything,' he said.

'That's because I'm invisible. You can stand on me, but can't see me. I'm frozen.'

'Are you the water or ice?'

'Ice. I only form when I freeze. I'm an ice square camouflaged in the frozen water.'

'Where does the river flow to?'

'When flowing, we make it all the way to the Valley of Triplock. None of the water carriers, droplets or ice squares, ever want to return from there. There we can be drunk, washed in and provide life to growing things. Here, we are mostly frozen. The dull, moist atmosphere and that dreadful mist have kept us solid. There isn't much fun here.'

'How far is it and will it be safe?'

'It will take one dark and one light. It is dangerous. Irrids are everywhere.'

'Could I defeat an Irrid in battle?'

'Run. It's the only safe way. Remember, The Waterfall of Wetness must be passed through on the journey. It is the entry to the Valley of Triplock.'

Grunt acknowledged the advice by running a warm hand over the ice square. It gave off a few melted drops of moisture. The ice square appreciated the gesture. It had been a long time since the river was free flowing and had experienced good things. The cold returned. Batbit was warming up. Davidia was deeply unhappy. The trio decided to follow the frozen river to The Valley of Triplock.

'How far is it?'asked Davidia. She was surprised that she wasn't frozen solid as she was only wearing a frock of thin fabric.

Unbeknown to her, Grunt had planted a warmer in her hand when they flew across the trees. It was a protective film that would spread and cover her skin. Grunt was beginning to learn that he had some unusual abilities.

'We must follow the frozen river. It may be our only escape. I have a feeling that there are no ejector stones here. My necklace isn't reacting when I touch the last letter. Maybe there is a communication blockage by being in this place.'

Visibility didn't improve. The banks of the river were wet and slippery. Batbit was warm again and enjoying the ride. Being nocturnal, he actually slept, thinking it was light. They pressed on. Furtive eyes darted between each shadow that materialised, then faded, as they passed. It was eerie. Vegetation was stunted and suffered nutritional deprivation.

The breeze that occasionally accompanied them felt like a spy had been sent to report on their movements. It came close enough to brush their bodies with a shiver. A hollow, echoing voice whispered, 'lunch.' It then vanished.

It was a warning that the Irrids had been sniffing for them. If captured, then there would be no more adventures.

The closer they walked toward the Waterfall of Wetness, the more erratic Grunt's behaviour became. He would suddenly stop and run off into the trees. It was assumed that it wasn't for a personal water stop. He would then reappear on the other side of the river. His eyes rolled in their sockets like roulette balls. They held fear, uncertainty and a glow that Davidia hadn't seen before. When he returned all his fingers would be crossed. It might be a secret society handshake. Davidia watched stunned at the transformation of her friend with his idiotic behaviour. As quickly as it had occurred, Grunt would return to normalcy.

'Are you alright, Mr Grunt?' asked a concerned Davidia.

'I do feel a little light-headed. It must be the cold.'

Grunt had no explanation, but he knew his actions weren't harmful.

'Please don't leave me alone.'

'You are safe with me.'

The two friends were becoming depressed with the boredom of the landscape. It was like a photo, encapsulated and frozen in time. It didn't change.

'Shush. I hear voices,' said Grunt. Davidia noticed that his body tensed up like a spring. 'Let's become shadows and hide over there.'

'I love hide and seek. At home, I played it with my brother, Dan. I'd hide and he couldn't find me for hours. I never knew why he couldn't find me. He had a playstation in his room and that was where he was when I couldn't be found.'

'Our visitors might be more dangerous than a game. Be quiet.'

They squinted through the mist. Four shadows flitted between the trees. Were they playing hide and seek? The only life forms were the Irrids. It might be a scouting party trying to locate them. They watched carefully.

'Where have they gone? I sniffed them to this place.'

'Is your sniffer clear of clogging?'

'I cleaned it out before with my toes.'

'Where is them?'

'I want to lop off an arm.'

'I want to lop off a leg. Then we'll see if they can run in a circle.'

'Sniff harder all of you. I can't see them.'

Four sets of snorting, flaring nostrils faced upwards, sideways and downwards, in all directions, trying to catch a whiff of any body odours. The cold, moist atmosphere often clogged up their sniffers and, with all their snorting, offensive particles were often exhaled. It didn't pay to greet them with a hug.

'That ice is frozen. Ya can't get a good sniff on that.'

Their weapons were ready for battle as the hunt for body smells continued. Both Grunt and Davidia realised that passing wind at this point, even though there was a strong urge, was too dangerous. There would be no humour accompanying the delivery.

'What's that bad smell?'

'Was it you?'

'No. It was you.'

'It was all of us. We all stink. We've been sniffing each other. Get away. I don't want those nostrils near any part of me. Go and locate those life forms.'

Just as they were about to move on, Grunt revealed himself like a fool from his hiding place. He hadn't been sniffed out, but an urge within him had forced the issue.

The four Irrids stumbled in fright. They hadn't seen such an odd looking life form, who was stranger looking than themselves.

'I mean you no harm,' Grunt said calmly.

'We do. Off with whatever you can get.'

The four scampering Irrids with their weapons raised, charged Grunt.

He stood there defiant like an Easter Island statue. Davidia woke up Batbit, who peered out in fear.

'I saw them earlier. It's over. Shut your eyes,' he said.

A transformation came over Grunt. Two of his five legs began to twist and turn like a corkscrew. They disappeared into his body and then in a flash, quicker than a wink, out came two huge, chubby, club-like legs. He waved them about his body, ready to bat his attackers. The fingers on all his hands became stretched, with each fingernail turning into an ice pick with four razor sharp edges. Grunt didn't want to kill anyone; he had no argument with any attacking life form.

The four Irrids, having seen the horror life form transform before them, slowed down their approach. The leading Irrid swung his razor-sharp weapon with the force of a hurricane at Grunt. A chubby, club leg took the full force of the blow. It had no effect. Grunt then kicked him in the unmentionables. He slashed his hands across his legs leaving a series of bleeding scars.

'Who's next?' he calmly asked.

The second Irrid came from behind. Grunt spun into invisibility and then at the moment the Irrid swung his weapon, Grunt's twirling legs kicked and clubbed him senseless. It would end up with nothing more than a bad headache and bruises to brag about.

'Do you want more?' he goaded.

The brainless, trained Irrids knew nothing but attack. The final two teamed up with one on each side of Grunt. They ran at him at full express. He suddenly withdrew all his protruding bits into his body and rolled out of harm's way. Only two Irrids would return from the skirmish. The two injured Irrids were left to consider their good fortune.

'Mr Grunt. That was horrible,' said Davidia, crying. She hadn't actually seen anything. Her eyes were tightly shut.

'I meant them no harm. They must have been programmed to fight.'

The two injured Irrids fled. The two left behind dissolved into dust, but before doing so, a glimpse of who they really were appeared as a vision. It then faded.

'It's not safe here. We must continue following the frozen river.'

'I'm not flying anymore in case it's my last flight,' said Batbit. However, he now sat on Davidia's shoulder, using his senses to warn of any pending danger. Grunt was on high alert.

'How do we tell if it's a dark or a light? The weather here so far has been uniformly monotonous, so we won't know how long a dark or a light is. There must be a way of knowing; otherwise we could end up on a never-ending journey. I wonder what the indicators would be that we are nearing the Waterfall of Wetness. Any ideas?'

'They don't exist here,' said a soft, lilted sound.

'What doesn't exist?' asked Davidia.

'Ideas. Nothing can possess one. They aren't allowed. They are too dangerous in anything's possession.'

Grunt, Davidia and Batbit searched the area for the source of the sound. They stood at the edge of the frozen river. Nothing moved.

'Will they hurt someone who has one?' asked Davidia. At home she was often told not to have such bright ideas, as no one would understand them. She ignored that advice and kept producing as many as she could. At school they were very useful.

'They will be discovered. Nobody can be brighter than the leader of the Irrids. If any idea is found with one of them, then that's the last one that they would remember. There would be no more of it.'

'But we have new ones all the time,' replied Davidia. 'We can't stop them because that is how we think.'

'If you have too many it's too confusing.'

'Who are we talking to?'

'I'm known as Clod. My family are scattered everywhere. I'm on the ground in that big lump of dirt that you are looking at. We whisper. My relatives have been sending signals, but not ideas, so we remain undiscovered as a communication highway.'

'Everything seems to want to help us,' said Grunt, marvelling at the ability of the landscape to react positively to them by communication.

'We have no other activity or purpose other than to sit motionless and clog together. Once we were tilled and toiled over, grew food, were jabbed with tools and underground life forms lived amongst us, but now we have no use. We are no longer required.'

'You should grow crops and trees and things,' said Davidia. 'At home we had a vegetable garden with all types of edible plants. Mum occasionally growled at me as I often dug up the wrong one to eat.'

'That's not possible here. Nothing grows.'

'How does anything eat?'

'It is stolen from other nearby valleys. My relatives signal the results, as they are often left barren afterwards. We clods of dirt no longer receive the respect in this valley of being a productive organism. We all wish to be useful once again.'

'Is there any way we can help you?' asked Grunt.

'The badness in the valley must be removed. Only then do we have any hope of becoming nutritious again for plant life to thrive.'

'This isn't a happy place, is it?' said Davidia surrounded by gloom.

'We wish it wasn't so. Once it was different,' the voice began to fade.

'Do you know where the Waterfall of Wetness is? How far is it in time that we'll understand?'

The clod had used its last nutritious elements to speak to them. It was now drained of any goodness. The soil had hardened under foot.

'Keep moving,' ordered Grunt. 'We will find this waterfall.'

'There wasn't any chance to retaliate properly. We were ambushed by a dozen strange life forms, none the valley has seen before,' explained a wounded Irrid.

'Is this how you repay me, by being beaten in battle? You are one of my finest nasties and now there are only you two left. Summon the elite Irridicators at once. I fear we have a problem. Get out of my sight. A dozen you say, mmm.'

Irridia knew her battlers weren't the cleverest of fighters, but they were loyal. All their ideas had been extracted from their minds so they only followed her directions. She was the ideas leader.

'Irridia, the Irridicators are here,' said a lowly Irrid, who was nasty, but hadn't been battle-hardened.

'There is an intrusion of immense danger to our land. You must rid these pests from my, I mean, our, lands. Extermination is what I want.' A fist thundered into the palm of another hand with such force the burnt skin squealed in pain.

'Do you want a trophy from them?'

'Their feet, so they can't walk anywhere. There is trouble here. I feel the danger is the most fearful. I will stamp out any challenge to my authority. Take Irritron with you. You will not fail with it. Go.'

The Irridicators left, snivelling amongst themselves. They were twelve strong, expert swordsmen and athletic strongmen, who acted unemotionally. Irritron was a tracker, gifted with the art of being able to follow any life form over any surface. Its nostrils were twice the size of a normal Irrid and more highly sensitive. Fear was one trait he easily sniffed out. A few snorts and he was clean to go. They returned to the last encounter where the "dozen" dangerous life forms had ambushed the finest four.

'Put your sniffer on that,' directed the head Irridicator.

Irritron sniffed inquisitively and spat in disgust.

'These smells are highly offensive, the worst I have ever inhaled. There is mortal danger amongst them.'

With the sniffer tracker Irritron in pursuit, the skittish, elite Irridicators followed like trained seals, often also sounding like their barks.

'This Waterfall of Wetness might be a myth, Mr Grunt,' said a highly sceptical young girl, not knowing where she was going. She wanted a shower with clean, hot, running water cascading over her and the softest, mild, bubbly soap to deep cleanse her pores. Instead, she had to contend with a miserable walk in a cold, mist-riddled, depressive landscape with no end in sight. It was what bad dreams were made of, or at the least the beginnings of them – her eyes flashed open, her body sprung off the bed like a tensioned spring and hugged the ceiling in a flat embrace; then she awoke – Davidia shuddered at the thought.

'We have to believe that the land life forms have directed us correctly. It would be almost impossible to track through this land in this mist. It isn't my favourite "what to do" pastime either,' replied Grunt, eyes peeled for any shadow-hoppers.

The frozen river began to dip downwards, refusing to release any of its icy components. The ground was still frozen solid, which made for slippery footholds. There were occasional patches of green growth clinging to a few paltry rocks on the last vestiges of their survival. The atmosphere hadn't improved. There were fewer trees here to hide any shadow-hoppers. If any attempt to attack was made, they would see the outlines of the antagonists much clearer. It gave some hope, but not much. Grunt toyed with his necklace again, especially the letter T, the final letter of the message.

He began to hum to himself. His body had a jaunty gait about it. The letter T clearly had a positive effect on him. Perhaps the Valley of Triplock was a happier place. He would soon find out. Batbit moved nervously on Davidia's shoulder.

'Your nails are digging into me,' said Davidia, as Batbit tensed up.

'There is evil lurking behind us,' he said. He flapped his wings in preparation for a quick getaway.

'Mr Grunt, Batbit is restless.'

'I sense something also. We might not make it to the Waterfall of Wetness.'

It was deathly quiet. They moved away from the river a short distance and rested. Their exhausted bodies had battled the light and now it was the dark that disturbed them. They sat down on a set of rocks covered in a flimsy, green mat of growth.

'Are these ejector stones?' asked Davidia. Before her question could be answered, a calm, whispering voice sprung up.

'We hold the secrets to the Waterfall of Wetness. There is a safer, short route to pass through. Only the bravest or stupidest of life forms have ever attempted the Path of Slip. If you don't damage us, we can help you.'

'How do you know anything about what we are doing?'

'Clod and his brothers have sent a message: the salvation of Irridon rests with these weird life forms. There are no other life forms here except the Irrids, so our guess is it must be you. None of you look like you could save anything much. There isn't a warrior amongst you.'

'But we are full of ideas though. We have lots of those,' replied Davidia.

The sparse, green mat almost shrivelled into a ball on the hearing of the word ideas.

'They might be too dangerous to handle, having so many.'

'The more the merrier. This is how we live. Ideas are problem solvers. Where are you?'

'You are sitting on us. We are the last gasp of growth before the valley ends. The Valley of Triplock is nearby. Remember, the Path of Slip is the way out.'

'Where is it?' asked Grunt, seeing that he would have to lead the small expedition.

'Find a slippery surface amongst the rocks. You will know.'

'How can we thank you?'

'Turn the river into running flow again.'

'How?'

'Use one of those many ideas you brag about. A problem shared is a solution halved, a problem solved is an achievement and a problem unsolved is a disaster. You have to select whatever works for you.'

'If we escape, who shall we thank?'

'Your father.'

The moss fell silent. It had become exhausted with the exchanges of sound by sacrificing its nutritional value to pass on details about the path to freedom.

'I didn't quite hear what it said,' said Grunt, who wasn't paying attention at that particular moment. Neither did the others. 'Rest. The light will show us the way.'

Irritron's fully flared nostrils sucked in the air at an amazing rate. Its smell centres translated the oxygen into identifiable patterns, particular to individual life forms.

'There are two definite recognisable life forms; however, there is a non-recognisable finer smell. It might be another. They are nearing the Waterfall of Wetness. If they escape, we might all be smelling an unpleasant part of our anatomies.'

The group "ooh ah'd" at that comment.

'Are we near them?' asked a battle-hardened Irrid, who had been in battle mothballs for quite some time. It wanted some hunting exercise and couldn't wait to flex its bad attitude and weapon.

'The dark has protected them so far. When it is light, we will strike with such ferocity we will enter the annals of folklore.

There must be dozens of them. The finest four nasties might not have told the truth just to give us the surprise of a larger challenge.' The leader was known as Irriot. His behaviour at times tested the saneness of his decisions. 'In the light we can lop off what we like.'

At light, the miserable landscape hadn't improved.

'Time to find our way out of here,' said a yawning Grunt.

'Is it early or late?' said Davidia. There was no way in telling whether it was or not.

'It makes no difference, we must go.' Grunt fiddled with his necklace again. His hand seemed drawn to it. The T began to twirl. He grabbed it. A darkness consumed him. 'It's time,' it said. Grunt saw vast fields of healthy crops, when suddenly it was slashed in half. From the cut emerged a nasty figure. It was about to speak, when a child's voice interrupted the dream sequence. Grunt awoke with a severe jolt.

'I hear snorting noises.'

'Hide behind those rocks over there.'

Davidia and Grunt ran quickly into a huge cluster of smooth rocks. They slipped at first, until they steadied their pace to gain a safe foothold. They looked behind them and could see many shadow-hoppers, who were running erratically. The stooped Irrids were in irridication mode, waving their weapons with expectation and authority.

'I sniff them. They are here,' yelled an excited Irritron. He pointed his nose upwards for a massive whiff, which would indicate exactly where their prey was hiding. Batbit had only been a mere observer until this time and suddenly he saw his chance to be a useful pest again. He flew directly at Irritron.

His sharp claws slashed at his flared nostrils, resulting in a squeal of pain. The other Irrids were transfixed with surprise.

'My face is leaking,' groaned Irritron. His sniffing nostrils were now so tender he could no longer perform properly. He suffered excruciating pain each time he tried to flare them for a huge sniff. His mind was elsewhere. 'Something has damaged them. Look,' he said, pointing at himself.

'Is that what is inside us?' asked Irriot, the leader. 'Let's hope we don't all leak that mess. Where are those life forms? There must be dozens of them nearby. They can't all hide.'

'My nose is too sore to locate them. I wonder what scratched me?' In the dark mist it is difficult to see anything clearly.

'Spread out. They might be able to hide, but they can't stop smelling. Prepare your sniffers.'

The Irrids went into vacuum cleaner technique, noses just above ground level, identifying any locatable scent. Nothing was left unsniffed.

'Over here,' called an excitable irrid. 'They were here at this spot. That green moss substance has their smell. Take a sniff.' All of them took a compulsory whiff.

'That's not so offensive,' said a mild sniffer. 'The dozens of them must all smell the same. There are only a few different scents.'

'It's their plan to confuse us,' said Irriot, wondering where they had all gone. 'Be ready for any attack.' The Irridicators milled uneasily.

⁂

'Well done, Batbit,' said Grunt, beaming with pride at the cleverness of his little friend. 'They will be occupied for a short time. We still have to find that Path of Slip.'

'All these stones have slippery surfaces,' said Davidia, as she tried to remain upright. They walked carefully in the dimness, further into the centre of the huge rock formation. Nothing guided their way.

'Look,' said Davidia. 'That rock over there has a smiley face. It must be misplaced. There's nothing to smile about here.'

'It's not a face,' said Grunt. 'It looks more like a scarred opening across the rock face.'

'It's a smiley face.'

'No it's not.'

'It is.' Davidia was becoming upset.

She let a gentle teardrop fall. Nothing impeded its gravitational drop. It hit the rock surface and spread like a squashed lemon. The teardrop had splattered into even smaller water droplets with each one trying to escape down a crevice. Gravity was sweeping them up. Grunt closely observed their behaviour. At first, it was a caring look that Davidia was upset enough to release her own water from within, then later it turned into a quizzical one as he noticed that the slippery land surface had tried to rejoin them into the original teardrop, with all the droplets rolling along towards the one crevice in the scarred face of the rock. Surprisingly, the teardrop was whole again. Then it vanished.

'Batbit, can you take a closer look?' asked Grunt.

'You want me to fly into a dark cave?'

'You're a bat. It will be like going home.'

Batbit had almost forgotten what he was.

'That's right.' He tweaked his sonar and rocketed into the darkness. He soared through the dark caverns. They all sloped downwards. The inside rock surfaces were all slippery looking. Any light reflection indicated it was so. He stopped a few times on the cave floor, only to be instantly hurtled downwards. There was nothing to grip onto. The floors were slippery. After a few minutes he returned to the surface. He impulsively screeched with delight at his little adventure as he flew out of the cave.

'That was so refreshing. It was like old times again,' he said.

'What was in there?' asked Grunt.

'Darkness and more darkness. It was bat heaven. It's an ideal place to take Mrs Batbit for a holiday. There were so many caves to explore. If only I had more time.'

'Should we dare venture in?'

'The rock surfaces were all shiny and smooth. The cave floor is slippery.'

'Do you think it could be the Path of Slip?'

'It's possible, but without a guide book, clear directions and better light, it's difficult to tell.'

'Let's take a closer look.'

They had almost made it to the cave's entrance, when the bloodcurdling screams of the Irridicators echoed off the rock surfaces. Batbit's impulsive scream of delight had told the Irridicators where they were. They had hopped towards them as quickly as they could. Only the slippery rock surfaces had delayed them pouncing on them earlier. Footholds were uncertain accomplishments.

'There they are,' boomed the voice of Irriot. 'Cut them down into smaller pieces. Let's lop off what we can.'

It was a frightening scenario that followed. Grunt knew that they were in mortal danger. None of their limbs would regrow if they were removed.

'I'm not afraid,' said Davidia. 'I have played Dan's horror vampire videos. It's all make-believe.'

A weapon had been thrown at them, with the sharp point embedding itself in a crevice. It clanged with such a strong vibration, the rock crumbled.

'We have no choice now,' said Grunt. 'Go.'

He hurriedly pushed Davidia into the cave. He was just in time as the Irrids had almost made it to the entrance and were within striking distance. Irriot swung his weapon at Grunt with full force. It just missed him and banged against the rocks. Grunt took a step forward and one of his legs exploded like a cannon ball. It hit Irriot in the stomach so powerfully it repelled him into his nasty band of Irridicators. In the ensuing mayhem, Irridicators accidentally lopped off some of their own body parts and were left languishing in a crumpled mess. Irriot was last seen berating his band of reduced Irridicators.

Inside the cave, Davidia slid downwards all alone into an abyss of darkness. All she could hear were the screeching sounds of a bat. It reminded her of the big slide at Wonderworld, when her dad had accidentally pushed her and she had a scary ride. Her eyes were shut tight. The Wisp of Wischink appeared in her mind. It smiled a comforting smile as she plummeted downward over hard, bumpy rocks. Would it ever end?

Grunt followed and he too disappeared into the bowels of the earth.

Had they accidentally found the Path of Slip?

Irridia, the leader of all Irrids, was incensed with the failure of her Irridicators.

'These life forms seem to be far more dangerous than I

had given them credit for. There must be an army of them to decimate my elite squad of Irridicators like that.'

She felt that her world was now under serious threat. A showdown would determine whether the life forms were strong enough to challenge her. It would be the final battle for some-one. Irridia had never lost a battle or a challenge. She thought that "someone" loser wouldn't be her. She stared over her mist-covered lands, safe in her stronghold hidden high in the mountains. 'I must give those intruding life forms a series of nasty surprises. They were fortunate to escape this time.' Her brooding mind was a steel trap that nothing had ever tested. The coldness of her eyes held fear because of everything they saw. There was an absence of any goodness. Once, it had been different.

9. VALLEY OF TRIPLOCK

'That hurt,' complained Davidia, as she landed in a river bed at the bottom of a huge water-fall. She was spat out of a rock formation, as if expelled from an individual's mouth as an inedible, cherry pip. The river bed was dry and littered with pebbles, stones and rocks of all sizes. Age had worn many of them into round, smooth shapes. Not one droplet of fresh, running flow cascaded over the lip of the falls. 'Am I bruised?' She checked her extremities. There were no bluish markings on her body to suggest bruising. 'My dress is ruined.' She shed a few tears. Frayed edges had formed at the base of her dress. The cotton had begun to unravel. 'I don't want a mini skirt. Where am I?'

She thought that she was alone when she heard a familiar, high-pitched shriek. Batbit went shooting by as if shot from a cannon. He was trying to regain control over his batwings after the fantastic ride he had just experienced. He thought that the next time he did that he'd bring Mrs Batbit along for the ride. What exhilaration!

'Davidia, it's me,' he yelled breathlessly. His adrenalin rush hadn't subsided.

'I'm so glad to see you,' she said. 'Where's Mr Grunt. We haven't lost him, have we?'

Overhead, something that looked like a hot air ball momentarily blocking out the sun, floated by.

'Is that Mr Grunt up there?' she asked. 'It certainly looks like him. He might be playing the balloon game. You know, the ones filled with hydrogen and released to float skywards.'

Batbit flew up to investigate. Sure enough, it was the huge puffball himself. He slowly floated to the ground. Pop. All his external pieces suddenly reclaimed their site on his body.

'That was close. The Irrids almost caught us. Where are we?'

'We don't know. The sun is shining. There's green on either side of the riverbed and we can see clearly at last,' said Davidia. 'I'm not going back to that other awful place again. I like it here.'

'If we follow the river bed it must eventually lead us to a town. Batbit, you can act as scout again.'

Grunt nervously surveyed his surroundings. A comfort blanket of good feelings wrapped itself tightly around him. He remained nailed to the spot. His body relaxed completely as he flopped to the ground like a sack of potatoes. The pebbles beneath embraced themselves in anticipation of a crushing.

'Get off us. We don't mind being brushed with running flow, but to be covered with such a large, heavy outer? It's not acceptable,' said a pebble, or was it a stone?

'It's pitch black now. What an impertinence to cover us without permission,' said another pebble ... stone ... or was it a small rock?

Grunt couldn't hear the protests. He was experiencing warm emotions denied to him long ago. This valley seemed very familiar and messages from the past were twirling inside his head. Uncertainty reigned about what they meant. He was in a world of his own.

'Mr Grunt, are you awake?' asked Davidia as she prodded him.

Grunt returned from dreamland to confront more pressing matters.

'Uh! What's happening?'

'You had an "older life form moment." You fell asleep,' said Davidia.

'I had some strange things occur inside my head. A confusion of thoughts.'

'Do you know where we are? It looks like a nice place to enjoy.'

'I think I have been here before, but can't remember when. Did we pass through the Waterfall of Wetness?'

'There isn't any waterfall. See, it's empty.' Davidia pointed to where they had exited from. It definitely was once a waterfall, but now it was dry.

'That's the border between the two valleys and an entrance through which I must return.'

'What are you rabbiting on about now? We just left that dreadful place and were almost lopped up.'

'I don't understand why I said that, but something made me say it.'

A loud squawk split the ambience of the day. They looked up. High above the Waterfall of Wetness, sat two large, feathered life forms with huge beaks, ideal for ripping apart their prey. Two sets of eyes bored into them. Suddenly, one took flight and landed nearby. It sat ungainly on its clawed feet, eyeballing them cautiously. It was as tall as Davidia.

'Hello there,' it said. The ground communicated the thoughts of the visitor.

'Hello to you too,' replied Davidia.

'May I ask the reason for visiting this valley and why you came via the Waterfall of Wetness?' It tilted its head to one side as a form of habit. It became light-headed once a few words had been spoken.

'It's all his fault,' replied Davidia, pointing a finger at Grunt.

'Me? You hit the ejector stones first to send us hurtling everywhere,' said a defiant Grunt.

'Tut, tut, now. We mustn't display any hostility in this valley. It's not the right thing to do. This is a peaceful place. You still haven't answered my question. Try again.'

'We were chased by shadowy, crazy things called Irrids. The ground directed us to the Path of Slip and here we are.'

'You haven't changed life form to infiltrate the valley, have you? Mmm!'

'Certainly not! I'm a girl. My name is Davidia. What's yours?'

'I'll ask the questions, thank you. What is your purpose here?'

'My tourist visa ran out and I'm going to apply for another,' said Davidia.

'Don't be so silly. There are no tourists here, whatever they might be. I need to know your purpose. Nothing that has ever come out of the Waterfall of Wetness has been good to anything. You may be a spy in a different life form.'

Grunt stepped forward.

'We definitely are not spies. For some unknown reason that we haven't quite worked out yet, we have been sent here from many valleys away. I hold this unusually shaped form for a reason even I don't understand. Are you a guardian of sorts?'

'I can answer that question. Yes. We protect the valley from the bad that can escape through the Waterfall of Wetness. Nothing is as it seems.'

Grunt almost fell over in disbelief. That phrase was one that kept ringing in his head on many occasions. Had it emanated from here? The huge, feathered life form was an imposing figure. His companion tensely watched proceedings from its safety ledge.

'Where are we?' asked Grunt.

'Who will you tell?'

'No one. We want to know where we are. It might mean something.'

The feathered life form abruptly took flight. Dust particles tried to follow, but it was only the instant flurry of flapping wings that momentarily encouraged them. It flew up to its companion. The two of them nestled for a while, discussing the ground-based life forms.

'Are they a threat?'

'I don't think so. They seem acceptable for entrance into the valley.'

'They don't have the smell of an Irrid. Besides, the ground and plants in Irridon wouldn't have directed them safely here if harm was their intent.'

Both feathered life forms lifted their huge claws and gave their chins a scratch. It was the signal that they had agreed on something. The feathered life form with the questions flew down again.

'It is agreed that you can stay. This is a peaceful valley. Make sure you obey the rules. There are other life forms that way.'

'Thank you, Twit,' blurted out Grunt, without thinking.

'What did you say?'

'Mr Grunt called you Twit. Is that your name?'

'How do you know that?'

'It just came out. Is your friend up there called Twirp?'

The huge bird was amazed that any life form entering the valley would know their names. It thought that there must be a trick to it. Once, only a small Igloid called Ignatus, who had played near the Waterfall of Wetness when it was free flowing, had ever known their names, but that was long ago.

'Who told you?' Twit didn't know if he was a Twirp, or was it that Twirp didn't know he was a Twit.

'A thought from my past. I keep having these weird thoughts, ideas and visions filtering through my mind like fine mist. I can't understand it all yet, but they seem to be stronger in this valley.'

Could it be that the oddball-looking life form, in a shape never imagined, once knew them? It was very unlikely. Something must have told him.

'This is the Valley of Triplock inhabited by friendly life forms. Keep to the rules and you will be safe.'

'How do we know what the rules are?' asked Grunt, feeling empathy with the two huge feathered, and to him, cuddly, life forms. In Davidia's world they were known as birds of prey.

'They have a habit of following you. Be safe.'

Twit flew up onto the ledge again to gaze over the valley it protected. It wondered again how the funny-looking life form knew their names. Grunt didn't represent their memories of a small Ignatus playing freely under the care of his parents. The two life forms bore no resemblance to each other. It must have been a mistake or coincidence that it knew their names. Their world resumed its quietness.

Grunt, Davidia and Batbit headed off towards where it was assumed a town and other life forms existed. They were oblivious of an important role that they would have to play out one day soon. The river bed was their guide. The running flow had stopped flowing as its origins were from Irridon where it had been frozen. This was cause for dissent in the Valley of Triplock against their neighbour. Irridon was growing more powerful and its aim was to capture Triplock when they were of sufficient strength. It was nearly that time now. Irridia had been carefully enhancing her army of Irridons for that final push into Triplock. She would then, hopefully, savour the thrill of total victory. If she succeeded there, then the other four valleys, which Grunt had passed through, would collapse like dominoes. The act of revenge had been a long time in the planning. Sadly, she was once a loving and caring life form, but a chance meeting after the Great Split with The Murmur, determined her future, destructive course.

'My feet ache,' complained Davidia. 'These stones are too hard to walk over. When are we resting? Mr Grunt, you have many more feet than me to use.'

'Those small growths over there are waving at us. We'll rest there.'

'I didn't see them waving.' They were all perfectly still according to Davidia.

Batbit flew over them. Nothing stirred. Was anything hiding there? Batbit again flew over the small, stubby growths. Nothing stirred again. As they approached, they felt many eyes were observing them. A comforting rock offered the premier seating available. Davidia wasn't waiting for the courtesy of "old age first". It was her spot. Grunt made do and Batbit nestled on a small branch.

'Are you one of them or one of us?' It was a tiny voice whispering.

'One of what?' replied Batbit.

'A Twixer.'

'I don't know what a Twixer is.'

'It's one of them or one of us,' whispered a chorus of tiny voices.

Batbit looked through the branches and couldn't see anything at all.

'Who's whispering to me?' asked Batbit, alarmed at the lack of any visual contact.

'We are.'

Suddenly, from underneath the tree branches out popped many sets of eyes all facing upwards. They were all attached to long, thin bodies clinging to the underneath of each branch. No wonder they were invisible. Batbit almost lost his grip.

'What are you?' he asked.

'We're Elongators, but sometimes we are known as Stretchers. Our bodies extend like so,' they answered, stretching their bodies to demonstrate. 'We wriggle along branches from underneath, trying to avoid being a food source for other larger life forms. Two large feathered life forms that live that way often eat our relatives, so we climb upside down to avoid being consumed,' they continued, pointing to the direction that the three of them had come from.

'Are you delicious to eat?'

'We think so, otherwise there wouldn't be such an intense interest in our wriggling abilities, would there? We don't do anything else but eat and wriggle.'

Batbit's stomach writhed in pain at his mention of the word delicious. Could he consume any of them? He was terribly hungry. For the moment, he would have to forego his personal needs.

'I would love to sink my teeth into one of those delicious elongators,' he said to himself. His bottom lip trembled at the thought of the opportunity for food that he had just lost.

'Where are you headed?'

'Along the river bed to wherever it leads,' replied Batbit.

'The life forms are larger there.'

'Is there any danger on the way?'

'Can't say whether there is or not. Twixers are everywhere. You have to choose the right one each time you meet them.'

Suddenly, the sky went momentarily dark as two huge-winged shadows crossed the landscape. Twit and Twirp were out hunting and landed closely to where Batbit was resting. He peered out from his vantage point and noted their hunting technique to eat elongators. They shook a branch with their huge talons and the elongators fell helplessly to the ground. Then it was a mad scramble for survival. Their huge beaks shovelled in the frantic elongators. 'Yum, yum,' they said. Batbit clung on tightly in case he was mistaken for food. Soon, they were gone.

'Our relatives have gone. We told you so. Must go. We need to produce more elongators to replace our losses. We'll be busy for quite some time.'

Batbit saw a long line of elongators trail into the distant woods. He had just seen breakfast, lunch, dinner, a late supper and snacks wriggle out of sight. In the meantime, Grunt and Davidia had recovered from their tiredness. Batbit dropped down to join them.

'Do you know what a Twixer is?' Batbit asked Grunt.

'Should I?'

'Those elongators said that they live in the valley and that we might meet them on our journey.'

Grunt had no idea what they were. Davidia was clueless and Batbit's knowledge wouldn't make a dent in a pea.

'There must be a town around here somewhere,' said Grunt, wistfully.

The three friends arose and followed the river bed, traversing from side to side to avoid the large boulders. They rounded a corner and there they saw it. A fortified wall. It was in the process of construction from dirt and large boulders. It seemed there was no unemployment here. Many life forms were busily adding their efforts. They watched safely from a distance and wondered what all the frantic commotion was about. They were completely ignored.

'Mr Grunt,' said Davidia, 'do you know where we are?'

'Not a dropsy, dripsy or drapsy,' came back the unusual reply.

'That doesn't make any sense. Are you confused?'

'This valley is affecting me and I don't know why. Perhaps those life forms over there might make it clearer.'

'Shouldn't we ask someone?'

'Those two are taking a break. Let's see what they are up to.'

The three friends walked directly over to them. The two startled life forms jumped up in fright and stood ready with their arms. The friends stopped dead in their tracks. No prong was worth poking into their bodies no matter how well it was made.

'Stay and state your piece, otherwise you will be full of skewer holes and aerated in a series of thrusts,' bellowed the closest one. The other life form ensured they didn't move by placing his pronger point into the ground in front of them. The fierceness on their faces upset Davidia. She began to sob.

'Is that running flow?' asked one of the life forms, surprised.

Davidia nodded slowly.

'We must tell King Iglandus at once that there is a life form that leaks running flow. You must stay here. Any attempt to escape is impossible.'

'But they are only tears,' she sniffled.

'Have you many of them?'

'Only if I cry a lot when I am upset. That's all.'

'We might need every one of them. Have you given them to anything else?'

'Certainly not! I don't like crying.'

Grunt also thought that it was a strange phenomenon that Davidia could make these water droplets seemingly from nothing. It was perplexing to understand. He thought this human girl life form was certainly an oddity.

'Is there a panic on? Why is everyone working so hard?'

The two armed life forms refocused on Grunt.

'Our valley will soon be attacked by an insidious, evil force from Irridon. We are building defensive walls to protect ourselves.'

'We have just come from Irridon,' said Grunt.

Two prongers were suddenly thrust at Grunt just touching his circumference. It was a defining moment in survival.

'Could either one of you be called Prongsy or Poiksy?' Grunt questioned them, while one hand held his necklace. His fingers felt like they had been burnt.

The two life forms looked at each other in amazement. How was it possible he knew who they were?

'Are you an Irridivisor, trying to pass yourself off as a new life form and infiltrate our valley? Explain quickly, otherwise its aeration for you.'

'We entered the valley via the Waterfall of Wetness after escaping from the Irridicators. The ground, stones and foliage guided us safely to here. Without them, we would have been destroyed,' explained Grunt.

The life forms thought for a moment. They had never heard of anything ever making it safely through Irridon and no one outside of the valley would have any idea about their names. Further investigation would be required. The Irrids were experts at camouflage and no risk was worth not investigating.

'You need to be taken to King Iglandus, who rules the valley. He will know what to do with you.'

'What sort of king is he?' asked Davidia, now that her running flow had stopped.

'Wise and caring,' replied Prongsy, or was it Poiksy?

'At home, mum and dad always talked about a king. His name was Elvis. I didn't know who he was. Apparently he sang songs and played a guitar. Mum said he often acted as stiff as cardboard in films,' said Davidia. She knew they didn't understand what she meant. They wouldn't have any of his records.

'This way.'

The three friends followed the plodding Prongsy and Poiksy, whose legs were like stunted elephant legs with huge, soft pads for ease of walking. They were so quiet whilst in motion that it felt like they were in a silent movie. The landscape everywhere was still a flurry of activity. Preparations were being made for the great encounter yet to eventuate. Grunt noticed that he had no resemblance to any of the life forms here. Somehow, he thought that it would be different.

'I don't look like anything here,' he said.

'Don't worry, Mr Grunt, all of us are different.'

'Back in your world Davidia, others look like you as if you all came out of the same pea pod. Nothing looks as ballish and unpleasant as me.'

'You have extra legs, eyes, ears and noses we don't have and you have special powers too. You should be proud to be what you are. An Igloid, isn't it? There could be some more here in hiding. We just haven't seen them yet. Cheer up.'

Davidia had a way of uplifting a sad moment.

'You're right. I am important. I got us all here safely so far. Our physical differences shouldn't be what we are judged by.'

'Did you say an Igloid? How ridiculous! He doesn't look anything like those ancients. Who is he kidding? One of our rules is to tell the truth and this time to say you are one of them is an insult to our king. He is an Iglood from an ancient race that oversees the valley. They live up there in the mountains and protect us all. You don't look anything like them,' said Prongsy, with a look of disbelief.

'He might be on that imaginative juice,' added Poiksy.

They both grinned through their thick beards. Their day had been made.

'Mr Grunt,' said a stunned Davidia, 'why don't they believe you?'.

'Maybe I got it wrong after all that time inside the Rock of Yocklaw. The memory that I took with me said I was one. I've never seen, nor remember any similar life form members. Maybe there aren't any others like me.' Davidia noticed his skin pores all moisten up. His emotions were trickling out. Davidia shed another tear or two.

'Don't waste those running flows. They might be useful,' said Prongsy. 'You won't run out, will you?'

'And if I did?' Davidia was catching on that they might be important.

'We haven't had any running flows for quite a while. The Waterfall of Wetness used to provide plenty of running flow, but now it's dry. Any running flow is precious. If it doesn't start again soon, the valley may be lost to the evil of Irridon.'

'Oh! So we are important then?'

'Maybe so, maybe not. King Iglandus will determine your fate.'

'I bet he can't sing,' said Davidia, humming to herself.

The trek was long and mostly uphill. On the side of the roads, heavy wooded areas flourished. Life forms seemed to thrill at their freedom. Batbit kept an eye out for any dangers. Grunt's sense of smell made his finely tuned air receptors twitch endlessly. The journey made them all perspire. Their body odours danced on the breeze. Prongsy and Poiksy carried a lot of body fur, which made them perspire at an accelerated rate. Poiksy kept nervously turning his head toward them. He played with his pronger, seeming unsure what to do with it. Grunt's nasal detectors gradually filled with an insidious odour. Grunt wondered whether someone had forgotten deodorant that day. The smell was somewhat familiar. Batbit's nostrils also became agitated. He stressed out at the offensiveness of the smell. What was it that made his ears stand upright like steel spikes? He hopped onto one of Grunt's arms. Davidia was blissfully unaware of the growing strength of the odour. She was walking quietly enjoying the greenery.

'Can you smell that?' Batbit whispered.

'Yes,' replied Grunt, 'it's not pleasant, is it?'

'Haven't we smelt that before in the valley of Irridon? Those Irrids possessed that very same smell.'

'They might have relatives here.'

'That Poiksy seems unsettled. Maybe it's him.'

'Or, it could be they all smell like that here also. Get a closer sniff.'

Batbit flew above Prongsy and took a few real deep breaths. Not bad, considering all that fur it carried. The smell almost choked his ability to continue breathing.

'Did you get a whiff of that? It was fearfully awful. I couldn't do any form of embrace with that swirling around me. Yuck!'

'Do you think he is for real? He couldn't be an Irridicator could he, sent to destroy us?' Grunt was now monitoring

Poiksy's every move. Something just didn't sit right. Prongsy was walking confidently forward, not bothering with checking on them. The pressure of discovery often instigated errors if someone was an undercover agent. Grunt had to find out before they reached King Iglandus' home. Maybe he was the target and the means of access to him was via Grunt and Davidia. Suddenly, Davidia, sometimes not known for her tact, she was only a young girl, uttered the obvious. Prongsy was upwind so he couldn't smell anything.

'What is that awful smell? Pooh! My pet dog Hero used to make those when we chased him around the yard. He's not here, so it can't be him,' she said, screwing up her nose.

The group stopped. Suspicion fell on everyone.

'Let's rest for awhile,' said Prongsy, as he placed his large frame on a tree stump. Poiksy stood erect with a firm grip on his pronger. Grunt, Davidia and Batbit sat facing upwind for relief.

'We'll soon be there. Not much longer now.'

'Prongsy,' asked Grunt, 'have you ever come across any Irridicators in the valley?'

'Sometimes we do. They are dispensed with fairly quickly to avoid any trouble.'

'How can you tell one is in disguise? I assume that's what they do. Are they Twixers?'

'Where did you hear that term? It's not used here. It's dangerous. Once spoken of in a serious manner, you must prove what you have said is correct. They are the rules; otherwise untold punishment is dealt on the accuser. If you are sure of your comment, please repeat it.'

'Is Poiksy a Twixer?'

Prongsy fell off his tree stump with a thud. Poiksy stood firm with weapon raised.

'I am not a Twixer,' said Poiksy, with the conviction of a judge meting out a death sentence.

'Are you one, Prongsy?'

'Definitely not,' he replied calmly, because he said he wasn't.

It was a stalemate. There was no way of proving who was or wasn't because both had said that they weren't. Grunt had a dilemma. If one was a Twixer, how could he prove it? Davidia was restless.

'Let's keep walking. I want to meet a real king,' she said.

'Hold it,' yelled Poiksy.

He raised an arm to inhibit her advance when his furry covering accidentally flicked across her face. A wispy, thin, dry, fur hair flicked the outer surface of her eyes. They instantly revolted against the approach by becoming itchy. Davidia whined a little as she rubbed her eyes with a two-handed fist wipe. A few tears of protection formed on her fingers and she flicked them off. The teardrops made a small arc of droplets as they arched through the air. Splat, splat. Some landed on Prongsy who brushed them off. A few landed on Poiksy, who froze as if thrust into an iced bath. The droplets began to disintegrate his fur. It fell off in heaps to the ground. His outer covering was undressing him. Below the fur, it soon became obvious that he was different. He must have had iglood poo attached to his feet. They were stuck fast. The truth had been uncovered. The evil head, stooped body and rough covering were all revealed. He was an Irridicator impersonating as Poiksy. Prongsy was lightening fast. He threw his pronger at the impostor. It disarmed him and his pronger fell useless to the ground. He began to snarl. They thought it was in anger, but it wasn't. It was in pain. Davidia's tears were slowly destroying him.

'Mr Grunt, he's disappearing. Can't you save him?' protested Davidia.

'It's too late. He's an evil Irrid who wanted to destroy the king and this valley. Prongsy, did you know?'

'It is impossible to tell. A true Twixer is too devious to be caught out.'

'Where would the real Poiksy be?'

'If a Twixer takes over the life form of another then that life form ceases to exist. The real Poiksy is nothing but a memory.'

'Is a memory something that flashes into my head from somewhere else?'

'No. It is a thing that you have experienced regardless of the time you have already lived. We all have memories, but we don't always recall them to mean anything.'

Grunt quashed a few thoughts of his own. 'A true Twixer is too devious to be caught.'

'Why are we able to walk to the king's home without obstruction?' asked a curious Grunt. He had been holding the necklace. It tingled again at the Twixer thought.

'Free passage has been granted because of your group. Such unusual life forms have to be personally inspected by the king. Those two giant, feathered life forms have already advised him of your existence. His curiosity seized his better judgement.'

'Aren't you pleased to visit your king?'

'All life forms obey the rules. Enough of this, let's walk.'

The valley where King Iglandus resided was rich with life. It was enclosed by a high security fence, which was either to keep him safe or intruders out. As a ruler, there was always the inherent risk of assassination. As they approached the gates, a low moan echoed around the valley.

'What's that terrible noise?' asked Davidia.

'It's the Iglood greeting horn, which announces any arrival at the front entrance.'

'Where did it come from? I can't see anyone.'

'Batbit, do a quick flyover,' requested Grunt.

The small, missile-like snack whooshed over the wall. A large net, seemingly from nowhere, shot into the air and entrapped him. His sharp, spiky teeth weren't strong enough to chew his way to freedom. The net with him in it fell to the ground. No one was injured. His struggle was in vain, but a huge hand gently picked him up. It turned him over. It provided no threat.

The front gate opened automatically.

'Identify yourself,' said a loud voice.

'I'm Prongsy, in the king's service.'

'I'm Davidia, in no one's service.'

'I'm Grunt, at the service of good.'

'Is this black life form with you?'

'That's Batbit, a friend of ours.'

'Next time, be aware that it's dangerous to snoop. What's your business here?'

'They have been summoned to King Iglandus,' answered Prongsy, appearing slightly nervous. Grunt sensed a constriction in his vocal chords as he expelled his words. He wondered why?

'Is your name Igloo?' Grunt's question surprised everyone.

'What sort of silly name is that?' Davidia was amused.

From behind the wall out stepped a huge mountain of a beast, taller than all of them.

'Who told you? Prongsy, have you been opening your word gapper again?'

'Me? How could I? I don't know your personal name,' Prongsy indignantly replied.

'Yes, you do,' said Grunt, incensed for some unknown reason. 'You called him that on many occasions when play was allowed inside the walls.'

'I did not. Playing inside the walls has been banned for a long time.'

'Remember that pet name you called a young life form.'

'This is ridiculous ranting. I have no idea what this life form is on about. The sooner I get him to King Iglandus the better for all.'

'Prongsy, answer the question,' demanded the tall life form. 'His pet name is ...'

Prongsy knew he was standing on spongy toast – one slip and breakfast was over.

'It was Iggy.'

'Try again.'

'It was Ignam.'

'Once more.'

'It was Ian.'

'You really have no idea at all, do you?'

'I told you so. Now let us pass. The king will be angry if we are too late.'

'There's no hurry.'

'Prongsy, how is it you don't remember? The real Prongsy was a guardian over a small life form. His pet name was Ignus.'

Igloo was stunned. How did this strange life form know so much from the past? He had been correct with the names.

'How do you know this?' The tall Igloo needed to know.

'I don't know. I was holding my necklace when a flood of thoughts crept into my mind and that's how they came out. Weird, isn't it?'

'Have you ever been to this valley before?'

'Not that I can remember.'

'Let's move,' hustled Prongsy.

'There's one more question I want to ask to prove that you are the real Prongsy,' said Grunt. 'Say the Igloodian alphabet backwards.'

Prongsy had no idea at all. He stammered a few sounds and syllables, not in Igloodian, but in Irridion.

'You can't be the real Prongsy. Who are you?'

Prongsy raised his pronger and threw it with ferocity at Grunt. Fortunately, Igloo was endowed with special powers and caught it exactly at the moment penetration began. He turned the pronger around and redirected it at Prongsy. It hit the mark. Suddenly an evil snarl emanated from beneath all that fur. Another evil Irrid lurked beneath the covering as his outer opened up. Soon he was another bad memory.

'Mr Grunt, I don't like this,' said Davidia becoming upset. 'At home this only happened in video games. My brother Dan used to tell me all the figures were make-believe digital dots. I'm not in a video game, am I?'

'Davidia, you are safe now from all those digital dots.' Grunt had no idea what he was saying, but it calmed her.

'What exactly are you?' asked Igloo, unaware that Grunt was one of them, but in a different body.

'I'm an Igloid.'

Igloo laughed as he shook his head. Humour wasn't a part of his normal demeanour, but for some unknown reason it had been triggered again. It felt good to laugh and smile.

'Follow me.'

'He's tall, Mr Grunt. My dad has a ladder that high. Sometimes he lets me climb it. It's a long way to the top, isn't it?'

Batbit was still netted. He was being carried up. The gates closed. They couldn't see any Igloods because they were usually invisible, a trait that Grunt possessed, but only in short spurts. His memory was generating a familiarity with the landscape, which he didn't yet fully understand. He felt he was a part of something, but what?

They trekked up a long pathway to the base of a huge tree. It was so huge that it took ten adult life forms holding hands together in a "hug me" position, to span its circumference. It was up against a rock formation, which seemed to go on forever. Igloo tapped a few times and slowly a door opened. They entered through the tree, then another door inside the rocks. Grunt felt at home as if he had come back to the Rock of Yocklaw once again. The interior hallways were rather plain, clean and symmetrically perfect. This was the home of King Iglandus, which he shared with the ancient Igloodian life forms that he was leader of. The ancient Igloodians had ruled the Valley of Triplock for a long time. The valley was healthy, its inhabitants were friendly and life was a well-mannered, pleasant experience. Nothing had ever had the audacity or strength to attack their valley before, but King Iglandus knew the time for conflict was near. With all his powers, he couldn't stop the forces of evil. He knew this time that the valley would have to defend itself. Would all goodness disappear forever? He was formalising defence plans when Grunt, Davidia and Batbit were introduced to him.

'This intrusion better be worthwhile. My late-day food intake is about to commence. What have you brought to me?' King Iglandus was thinking of defensive issues.

'Your Regalness, these three strange life forms have made it through the Valley of Irridon alive, so they say,' said Igloo.

'Impossible. Nothing that has entered there has ever survived. Who dares to treat me as a fool? You there, with the round shape, what say you?'

Grunt eyed the king very carefully. He saw a tall, statuesque life form and looked older than anything else he had seen. It was an ancient of some sort. It had long flowing hair, legs as tall as a chimney, muscular arms – but only two – and the craggy features of a rocky outcrop. The deep blue eyes told a truth in its depths.

'Speak plainly when addressing the king,' said Igloo, observing protocol.

'Sir, it's true that we have made it safely through the Valley of Irridon. The ground and plants made it possible for us.'

'Who and what are you?'

'This is Davidia, a young girl life form; this is Batbit, a bat life form; and I am an Igloid.'

'That's preposterous. Imitating an Igloid means destruction for you. You don't look like one of us. How is this so?'

'I have always believed that I am an Igloid. I don't know any other name for me. My memory tells me I am one. I don't know why,' explained Grunt.

'Where have you come from?'

'Far away, from a valley that was overtaken by an evil mist, which I eradicated.'

'This evil you speak of, how did it arrive?'

'It appeared from nowhere in the atmosphere. It covered all the landscape with ice, freezing moisture.'

'Mmm. That seems to be a pattern. How did you get here? Who led you to this valley?'

Davidia had been quietly listening, but a precocious young girl can't stay silent forever.

'I did, Mr King,' she said proudly.

The king turned toward her.

'Come, come. A small thing like you did this, you say?'

'Yes. I pressed some ejector stones and we flew though the darkness.'

At the mention of the ejector stones, the king stiffened. He leant forward to scrutinise more closely the small life form.

'And where were these ejector stones?'

'In a wall, in a tunnel. I accidentally fell on them. Mr Grunt got angry as we didn't know where it tossed us.'

The king thought for a moment. His heart rate had hit the top of the danger scale. Did he dare to believe?

'You called him Grunt. Is that what you are called?' the king directed the question directly at Grunt.

'That is what I am called.'

'This valley you speak of, does it have a name?'

'It's the Valley of Preciousness. I was its guardian from inside the Rock of Yocklaw. I have protected the valley for a long time.'

'So you have,' mumbled the king.

Is it possible that this hideous life form was once … ? The king shook his head. He looked at the throwback in front of him; was it possible that it might be his banished son, Ignatus, who had been banned long ago by evil forces?

Many eons ago, King Iglandus was partnered to Queen Irridia and they had one son called Ignatus. Life in the valley was happy then. Life forms, Igloids and Igloodians enjoyed harmony with their neighbouring valleys. It all changed during the dark of the Great Split. Quietly and insidiously that dark, an evil demon known as The Murmur slipped unnoticed into the Valley of Triplock. Queen Irridia was walking outside the safety of the palace walls when they met. The Murmur whispered that ideas of grandeur and absolute control could only be gained by being infected with evil. The Murmur somehow knew of the power struggle between the king and queen over how Ignatus should be raised. It knew that to gain control of the valley, Queen Irridia had to be swayed to embrace its evil demons. It also knew that King Iglandus would never give up the valley to evil, so a new valley had to be set up, the Valley of Irridon and that they would have to bide their time. Queen Irridia was incensed that the young Ignatus would rule the valley after the king's passing or right of passage, whichever occurred first, when she believed that right should pass to her. She couldn't risk direct confrontation with the king, so that dark she left the palace to pursue her own selfish and powerful goals. She wanted to rule a valley in her own right. In doing so, she encouraged Ignatus to meet her outside the palace walls under the pretence of telling him a special secret. The Murmur then kidnapped him. He was taken to Irridon and visited the Cave of Murm where The Murmur lived. A special banishment spell was cast on Ignatus, never to return. The Queen, probably now ex Queen Irridia, had rid herself of any competition for the top spot. Her actions had left her short of followers, but in time her evil force, with the guidance of The Murmur, would gain sufficient strength to overthrow the Valley of Triplock, which was the prized valley at the time. Ignatus hadn't grown old enough to be immune from banishment as he hadn't reached the age of "no effect" where an Igloid becomes an Iglood. King Iglandus heard of the disappearance of his son and sent emissaries everywhere to locate him. Twit and Twirp found him near the Cave of Murm and reported it to the king. In haste he sent them back with a powerful tool in the form of a necklace in a battered tin. They were instructed to place it in his son's clothing, which miraculously they did at great risk to their own feathers. Ignatus was outside the Cave of Murm when the two feathered friends located him. They quickly tucked the tin inside his pants and escaped with their existence. Shortly thereafter, he was banished elsewhere in an unrecognisable form. No one knew where. The king was devastated at the loss. Irridia smiled a revengeful smile of satisfaction. She had taught the king a lesson that she should be the rightful ruler and not their son. Ignatus was banished with loss of memory, so that he could never become a future threat. Smug satisfaction grew across Irridia's face. Together with The Murmur, they plotted the future downfall of King Iglandus. The time of the Great Split the dark cast doom everywhere, except in the Valley of Triplock. It had been too powerful to fall under the spell of evil. However, it was nearing time where this would not be so. Only the return of Ignatus would stem the tide of evil. Irridia had ensured that it was never going to happen. She had made a complete success of evil. The necklace that Ignatus was banished with, known only to the king, was the only window of salvation and the path back to the past, if it was ever found. It seemed that evil would win over good.

Davidia had unknowingly opened up the path to the past by discovering the necklace in the battered tin and accidentally pushing the ejector stones. Fate had another exercise in store for Grunt.

'May I see the necklace that you speak of?' The king knew that if it was what he thought it was, he had found his long lost son. It would be a defining moment for the valley and his kingdom, if it were true.

Grunt slowly took the necklace off and showed it to the king. His eyes lit up instantly like a flare, with instant recognition. He couldn't believe his eyes. This was the necklace that he had sent to Ignatus all that time ago. Could this life form actually be him? The king's head pounded heavily. 'I don't believe it, I don't believe it,' he kept repeating to himself.

'Where did you get this necklace? Did you steal it or did something give it to you?'

'Mr King, I found that necklace in a small tin hidden in a cave wall, just as I have already told you. My mum always taught me to tell the truth. Mr Grunt has taken us through many valleys to be here,' expressed Davidia.

'I want to be sure what you tell me is correct. The future of Triplock may depend upon it. The wearer of this necklace, if it be true, is my son.'

The revelation hit like a thunderbolt. Grunt fell to the floor in shock. He had found his daddy. The pain of relief and dis-belief oozed out of his every pore. After the initial shock he regained his composure.

'Is that correct? Could I be your son? I don't look anything like you, though. It can't be true, can it?' Grunt was suffering from an emotional upheaval and the shock of an instant family.

'It is true. You are an indifferent looking life form, but banishment can do that to you. It's obvious it was meant that you would never really discover who you are. Do you have any memories of the past?'

'Very few. Sometimes things fade in and out without mak-ing any real sense.'

'This necklace was sent to protect the wearer and provide a pathway back to its past if it was ever discovered. However, before the wearer, which is you, could have succeeded in this quest, it was necessary to experience what evil can do. It is called character building. It was also in preparation for the real quest that you had to undertake; the destruction of the evil within the Valley of Irridon and its return to peace and harmony. It was an extremely difficult task. Impossible, some would say. The danger is that valley is everywhere. Only a true Iglood can combat such evil. You are not that Iglood in your present shape,' explained King Iglandus

'I remember that the Waterfall of Wetness is important

and that if I were to enter the Valley of Irridon, then that is the chosen path. I don't know why,' said Grunt.

'There is no running flow to cleanse you so that path is unavailable.'

'That imposter, Prongsy, said that running flow was needed to release the flow in the Waterfall of Wetness. Davidia possesses that running flow. I've seen it. Is it important?'

King Iglandus sighed a "waste of time" sigh and smiled sympathetically at Grunt. He thought that it was inconceivable that Davidia's small frame could possess such important wet matter. Were they humouring him? Mmm.

'It is said that wet matter is required to recommence the running flows again, which once made the valley more fertile, but alas, there hasn't been any flow since the Great Split. There is none to be found,' said King Iglandus.

'Mr Grunt is right. I do have running flow, but they are called tears. Would you like to see them?' said Davidia. 'I have to feel sad or hurt for them to occur.'

The king was astonished at the impertinence and confidence from such a life form.

'Please show me your wet matter,' requested the disbelieving king.

Batbit suddenly dug his claws into Davidia's shoulders much harder than usual. The suddenness of the pain made her cry. Batbit felt awful that he had hurt his friend, but the surprise pain would increase the potency of the tears. Davidia's eyes welled up into two small pools of moisture. Gravity gave them a boost by forcing them downwards. Grunt cupped two of his many hands to catch the precious moisture. The king sat down dumbfounded.

'Well, I never,' gurgled from his throat. 'Save it, please.'

A small container was brought out and Grunt tipped

the tears into it. A small pond developed in the bottom of it. Davidia stopped crying.

'There, I told you,' she said, sniffling a little. 'That really hurt, Batbit.'

The small bat sat sullenly; however, his instinctive reaction might save the valleys.

The king admired the fantastic ability of Davidia to leak. With all his fabled powers, he did not have the ability to create pure, wet matter.

'This moisture must be saved. In the next light, we will call the great archer Imagoodshot to prepare for us. That is enough for this dark. At next light, we travel to the Waterfall of Wetness. An important task lies there. Igloo, see that they have comfortable quarters. May the next light shine on your eyes.'

'Do you have anything to eat?' asked a ravenous Davidia. 'I don't want grass, insects, goo or other small life forms.' The pained expression on her face relayed the message well and clear.

'Igloo, take them to the open gapper inhalation room. There they will find a range of items that they might enjoy.'

They entered a large room containing a solitary, bare, large table.

'Please sit,' said Igloo.

'There's nothing here. We can't eat fresh air,' complained Davidia.

'Place your face on the table, close your eyes for a moment, dream of food and then open them.'

Davidia wasn't convinced. She was too tired to disagree. She did as she was told.

'This is ridiculous. I might fall asleep.'

She opened her eyes and there on the table sat a bowl of what looked like various types of fruit. Davidia's small hand grabbed the first item, which disappeared at her touch. She tried again. Same result. Her frustration grew like an air bubble, ready to explode.

'Where is the food? It runs away each time I touch it.'

'It's fast food,' said Igloo smiling.

'Mr Grunt. Are you eating anything?'

'I'm already full,' he replied.

'Batbit, what have you eaten?'

'The most delicious, chubby elongator that I've had the pleasure to swallow. Mrs Batbit would be so jealous. We don't eat gourmet insects at home.'

'Where's mine? I don't see anything.'

'It's right in front of you. Remember; turn your head the other way.'

Davidia finally did the reverse and saw a round, red object. Her hand brushed it lightly. It was solid. She picked it up carefully. It didn't try to escape.

'What's this called? It looks like an apple.'

'That's a Rotunderer.'

Davidia planted her set of small chompers on the Rotunderer and enjoyed an edible experience. It was quickly eaten.

'Have a drink of Tremature to accompany all that chewing.' Igloo was good with the advice.

Davidia enjoyed her first burp in the valleys and rested well that dark.

That dark, in the Valley of Irridon, agitation grew throughout. Her feminine intuition told Irridia that the next light was fraught with danger. Her attempts at controlling all valleys had been upset by those strange life forms that had outwitted her evil at every turn. Even in her valley, right under her evil nose, they had escaped via the Path of Slip. She didn't believe that she had seen the last of whatever they were. She ordered her Irrididominator force to prepare for a mass incursion during the next light. The snarling, nasty, smelling Irrids snorted grossly at the thrill of a lopping. No one would go hungry in the next light. The valley didn't sleep that dark. Irridia had no idea in what form an attack would manifest itself, but she was prepared to battle to the finish. She thought that her kingly ex-partner would rue the day that he interfered with her child and denied her what she perceived to be her rightful leadership honour. That dark, Irridia visited the Murmer in the Cave of Murm with her senior nasties. The battle plan was under foot. The magical powers of evil would feast this dark.

The next light came early, shining brightly and teasing the valley inhabitants awake. King Iglandus was waiting for the arrival of his great archer, Imagoodshot, whom he had summoned to the palace. Grunt, Davidia and Batbit sat on the stone seats with the king too. Grunt had retained his necklace, which had provided great interest the previous dark, and kept incessantly fiddling with it.

A loud horn sounded the arrival of Imagoodshot.

'He's got bows and arrows,' said Davidia. 'What is he going to do with them?'

'The king will explain,' replied Grunt. 'They are enormous, aren't they?'

'I don't suppose he would give me a free ride on one of them,' said Batbit, now fully confident of any fast ride.

'My faithful warrior, your special services are needed immediately.'

'Greetings, Your Highness,' said Imagoodshot, bowing to the king. 'What is your request?'

'Two flighters to be shot over the Waterfall of Wetness into the valley of Irridon with each flighter carrying one of these two containers of pure, wet matter. They are to land on the frozen river and be dispersed. If I am correct, the Waterfall of Wetness will then recommence its running flow. I cannot stress the importance of this task. The valley depends upon its success.'

Imagoodshot was a very tall Iglood with the strength of ten of them. His muscles bulged from his arm, as if there was no room left for anymore. He wondered what the three odd life forms sitting there had to do with anything.

'At your service, sir. I will meet you at the Waterfall of Wetness shortly. I must prepare two of my best flighters to successfully carry out your request.'

Imagoodshot left. The king motioned to the others to follow him. It was strange that he didn't have any bodyguards with him as they walked to the Waterfall of Wetness. Grunt thought he was either brave or very foolish. Remember that an Iglood had the power of invisibility. At the location, the two large, feathered life forms, Twit and Twirp, flew down to greet the king, who whispered something to them. A wild shriek erupted as they flew off at a fantastic speed over the waterfall and into the deadly Valley of Irridon.

'Will they return?' asked Grunt.

'One can never be sure if anything will return from there,' replied the king.

'Then they are doomed.'

Davidia began to sob again at the realisation that the two

lovely, feathered life forms might never be seen again. Frantic efforts were made to save her tears in case the extras were needed. The invisible Igloods all carried a small container in which to catch the drops.

'How can you be so cruel?' she continued, sobbing. A few of her teardrops fell to the ground. Miraculously, tiny ponds formed from the fallen teardrops. They all stood amazed and thought that the small life form must be very powerful.

Imagoodshot strode along the riverbed. He held an almighty propulsor and two equally impressive flighters in his hands. The precious pure, wet matter was securely attached within a shatterable point that would disintegrate upon impact, but only with a hard surface.

'They are known as bows and arrows in my world,' said Davidia. 'My brother Dan and I often played Cowboys and Indians and that's what the Indians had. He was always the Indian so he could fire the arrows at me. They sometimes hurt and I would cry. He grew up, so we don't play that any more. Besides, Miss Percival was tired of bandaging my wounds. I actually told mum about him.'

'Prepare for flight,' said the king.

Imagoodshot lay down his tools in the riverbed. From out of nowhere, two assistant Igloods appeared out of a deep hole into which the propulsor was firmly placed. This was to give added strength to the tension power of the propulsor. Chattering voices, waving arms, pointing fingers, sighs and eye-level management all culminated in the precise location for the propulsor to be placed for the flight path the flighters would take. The intention was that they would hit the iced river. This had never been tried before. Would it succeed? All was in readiness.

'Shoot,' commanded the king.

The propulsor was drawn back taut, the flighter was

wavering with a nervous movement and at the precise coordinates of pull and angle – ping, Imagoodshot let go and the flighter disappeared over the waterfall high into the unknown. He repeated it with the second flighter, but made some minor adjustments. It too, flew on its one-way journey. Only time would tell if they had been successful. The Valley of Triplock was now in limbo. The wait had begun.

'We must move out of the riverbed for safety.'

'What if it fails?' Grunt wanted to know.

The king sighed uncomfortably. Only he knew how close the Irrids were to invading his valley. By the time this best kept secret was disclosed, the king hoped he would have an answer to the invasion. He didn't. This was his last hope of saving his valley.

Irridia felt the weakness of Triplock. It was almost time.

10. THE CHALLENGES

'I don't like the feel of his place,' said Twit. 'It's dark, wet and ever so cold. Nothing could be happy here, could it?'

'This is my first visit in years. There's probably no politeness here. My, how it has changed,' replied Twirp.

'Where are we supposed to fly to?' Visibility was very poor and the mist discoloured everything to be a uniform grey. Landmarks would be hard to locate and recognise.

'The king said, follow the grey-streaked light just above us for fifty-seven flaps and we should land on a tall tree which pierces the clouds. Down there, we couldn't fly safely. It would be too dangerous. Look, there it is.'

Twit and Twirp were the flying scouts of the king and loyal to their last feather. They were sent as forward reconnaissance and to wait for the signs of the two speeding flighters. They were each to follow a flighter on its path into the mist and ensure that the pure, wet matter was successfully dispersed at all costs, even if it meant the loss of all their feathers, a lopping and no return.

'How long must we wait here? We can't see the ground from here.'

'Shush,' whispered Twirp. 'Keep that beak of yours closed for a moment. Can you hear that snorting?'

Twit tilted his head to one side. It detected the sounds of a huge number of snorters.

'They must all have a case of bad breath with that nasal activity, mustn't they?'

'I don't think they appreciate good manners in this valley.'

'Quiet. Listen. I hear a hissing sound. It's a flighter. Be ready. Look, there it is. Go. Follow it down,' ordered Twirp.

'Why should I go first? You're senior to me. You should go,' whined Twit, a taxidermist's dream.

'I haven't got time to argue.'

Twirp chased the flighter down through the layers of mist into an uncertain future. As he got closer to the ground, the coldness intensified and his flapping rhythm increased. Another sound grew louder also. It wasn't the cold that sent shivers through his spine. It was the sinister snorters, revelling in the chances of a lopping. The flighter sped through the mist, heading straight for the iced river. Suddenly, an unexpected gust of wind blew it slightly off course and it landed on the edge of the river a few metres short of a band of Irrids. The clattering noise attracted their attention. The flighter hadn't broken the small container of pure, wet matter and so it was there for all to see. Twirp halted his descent and took refuge in a small tree just above the Irridion eyeline.

'Who threw this long twig?' An Irrid leader screamed. Their IQ might be equal to what can be found at the bottom of a fish bowl, but when it came to loud language, nothing could compete. The louder they yelled the higher up the idiot chain of command they were. Everyone robotically shook their heads. 'Who's pulling my tree stump?' He yelled louder. Again, a unanimous shaking of the heads. The leader went over to inspect the lost tree twig. 'This tree has grown perfectly straight. Do we have any trees in Irridon this straight?'

'It fell from the clouds. It must be a sign of good fortune. Maybe Irridia sent it as a "thank you" message.'

The leader wasn't sure who said that and didn't quite believe its content. To add to the confusion, Twirp had landed on a thin branch of a tree and it cracked under his weight. Bang! He landed on the ground. He let out a piercing, painful shriek. High above the mist, Twit heard the call. Just as he did, the second flighter hissed by and gave chase. It too went down deep into the mist and with all the warm air generated by all the snorting activity, a small warm, upward air current pushed the flighter off course and it also landed next to the iced river. However, Twit was in a downward spiral and he landed with a thump. The two large helpless, or so they gave the impression of, birds clumsily stood on their claws fussing over their feathers.

'I don't think they're damaged. Such feathered refinery wouldn't be appreciated here,' said Twirp.

'Don't fuss so. My feathers are as fine as yours,' replied a vain Twit. The two ego-driven birds were more concerned over their appearances than the immediate danger that they faced. The Irrids approached.

'Leader. A second straight twig has landed. There must be a forest of straight trees somewhere, all wanting to visit our valley.'

'We'll find that forest after we've dealt with these two feathery things. How did you get here?'

'We flew.'

Twirp was the brighter bird and gave the excuse that something fired a straight twig at them, trying to shoot them down and in the panic to escape, they landed in Irridon by mistake. The Irrids were itching for a good lopping and the best item to lop off was their heads. They were the easiest item to attack.

Thankfully, both small containers were still intact. Twirp edged closer to one of the flighters and took a firm grip on one of them with one huge claw. His pointy talon was poised to crack open the container. Twit had seen Twirp's action and mimicked it. The two clumsy birds were now surrounded by danger. They edged backwards onto the ice. The river was frozen solid. They suddenly realised that it was impossible to escape. Their fate was almost sealed. Maybe a plea for leniency would save them.

'Please, sir,' pleaded Twirp, 'We don't mean any harm. We're lost and want to go home.'

'Go where?'

'To the Valley of Triplock.'

'The what?'

'The Valley of Triplock.'

'That's an insane request. We're going there, but you aren't. Off with their heads.'

Twit and Twirp stood back to back with wings outstretched. This gave the illusion they were three times their normal size. It was just enough time to crush the wet matter containers onto the ice and spill the contents. At first, nothing happened. The Irrids by now were all on the frozen river.

'It's over. Dinner will be served,' yelled the leader, waving his lopper in its favourite strike position.

Before he could strike a fatal blow, his foot sank into the ice and he was trapped. This halted the Irrids' advances toward Twit's and Twirp's possible last outing. A rumbling noise grew from under the ice. Another Irrid's foot sank, then another and so on. Not one of them could move. However, underneath, the ice was melting and the running flow had begun. Davidia's tears had freed the iced river and it started to flow once more. The Irrids screamed in fear. They had a hatred of water. It would wash away their smell. Suddenly, the top layer turned into running flow and they were all washed down the Path of Slip in a raging torrent. Twit and Twirp floated safely back into the Valley of Triplock and were ejected out through the Waterfall of Wetness.

The Irrids that were also washed down were captured by the Igloods and caged so they couldn't escape. The leader was incensed that two, dopey, feathered life forms had outsmarted him. There would be no more IQ schooling for him. Irridia would lop them for failure, if they ever returned.

'Hello there,' said Twit. 'This is my first time in running flow. What fun.'

'He landed on the ground, sir, so that may have unbalanced him,' said Twirp.

The two large birds made it to dry ground and flapped vigorously to release any clinging wetness. They bowed to the king.

'Thank you, my loyal friends. The running flow that has begun will once again nourish the valley. I can't thank you enough for your efforts. Davidia, it seems you are a powerful life form, which has surprised all of us. Imagoodshot prepare the archers for a firing, so that when the time comes, we are prepared to defend our valley to the last life form.'

The king knew that, even with their fabled powers, it might not be enough to defend the valley. If they were overrun, no life form would survive. The Irrids would decimate every form of goodness. The black heart that Irridia possessed needed a colour change. Once it was a bright yellow, but revenge had darkened it with evil. He wondered how his three odd visitors would play their part in saving the valley. Hope was not encouraged at the sight of a young girl playing with some pebbles, a small, black bat foraging amongst the rocks playing hide and seek with any insect and the out-of-shape Grunt, protruding everywhere with arms, legs and noses, pretending he was a powerful guardian. The king thought that Grunt may have been a guardian, but by the look of him doubted if his powers were strong. He thought that this team of misfits had no hope of succeeding against Irridon. Oh, how his aching heart would like to believe that Grunt really was his son. His physical form didn't quite fit with what he believed his son should look like.

'Mr Grunt, you need a bath. Phew! I can smell you from where I'm standing,' said Davidia. Young girls didn't perspire nearly as bad as larger life forms did. 'Mum made me take a bath every night whether I was dirty or not. Miss Percival wasn't allowed to because she was a doll. She always smelt nice. Go on, you need it.'

Grunt grumbled to himself. The Waterfall of Wetness was of great significance to his memory without him receiving any explanation as to why.

'Stand back. I might be messy. It has been a while.'

Grunt walked toward the waterfall. Its clean, running flow cascaded from above as a message of goodwill. In its waters was the life-changing power source of Igloodian strength. The king had almost forgotten its value. The necklace around Grunt's neck began to disintegrate one letter at a time, the closer he went. Soon it was a small insignificant chain any jewellery shop would sell to its customers and tell them it was a valuable item. He turned around to his expectant audience.

'Don't forget to wash under your arms,' yelled Davidia.

The five letters that had fallen to the ground from the necklace each reflected back at him all the powers that an ancient Iglood possessed. Only a royal Iglood had a chain with them.

Grunt possessed all of these powers. Had the Valley of Trip-lock found a new royal and future king?

'It's cold,' he complained.

'Don't be a scaredy cat. The water likes you,' encouraged Davidia. She was a wise young girl. The Wisp of Wischink who had escorted her in her mind this far, was pushing out of her mouth the intelligent words she was expressing. It was called development and growing up.

The running flow roared its welcome. Was it yelling at Grunt to come closer? Grunt stood mesmerised as the playful droplets danced over the rocks. This was his first wet experience. The downward force of the running flow held an enormously powerful weight which flattened anything beneath. As Grunt walked into the cascades, the middle parted so that he wasn't hit with the full force it possessed. Suddenly, it knocked off an arm, then a leg, then another arm, a nose and an ear. He was being progressively dismantled. His skin pores all rushed off his body in haste to escape a thrashing. All that was left was a round plain small rotating ball in the middle of the cascades. The small group of onlookers were aghast at the seeming loss of their friend.

'Can't we save him?' Davidia wailed.

'It's too late for him now,' replied the king. 'We must return to the palace and plan our defences.' He began to walk away. Twit and Twirp chirped in agreement. Imagoodshot had more strong flighters to prepare. Only Davidia and Batbit watched helplessly at the diminution of their friend taking place.

'Don't cry, Davidia. They don't need any more of your tears,' said Batbit. He squealed a stifled sob.

'Will we ever see him again?'

'I don't know.'

Sadness grew within them, but only for a moment.

Bang! Bang! A huge thunderclap struck the waterfall. Running flow sprayed everywhere. A brilliant, yellow light shone from the rocks covered by the running flow. The cascade became an enormous light show. Another thunderclap split the air. The yellow light contracted into a small, sun-like ball at the top of the waterfall. Twit and Twirp suddenly appeared at its edge with wingspans at full flapping capacity.

'It's your turn to kick it,' said Twit.

'Thank you,' replied Twirp. 'Manners are important, aren't they?'

The two flapping birds positioned themselves for the vital kicking. Twirp carefully flew over the edge, extended his huge talon and gently kicked the yellow ball, sending it on its final journey. As soon as Twirp touched it, it materialised into a solid, yellow shard of light. Down it went into the cascades, piercing Grunt. The cascades opened up like an unravelling carpet roll. Grunt began to unfold. He grew and grew and grew. Davidia and Batbit stood with mouths agape, but with no word offerings. The king observed from a distance. The noise had attracted his attention. All was silent. Without warning, a huge, new life form emerged from behind the Waterfall of Wetness. What was it?

Grunt had metamorphosed completely to become the great ancient that was his destiny. He was tall, strong, better looking than his previous form and walked with a royal swagger. He called out to the king.

'Dad.'

It was the treasured voice of his son, Ignatus, who had been lost for so long. The king came running to embrace his son.

'Son.'

It was the most important word that he had spoken in the valley.

Davidia and Batbit couldn't believe it. Grunt was someone else. They weren't too sure how to handle the change. Davidia ran to hug her new friend.

'Can I still call you Mr Grunt?' she asked, staring at him with her melting, blue eyes.

Grunt knelt down to hug her. He whispered, 'Yes, but only you.'

The king now felt confident that the valley would be saved with the return of his son.

'Ignatus, there are things that you must learn. Igloo, take care of these two.'

The king and his son, Ignatus, were once again united as one. Any foe now had a considerable enemy.

'How is it possible that the iced river is now running flow again?' demanded Irridia of her followers. 'Tell me, or you will be slit from your ugly face to your revolting smelly feet. Out with it.'

'There are no survivors. They all disappeared into the Valley of Triplock. It is said that two giant birds, five times larger than any of us, landed on the ice, cracking its surface and the running flow began.'

'What! Those two, slow moving elephants of the air got the better of my followers? They aren't bright enough to have a thought between them. Summon the army. We march at the next light to the Valley of Triplock. They are weak and we are strong. I will have my rightful place as ruler. Remember, the best loppings are the heads. King Iglandus, enjoy your last breaths. At the next light it will be a permanent dark for you all.' Irridia laughed insanely. Jealousy had suffocated her goodness and The Murmur had sucked dry any leftovers.

Hate ruled the Valley of Irridon. Would change be thrust upon them?

*

'Sir, the Irrids are forming for an attack above the Waterfall of Wetness. There are too many of them. We are all doomed,' reported a frightened scout.

'Dad, send Batbit to assess their strength. He was a bat commander in the cave we lived in. He's a fight specialist,' said Ignatus.

'Can I trust him?'

'You have my word of honour.'

'Send for the bat.'

Shortly, Batbit arrived for his orders. The king explained his mission.

'I'll need a full stomach if I am to succeed. You don't have any elongaters here, do you?'

A few moments later, three large, wriggly elongators were delivered. Batbit eyed them hungrily. He was about to chomp hard on them, when one of them spoke.

'Haven't we met before in the trees? I remember your tiny, spiky teeth. You don't eat friends, do you?'

Batbit dropped his intended meal in fright and it slithered safely away with its friends.

'I'll go anyway.'

The king explained to Ignatus the position he now held in the Igloodian community. He was to be its new leader. The king took Ignatus to a private part of the palace banned to everyone except royalty. There he practiced his new special powers such as invisibility, changing life form patterns using his indomitable strength and the skills of combat. However, the emotional side of his power was the most special and powerful of all. He was advised how to use it most effectively.

'It is surprising the effect kindness has on anything. Apply it liberally. A hug is for free. Those special glands on your wrists hold the key to our victory. They operate by rubbing your wrists against the wrist of an Irrid. It must be transmitted during a hugging session. Be subtle. If caught during the transmission, you might be lopped. The Irrids have lacked kindness from their emotional diet. Feed it to them and you may be surprised. You can transform into their life form and hug them by surprise. Once you have achieved your individual task that Irrid then becomes instantly paralysed as the process reconverts them to goodness and they leave their unsavoury past behind. They in turn can then perform the same task as you, but only once. We want the good returned to them, not the destruction of their existence. Once Batbit has returned, you must enter during this light, not the next one, and infiltrate into Irridon through the Waterfall of Wetness.'

Iglandus began redeeming his full set of memories one at a time. Would they hold any dangers and sadness for him that he should face? Did he have a mother and, if so, where was she? Now that he knew he was an ancient Iglood, real meaning had been restored to his existence. The change meant he was a something. He no longer required the necklace to feed visions and thoughts into his mind. Soon his memory would be fully restored.

The journey into Irridon would be fraught with unparalleled dangers. He felt that his new powers were more than capable of making a difference. This effort would seem to be the longest light and dark he would ever experience. This was the one journey he had to make alone. A leader must lead by example.

It was time to leave.

'Mr Grunt, be careful,' called Davidia. 'Miss Percival wants to meet you when you return,' she pouted. 'Why can't I go with you?'

'It's too dangerous for one so young and small. Stay here with the king and Igloo. I will be away one, maybe two, lights and one dark. Batbit, you come with me.'

Ignatus and Batbit headed toward the Waterfall of Wetness.

'What's with the new power trip?' asked Batbit, stunned that the giant he walked next to was once his timid, fellow cave dweller.

'I feel that this is my time. I finally know who and what I am. We have to save all the valleys and return them to good and harmony.'

'These Irridions won't let us near them. I'm too small to hug.'

'Leave that to me. When I was Grunt, I was so large and rotund I couldn't physically hug anything. Nothing appealed to me. Now it's a race of nasty, smelly, snorting loppers who care for nothing but destruction that I must embrace. Ugh! Their perspective needs tweaking. I only have one nasal sniffer now; what a beauty.'

Ignatus breathed in heavily. All sense particles were immediately identified.

'I can even smell those Irrids from Irridon. Wait for me at the top of the waterfall.'

Batbit flew upwards and out of sight. Ignatus walked into the waterfall. Running flow sprayed everywhere as he disappeared. Soap hadn't been invented yet.

'Get out of my way, you dirty mongrel, or you'll walk one legged,' threatened an Irrid.

'You piece of rubbish. I'll send you back to oblivion if you don't give me that sitting space,' snarled another.

'That's my rock. I'll crack your shell if you don't back off.'

'I'll toss you into the running flow if you don't obey orders,' yelled out a leader.

'You stink. I thought it was a passing phase, but no, it lingers with you. Keep away from me.'

'You're just as bad, you road-mapped weasel.'

'Come any closer and you'll breathe from a flat face.'

'Your stoop might be permanent if you don't perform in the next light.'

'It's your fault we're stuck here in this morass of detritus from Irridon. I want to lop something.'

'Nothing would miss your ugly head. I might lop it off myself if you keep your open gapper, gapping.'

'You and what army, you exaggerator?'

'That's my food. Drop it or I'll prong you.'

'I'm in charge of you ragged lot, so stop the whining or I'll plug you with my fist.'

'He's a yeller. All sound, but no grunt. The only thing he hurts is his vocal chords.'

'Where's Irridia? She should be here. Shirked it again, has she, when a real battle is about to start?'

'She'll lop you for disobedience, you crazy lopper.'

The restless Irrids often fought and argued amongst themselves prior to a conflict. It sharpened their senses. The Irrid army was at the confluence of a full-scale confrontation. Their thought communicators were all cross-wired for conflict.

Irridia was sitting quietly with The Murmur in the Cave of Murm, contemplating their next move.

'The Valley of Triplock is the prize for all of us,' said The

Murmur. 'We must wipe out all of its inhabitants as the path to evil for them would be too difficult to live with. We would always be under threat if that sickly goodness returned to them. Irridication or should we say, complete eradication, is the solution? Do you agree?'

Irridia had been planning for this moment for a long time. No ex-husband or king would "rain on her parade", once they entered the Valley of Triplock. It would be her personal pleasure to lop the king and his fellow Igloods. She knew the danger of their powers; however, with her superior number of stupid, selfish Irrids, who obeyed her every command without question, they would sacrifice themselves unquestionably to overrun the Igloods. She could smell victory if it actually had a smell. The two evil minds were inseparable. There was no barrier left to her success. Ignatus hadn't hit her radar just yet. What's another Iglood? Just an extra lopping.

'There should be no Iglood standing after the battle. It will soon all be mine.'

'It will be all ours,' The Murmur reminded her. His cold, wet tail agitatedly flicked with his response.

As Ignatus climbed up the Waterfall of Wetness, he noticed his body gradually change shape. After just discovering what he was, he had to undergo another, but this time, hideous transformation. It was enough to make him join a circus as a freak act. By the time he had reached the top of the waterfall, his body was now that of an unsavoury, hate-filled Irrid. Batbit stared in disbelief. Ignatus appeared to have become one of the enemies. Where had his friend gone? Ignatus emerged with a sourpuss face, acting like he was an evil Irrid. However, underneath his new outer shell he oozed goodness.

'The king explained to me what I am capable of achieving with my new powers. Transformation into any life form is high on the list, but can only be achieved whilst there is running flow through the Waterfall of Wetness. Igloods are peace-loving life forms who try not to exterminate opposition life forms for any reason. It's hard to believe they are a non-combat life form. However, they are called diffusers and endeavour to reduce all conflict to a minimum amount of pain and destruction. Sometimes when that action is impossible, casualties occur,' explained Ignatus. 'Now do you understand why my appearance has physically changed?'

'But you look exactly like them,' Babit said, looking worried. 'How will I be able to tell the difference?'

'Scent. By scent only. I don't possess a putrid smell. Take a whiff.'

Batbit hesitatingly sniffed Ignatus. 'Not bad, it's certainly an acceptable aroma.'

'That's the bait. I'm hoping to be sniffed. No Irrid will be able to resist the curiosity of a new, sweet-scented smell. When they approach me, I will subtly hug and do a wrist-rub without them noticing it. The hug is a shock mechanism that they cannot handle at all. It is their weak spot. They will in time return to goodness again.'

'You won't have time to hug a whole army. It's an impossible task,' said a doubting Batbit.

'Ah! However, there is a secret effect. Once they have performed their one hug and wrist-rub during the next dark and light, they will return to their original life form they were before conversion. Also, they will fight the evil Irrids who persist on continuing that path, if necessary. It's like growing an own army of mine. The two major antagonists that I must locate and destroy are the Murmur and Irridia. I'm told that they are relentless in their evil pursuit, much like litigious divorcees. We must begin at once. Fly nearby and remain out of sight. It always seems to be cold here.'

Ignatus was aware that his chances of success might be compared with pushing a jumbo jet uphill with a toothpick. Unfavourable odds existed in any two-horse race. He sniffed the air with his new, beaut, snort sniffer. He humourously thought to himself, smellus, nastus, irrustus, as he inhaled the most offensive odours wafting on the air. Behind a few rocks nearby, a group of Irrids were enjoying lopping practice on the remnants of a tree stump. It groaned with each slash. Ignatus jumped out like a jack-in-a-box from behind some rocks, startling the dimwitted Irrids. Would he pass as a real Irrid? Would he be discovered and lopped from ear to ear? He felt he was bullet proof in his almost perfect disguise. Would they be attracted to his sweet smell and could it cause his downfall? He cautiously approached them. Grunt could communicate by thoughts with them. He possessed their similar telepathic airwaves.

'Hello there. Can I join in?' he asked. 'I want to lop something.'

The small group scattered in fright like confetti in a wind gust at the sudden intrusion. They were skittish because of the impending fight with Triplock.

'Who are you?' One of the Irrids spoke. 'We haven't seen you before.'

'Let me lop a leg, I need the practice. He'll have to hop after that,' sneered another.

'I've recently arrived from North Irridon ready to fight and toil for the greater bad.'

'Let's see your moves first. Wait a minute. What's that sickly, sweet smell. You don't sniff right.'

Ignatus knew this was a risk, but he had to prove if he could genuinely infiltrate them. His next answer might be the catalyst for his doom.

'Up north, we consume a special sap from the stunted Irritree where it grows in abundance. It sometimes changes our odour. Not all wind passes at the same odour capacity or density.'

'I haven't heard of it.'

'You wouldn't know about it unless you were from there. In times of conflict it becomes noticeable when all Irrids join together.'

'Where's the rest of your mob?'

'They arrive at the next light to finally irridicate Triplock.'

They all snorted a form of laughter.

'Swing your lopper and I'll show you my skills.'

'This is to your death, you impostor. No Irrid in my experience has ever smelt that good.'

'I'm as nasty an Irrid as you are. I'll prove it to you.'

Ignatus took one powerful swipe. His opponent's lopper fell useless to the ground. He feigned a trip and fell on top of the crumpled Irrid. He had it pinned to the ground as it writhed in defiance. It bit, scratched and kicked, but Ignatus overpowered it. Quickly, he wrist-rubbed it and stood up beating his chest with the sickly look of success, slobbering from his bottom lip. A saliva pool instantly formed. It was the victory dribble. The defeated Irrid finally stood up. It felt light-headed as goodness began to seep through its body. It attained the same sweet smell as Ignatus.

'Damn you,' it protested. The transition was painless.

'Who's next?' teased Ignatus. He was on a roll.

Another tried trickery and deceit by gaining Ignatus's attention, while three other Irrids tried to ambush him from behind and at the sides. The same fate befell the group. He was fleet of foot, far too strong and could jump three times his height while standing still. His outer casing had a special hardness none could crack. He twirled, danced and swung his lopper with such relish, he felt good about being in battle. His classy skills were too much for the slower moving lot. All were wrist-rubbed and each slowly changed and smelled sweet. They had finally awoken from the dark haze of evil that they had existed under for so long. Ignatus observed each transformed Irrid, looking for signs of continued evil. There were none.

'Batbit, my powers work,' he exclaimed, excitedly.

The transformed, hateful Irrids had suddenly lost their purpose and focus and felt lost and emotionally abandoned. Ignatus realised that he must act immediately. Acting like a prophet he had to set the converted on the right path.

'Go, my brothers, redeem the lost.'

With these words, they scampered back to the main force looking for a friend. There were none there, so they had to create their own. Ignatus watched from a safe distance. The transformed, much to his surprise, repeated his identical actions on other Irrids. Practice loppers became a victim to goodness they also hadn't experienced in a long time. His success began to grow like fungus spores, spreading throughout the forces. The Irrids began to lose their zombie-like antics and embrace change. However, the rate of change to goodness wouldn't be enough to stop the attack on Triplock. As time went on, the odds of defence improved.

'What's that sickly smell?' One of the leaders sniffed a change and questioned some of his forces. The transformed Irrids were having an effect.

'There's something not quite right, leader. A few of our fellow Irrids have stopped snorting and acting nastily. They have been affected by something unusual,' commented a prospective nasty. 'It wouldn't have been anything intelligent you said, could it, that has caused such irrational behaviour?'

The incensed leader swung his lopper and one headless, lifeless Irrid was left speechless.

'Is there any more dissension or cleverness any one of you is endowed with?'

Silence. No one dared cross this lunatic. They all wanted to continue with the chat.

'Find out the cause of this irritating behaviour. You, yes, you, with the dribbling jowls. Go and tell Irridia that disharmony is occurring within our ranks. None of us can stand good behaviour. Go! If this sickly smells reduces our nastiness, it could hinder our ability to conquer. We don't need any new friends because we didn't have any to start with in the first place.'

Dissension began to grow like a flea challenging an elephant. Goodness wasn't acceptable in a nasty environment. Conflict broke out in small pockets. The once friendless Irrids now had amongst them a few who, surprisingly, tried to hug their fellow Irrids. It stunned them all. This wasn't Irridion behaviour. They hadn't experienced such warmth from another Irrid for so long. It was almost a forgotten emotion that their change had definitely hidden.

When the Great Split occurred, Irridia fled, spouting revenge for her loss of title and opportunity to rule the Valley of Triplock. She set up the neighbouring Valley of Irridon. Unfortunately for her, the valley already had an evil inhabitant who was seeking growth for his evil ideas. It was during one dark that she sat alone in a cave where the induction to evil took place under his evil guidance. She was tutored and brainwashed by a mastermind manipulator. He possessed psychotic behaviour that, once transmitted to another, exhibited the same personality traits. Winds howled, murmuring words of revenge such as, 'rightful place' and 'Igloods are the enemy', and threats such as, 'torture is therapy for the soul' and 'death of another is success for an Irrid', were made. These were whispered all dark. Sleep deprivation was enforced by the cool, cold, circulating winds. These were mind games from which recovery was almost impossible. The Murmur knew his subject. Any goodness she possessed had been squeezed out of her like putting a lemon through a juicer. Once converted to evil, it was almost impossible to alter it. Irridia had succumbed because her revenge towards King Iglandus had overridden all her reasoning senses. She was easy game. The Murmur wanted to rule the valleys and watch evil flourish. Irridia believed that she was in control, but she wasn't.

To become a nasty, snorting Irrid, devoid of any warm emotions and full of negative traits, all captured life forms had to undergo a dark of Murmurfication – a terrifying, solitary ordeal in the Cave of Murm – and at the next light, a nasty Irrid emerged full of harm. Their senses were retrained and the transformation was complete. The capture of good life forms supplied the chaff upon which the army was built. The Irrids' strength just grew and grew and a vicious, nasty, strong fighting force of loppers was born. The Murmur's strength was harnessed by the evil mists he despatched from the Cave of Murm under the direction of Irridia, to wreak havoc, weaken resistance and finally take control of a valley. The Murmur and Irridia were driven by the same powerful aphrodisiac – power!

The dull, grey atmosphere of cold, moisture-laden mists and constant darkness were all part of a plan that never allowed an Irrid a good time. Life was normally morose and boring.

The scout reached the Cave of Murm. Irridia and her partner in evil, The Murmer, greeted it with suspicion.

'There is trouble in paradise.' A loose term if ever there was one. 'A strange smell and non-Irridion behaviour is occurring,' it said.

'This had better not be a lie or an exaggeration or a time waster,' answered Irridia, knowing exactly that the standard of Irrid explanation wasn't always above par.

'I don't understand it.'

'What are you telling me? Spit it out and not on me.'

'Some Irridians are hugging and fighting each other. A sickly smell accompanies each altercation. I've never seen or smelt it before.'

'Hugging each other? That's not possible. That's not a greeting used in Irridon,' she scowled.

'What is it? What does it mean?'

Irridia had forgotten many of the good things that she had once practised. Evil had replaced any good thoughts. If she had a memory of times past, she would have realised what good a hug did.

'A problem. Is the army ready to strike?'

'They are raring to have a lop-off against Triplock.'

'Have you seen any non-Irrid strange life forms?'

'Should there be? I haven't seen any at all.'

'I am expecting an attack, but I don't know in what form. It has been in the making for a long time.' Her voice trailed off as if discovering a new thought. 'King Iglandus can be very innovative. Let me deal with any intruder. I'll lop and tail them.' Irridia took a wild swoosh, which nearly lopped her scout. She enjoyed nothing more than a top class lopping or causing others to suffer pain at her hands. 'Are you coming?' She called to The Murmur.

'In a moment.' He dashed into the depths of the Cave of Murm to a special place.

'Coward,' Irridia yelled ferociously. She was ready for a serious stoush. Her evil eyes danced maddeningly. It was time to inflict pain.

'Nothing will double cross me,' The Murmur whispered to himself. 'You three come with me,' he ordered.

There were three vacant winds known as the Murmettes who had not yet been assigned to perform an evil duty. They were first-timers and eager to please. The plan was to use them in a crosswind to cause instability and confusion against the Igloods. If Irridia was turned to good, he would destroy her. Nothing would stand in the way of his evil rule. With friends like The Murmur for support, who needed enemies?

✧   ✵

The conflict was escalating. It was impossible to assess the damage done by Ignatus' intrusion effect because low visibility existed. The army was spread over a wide area and had to be drawn in to gauge their strength and be advised of the new danger they now faced.

Irridia arrived seething at the mayhem she saw. Spread out like locusts in a cornfield, her evil army seemed to be splitting apart. She was very powerful and, for an Irrid, had an air of beauty about her. Her finer exterior hid the deathly strength of her evil eyes. No one ever dared to outstare her. To try meant a shattered mind. In the case of an Irrid, that wasn't difficult.

The importance of the event was of an unimaginable scale of difficulty and stress level. Irridia stood out like a huge monolith on a flat, desert plain.

An excruciating sound blasted from the end of a shell calling the army together. Its awful blast was so piercing that all combat stopped between the transformed and the non-transformed Irrids. The leaders of each group signalled for a gathering and congregated on the Plains of Wetness to listen to Irridia. She gazed over the substance of her revenge, Triplock.

She paused and eyed her eager war fodder. Her mouth moved silently as if searching for a communication verb, vowel or sentence, and she sneezed.

'I've been blessed,' cried out a brainless Irrid, as splatter fell over the front of his torso. It writhed in wonderment at having received something from the honoured leader, even if it was just spittle.

'Get it out of here,' she commanded. 'Are there any more bozos out there?'

Nothing moved. They stood as still as a painting.

'The last dark before the victory at next light is at hand. Sniff your final smells, lop an imaginary opponent or any who are causing difficulty and think of the task against the enemy. It will be exciting and real. Imagine the most delicious loppings one could ask for. At next light, breathe it in. This is what we have planned and waited for ages for. I'm choking on expectation.'

Suddenly a gust of wind whistled through their legs. It was the Murmettes having a practice run at accessibility in a crowd. The Murmur wanted to ensure his trio of learners was up to the impending task set for them.

'Something is hurting us. I feel it. Search it out and then lop it,' said Irridia, as tense as a tennis racquet string.

'How will we know who to lop or not to lop?'

'Use your sniffers. Clean them out with a snort and use them. Find those that smell different and those that hug others. Be quick, otherwise you may fall under their spell. If you don't wreak and stink badly you aren't a true Irrid.'

A sea of blank zombie-like looks grew on almost every face. In fact, they could almost pass for normal.

'Hey, you, with the sweet, scented smell, come here,' demanded a leader.

'Do you like my new scented flavour? Would you like to share it?'

'Rubbish! You don't stink like me.' With that last word spoken, the leader lopped the sweet-scented one.

'Why did you do that?' another Irrid asked Irridia.

'It was an imposter Irrid. It smelt too nice. We're nasty, filthy, smelling and stinky. Anyone who doesn't smell that bad can't be one of us. You there and you there, if anything smells that sweet, lop it. Go sort it out.'

A wild group of insane, side-running Irrids whooped for joy. They could now actually use their lopping techniques. Practice was over.

Irridia watched in irritation as a larger percentage of her army began engaging in behaviour unbecoming of an Irrid. Hugging! Ugh! It was deplorable. Small battles erupted like an attack of hives all over the plain. It was a ghastly sight as her army began to self-destruct. Whatever had infected it was clever and dangerous. However, the nasties soon gained the upper hand and the leaders proudly returned to Irridia, who was grinning like a Cheshire cat.

'Try and destroy me, would they? I'm too powerful,' she said out loud.

The sweet smellers weren't all irridicated. A few were missed and survived because they weren't fully scented. They would form the basis of a fresh wave of dissension.

Ignatus surveyed the minimal success of his plan to turn the Irrids towards good. However, the remaining Irrid army was still far too strong. His plan had been detected early. Another approach of devious dimensions was required. He couldn't defeat them all single-handedly, even with his immense powers. The sweet smell he possessed would be easily sniffed out. Batbit had sat silently on a stunted tree branch and was calculating plans of his own, when Ignatus approached.

'Batbit. Fly around near their leader. That must be Irridia up there giving orders. She looks formidable.'

Batbit struggled in the cold mist. Moisture kept wetting his wings, making them heavy. For a small bat, it was like flying with a friend. He swooped and dived like a flyspeck, assessing the enemy's strength. He had the urge to shriek, but thought it better to be a "silent nothing" than a "known destroyed something". He returned to Ignatus.

'Over there, the leader is holed up. She can see everything. Her eyesight is far reaching, better than ours, I would suggest. The Irrids are snorting far louder. They sense a big event.'

'Did any of my plans work?'

'There seem to be a lot less Irrids now. The lopped ones suffered most. There wasn't a happy face amongst them.'

'What do you suggest we do?'

Batbit dropped to the ground. He extended a bat wing and

used his long fingers to draw a design on the ground. In the Rock of Yocklaw, he was a bat commander who planned the successful foray in the hunt for the juiciest insects each dark. He likened the Irrids to insects and devised a strategy of separation.

'Tease an Irrid group on the fringe of the army with the promise of an easy lopping. The operation would work like tugging the tale of a dog, then running. Whisper that the cause of the disruption is this sweet-smelling Irrid, who is hiding amongst that rocky outcrop. Imagine the kudos for Irridia and her fellow Irrids if they secured victory over the dissenter –they are all ego heads wanting personal gain – then jump them with your spirited hugathon and wrist-rubbing technique – they wouldn't know what hit them – then send them back to continue the transformations. What do you think? Ingenious, uh!' explained Batbit.

'Won't it be discovered? I tried something similar before.'

'Nah! Have faith. It's so dark here, their innate curiosity is to sniff smells and they are experts at it. They know where life forms hide just by taking a huge whiff; however, they are easily led. They don't have a lot of brains to affect their stupidity. A commander senses these things from observations. I can fly low and be used as bait. Chase me, and wham! Ambush! I can also pester them from above if necessary.'

'There aren't many of us here, so I suppose I'll shoulder the heavy workload.'

Ignatus felt empowered. As Grunt, he was given certain abilities, but now as Ignatus, his raft of possibilities had enlarged to almost limitless powers. They crept nearer to the force. Batbit selected a small group for harassment.

'Psst. Psst.'

A keen set of ears, probably not cleaned for a while, heard the sound.

'If you want to do that on my foot, I suggest you move. I don't need to smell worse.'

'Psst. Psst.'

'Turn off your moisture valve, you'll dehydrate.'

'Don't snarl at me. I thought it was you.'

'Me too. Who's the culprit?'

'Over here,' whispered a tiny voice, so small its vibrations almost couldn't be heard. 'I know who's causing the troubled loppings.'

'Who?' said a snorting snarler.

'It's over near those rocks. It's waving to you thinking you are friendlies. Go and stick it to them, tiger.'

'Tiger? Never heard of it.'

They couldn't see Batbit because of his size in the dark, but Ignatus stood tall, waving to them exactly as Batbit had explained. Six nasties leapt at the chance of a prized lopping.

'Where did it go?'

'Who's hiding it?'

'Let me lop something.'

Suddenly, a whirlwind materialised.

'It's not you, is it, Murmur, playing one of your tricks on us?'

It encompassed all of them. Ignatus materialised to hug and wrist-rub each of the hapless Irrids. After the quick encounter, the Irrids stood dazed.

'Whoa! Was that a trip and a half,' said one.

'Do I look normal to you?' asked another.

'Yes, but you smell different.'

'Thanks, I didn't think you'd notice.'

The trap had worked perfectly. The "hit and run" technique was put into place. That dark, they worked the perimeter carefully as the "cloak and dagger" thrill seekers. The Irrid army began to grow restless again. Its stomach for action was becoming hungry. Their sniffers were kept active all dark. By next light, a sickly-sweet smell, not evident the previous dark, wafted on the breeze. The effect had unsettled them.

Irridia awoke from a bad dream and flew out of her lodgings – a rock cave – to experience the same sickly smell that her army had spoken of. She scanned the valley below and could see tinted spiralling mists filter upwards. They were the wrong colour. Something was bothering her and it wasn't her lack of clothing or colour coordination. She watched intently for any unusual behaviour patterns. On the fringes of the army, small groups were again hugging each other. She detested any expression of emotionality. What was undermining her? From her vantage point, she strode boldly into the midst of her army. Being an ex Iglood, she towered over her force.

'I dare any of you to challenge me?'

No one rushed forward. The Irrids might be fools at times, but never stupid enough to answer this challenge. Lopping would only have one consequence, them.

'It's time.'

It was the beginning of the next light, the moment for attack. She instructed her leaders to organise their groups for the final push; however, there didn't seem to be as many as she had thought. Had some deserted their quest?

Ignatus saw the powerful leader take charge. She was as tall as him. He knew that he couldn't allow them into Triplock. It was his duty to protect it. As the army began to march, Ignatus walked out from behind a camouflaged rock and stood motionless in full sight at the front of the army. He was actually an

Irrid in appearance and they paid no attention to him. Being unusually tall wasn't necessarily uncommon.

'Batbit. Fly to the Waterfall of Wetness and bring back a mouthful of running flow. Do not drop any of it. Hurry, it's important.' Batbit did as he was told, unlike a recalcitrant child.

The Murmur and the Murmettes lingered above the clouds, ready to inflict their aggressive nature and destructive forces on the Irrids if failure was on the horizon. Ignatus sensed their presence.

'How do I shape my gapper if I want to howl?' A learner wanted to know what to do.

'As big as possible,' replied The Murmur. 'We are here to be dangerous and not to act as light, fresh winds to please anything. Keep alert.'

Irridia stopped dead in her tracks. It's rather odd that an oversized Irrid would impede her progress. Her dark eyes flashed angrily.

'Who are you and why have you stood directly in our path?' she demanded. 'Are you one of us? I haven't seen you before.'

Ignatus thought a little, whilst the mass seethed with agitation.

'I'm one of them. You will not attack Triplock. I'm here to protect it.'

'What? By yourself? That's laughable. You look like an ordinary Irrid. Get out of my way otherwise you'll be lopped. Triplock cannot be saved.'

'It will be. I am barring your entrance.'

A great roar of jocular disapproval filled the valley. It sounded like it was to be a good day for Irridon. Loppers swayed like a palm tree forest in support of Irridia and the reaction to what they thought was a humourous comment. The sound travelled through vibrations.

A small breeze was felt. Batbit was in sonic flight – well for a bat, that is! No moisture or dark mist was impeding his flight plan this time. He flew directly above Ignatus.

'Spit it to me. Spit it to me,' demanded Ignatus.

Batbit zoned in and spat out his mouthful of running flow from the Waterfall of Wetness and, mixed with his own spittle, it dribbled over Ignatus. 'Yuck,' was the expected response. Instantly, Ignatus the Irrid began to change and die a slow death. In his place, stood a tall, strong, defiant and confident Iglood. A great crowd 'ooh ah,' filled the valley at the transformation. No Iglood had ever dared enter the Valley of Irridon as it was usually a death sentence. Either he was exceptionally brave or very foolish. He now stood directly in front of Irridia as the only barrier to the demise of Triplock; one solitary Iglood.

The shock of seeing an Iglood in the valley scared the lights out of them. No longer would they be able to sleep without bad dreams. Irridia displayed an ugly set of dentures from a sneered mouth, with upturned corners in creases of rage. Did she dare ask the question that played on her mind? What is an Iglood doing here and is it lost?

'State your business. Only death waits you here in this valley. It's the rule.'

'I appreciate the advice; however, I am the protector of Triplock. My destiny is to repel and destroy, if necessary, any attack or danger to the valley.'

'You can't be the protector. Only King Iglandus has that authority.'

'It has now been transferred to me,' he said proudly. 'I must fulfil my duty.'

'Impossible!' screamed Irridia on the verge of a major hissy fit. 'It can only go to bloodline. He has none.'

'Au contraire. I am his bloodline.'

Irridia's heart almost exploded from her body in surprise. Her temperature soared. If this was true, she knew she had a powerful foe. Was this the moment she had always dreaded? The messenger sent to save Triplock. Only hers and King Iglandus' son could rule, but she had him banished a long time ago. Was it payback time? Had he another she was unaware of. Sentiments ran rampant in her emotional confusion.

'Convince me of your credentials. You cannot be related.'

'I was banished a long time ago to live as an unseen, unloved, hideous creature inside a rock. I had to guard the Valley of Preciousness from within the Rock of Yocklaw, never to return. The gods smiled on me. My return to the Valley of Triplock has unlocked my past. I now know who and what I am and my destiny. I have no particular beef with any life form; however, when Triplock is at risk my role is to remove it and that includes you.'

Irridia was dumbfounded, nonplussed and struck out with the truth. Was she preparing to fight her son?

'Move aside. One Iglood cannot stop the advance.'

'We'll see. Another step closer and prepare to be defeated.'

Ignatus was puffing with bravado. Irridia sensed a strength in him that no other Iglood had ever possessed. The time of his banishment had certainly developed his strength of character.

'For the final time, step aside or face eternity,' threatened Irridia, becoming tired of the verbal standoff banter. It was action she craved, not words.

'Batbit, send the signal to Imagoodshot,' instructed Ignatus.

A loud, piercing shriek split the air. The Waterfall of Wetness also carried the sound. Ping, ping, ping was heard, followed by a whooshing sound. Then plod, plod, plod and stick, stick, stick landed in front of Irridia forming a barrier of flighters.

'There are those straight trees again. We should have a forest of them somewhere. They must be stealing them,' suggested an observant Irrid.

'You idiot. These are the deadly flighters of Imagoodshot,' yelled Irridia, none too pleased at the intelligence level of the verbaliser.

'Do you know him?' asked Ignatus.

'I did, once.'

'His flighters will decimate your army. Triplock is ready to defend itself. Return to goodness and peace. There is no need for conflict.'

The Murmur had silently crept towards where he expected conflict to erupt. He wanted to be in on the decimation.

'Before you cease to exist, there is something that you must know. I am the ex-Queen of King Iglandus, your mother,' said Irridia.

Ignatus gasped. His airwaves were knotted. His body hardened like a stone. He had no instant strategy to deal with the emotions of such an instantaneous magnitude. This evil, unhuggable piece of detritus, full of venom and hate toward his father, was actually his mother. Ignatus felt lost. How could he destroy his mother? Another strategy had to be formulated. He had to think quickly on his feet. The suddenness of the change of plan left him in a dilemma – destroy Irridia and save Triplock, or don't destroy Irridia and Triplock is destroyed. Why wasn't there a simpler solution? The two combatants stood silently staring at each other as the family feud was about to explode. Ignatus steeled himself for his next sentence.

'Do you relinquish evil for good? If not, then we are enemies,' he bravely said.

'I've feasted upon it far too long to give up its succulent taste. It's an aphrodisiac for my soul. Yum, I'm hungry. It is also my chosen path. I am the rightful ruler of Triplock and nothing, including you, will deny me that right. Stand aside or face the Irridon wrath.'

Consultation had run its course. It was now as useful as watching grass grow. The transformed Irrids waited on the fringes of the army ready to inflict more hugging.

'Batbit, signal Imagoodshot.'

Almost instantly, a wave of flighters flew over Irridia into the heart of her army. They all hit a mark. Confusion reigned. The dull thuds and writhing agony was difficult to watch in the gloomy conditions.

Irridia screamed a hideous, vocal chant. She wasn't arguing with an ex-husband. The Irrids raised their loppers. They ran forward with maniacal intent to attack. Ignatus put up one hand – he still had all his fingers – and flashed his lazer frayzer at the first two dozen who froze solid like statues. The expression of surprise and dismay on their faces was captured forever. He turned away and slapped himself on the rump, disappearing from sight. He emerged in the middle of the fighting force. Once again, his lazer frayzer spurted out its immobilisation force, solidifying more of the hapless Irrids. In the meantime, the huggy Irrids pounced on the opportunity to hug and wrist-rub and help reduce the nasties.

Irridia raged. She found Ignatus and fired her lazer frayzer at him. He was alert for its devastating intent and met it with a burst of his own. Boom! There were sparks flying everywhere.

It lit the darkness to the brightest it had ever been. The battle had begun. Ignatus could see the fiery demons in her eyes. He kicked a soil thunderer at her. It hit her feet upending her into a horizontal position. There was no love lost for this relative. She raised her monster lopper and flung it at Ignatus. He ducked and jabbed out a long, spindley finger which grazed her leg and cut into it. Irridia screamed so loudly Triplock could hear her pain.

'It sounds awful, Mr King,' said Davidia. 'My mum and dad never yelled at me like that. She should meet my parents and they'll teach her not to scream. Close your ears Miss Percival, if you are here.'

King Iglandus and his Igloods were prepared to battle any Irrid that passed their way.

Ignatus was within touching distance. The wounded Irridia lashed out and caught him by the hands. The two formidable contenders gripped as strongly as any wrestler, each trying to subdue the other. They were evenly matched. Ignatus searched her eyes for redemption, but an evil veil had it well hidden. Her hands momentarily felt full of emotion for Ignatus, which infected his body with a good feeling although it was from an evil source. This was his mother he was holding hands with, even in the middle of battle. Suddenly, a strong gust of wind threw them off guard. They both scrambled for a vertical position. Irridia's fitness was in prime condition for a senior Irrid.

No life form could interfere as a secret field of particles prohibited entry into the circle of last effort. Only one would survive. They jumped, parried and slashed at each other. One was perspiring a rotten, dead smell and the other the sickly, sweet-scented one. Many felt safer on the outside. Phew!

They both used their invisibility techniques to gain the upper hand. There were high jumps to avoid the leg lopper, sideways bending so a spindle finger didn't probe too deeply, kicking to fend off the other body's nearness, firing of lazer frayzers to frizzle the opponent with frying potential, and a mass of other movements too quick for the eye to see.

Irridia was as cunning an opponent as she was a mother and suddenly stopped and pretended to cry and give up. Ignatus was sucked in with the seeming acceptance that all was lost. He bent over and, wham, a hand with the feeling of a death punch, landed squarely in his stomach and threw him backwards. He landed breathless and in extreme pain, his doom almost upon him. Stunned, he looked upwards at his opponent. In that moment, a slight eye-flicker caught his attention. Was she upset at hurting him? Did she feel sorry for him? No, it was a vision of victory that trembled throughout her body, looking at the hapless form of Ignatus. Was this his last light? Would he be banished forever to the dark if he lost?

'It's time to say goodbye to mamma, sweetie,' drooled Irridia – it was almost over, or so she thought it was – 'and I was just getting to know you,' she teased.

Had the new guardian of Triplock met his match? After all, he was only fighting a woman who it was assumed had less considerable strength than he had. Against Irridia, many of his powers didn't work because they were both from Igloodian stock and some of them had nullified the effect on each other. Had they both fought any other life form, their individual powers would be devastating in any contest. They seemed to have become two blocks of ice, one lasting slightly longer than the other, as they melted in the heat of battle.

Ignatus thought that the ground was certainly filthy as he lay there unable to continue the battle for goodness. His mother certainly packed a punch. He wondered what gymnasium she attended. Her pectoral muscles were strong and her lithe movements were deadly. Things looked as gloomy as the land of Irridon as he lay there wheezing and sucking in vital oxygen. It took a while longer to recover in Irridon as the air quality was a little short on goodness, just like its inhabitants.

'I'm sorry mama,' he emotionally spoke. 'There's not much time for a friendly relationship.'

'It's over. You, your king and the Valley of Triplock are mine,' she chimed.

Ignatus had been feigning injury to secure an advantage. Women's intuition, which every female possesses, had twigged her curiosity about Ignatus. She wanted to know at least something about him before the sentence was dealt and the opportunity was lost. Maybe that's why the death blow hadn't been dealt just yet.

Ignatus quickly rolled over onto his side like a playful puppy. He kicked out his legs at the advancing Irridia and fortunately clipped an ankle. She screamed a diatribe of Irridion abuse at him. He regained his feet and swung his lopper at her. Its intending damage was met solidly with a defiant lopper swing and a foot landed in Ignatus' special body region. Her movements were razor sharp. He winced in excruciating pain. Half doubled over, unable to straighten himself, he saw what he thought was to be the fatal blow. In his mind, a slow motion newsreel began to unfold. He saw elements of an early memory of his life, with two loving adult Igloods enjoying a playful session with a smaller, smiling version. Life felt good then. Visions flashed through his mind as if fast tracking to see them all before the permanent dark ascended upon him. His head would be separated from his body and Triplock would vanish forever. A cold, fear of loss and disappointment enveloped him. He was sad that he would no longer be able to see his friends, Davidia and

Batbit, and his new life would be cut short. It wasn't a good picture that was mentally presented. He looked up at Irridia in full lopping flight. She had no emotions except to ride the dark horse. Her face was contorted with rage. Victory had an uneasy facial grimace, when in one swing, all the dreams of power, planning and satisfaction materialise into a powerful moment. It was to be all hers.

Miraculously, Ignatus, who was also a lightening rod on two legs, was able to tumble roll like a bocce ball out of harm's way in that defining moment. Survival is a great driving force of the good. Irridia's lopper hit the ground so hard the clang could be heard valleys away. The ricochet sent shock waves up her arms with such force that it looked like she had been left shivering vigorously in a cold storm. Ignatus had been a breath away from extermination.

Her face reddened with rage. Her nasty, snorting Irridon behaviour exploded into maniacal rage. Her body hurt more from missing her target than the pain it gave her.

Her vocal sounds and thought rages sent vibrations of fear everywhere. Ignatus controlled his emotional feelings, as he now knew it was too late for Irridia to be returned to the path of goodness. He felt her pain. Evil had damaged her emotions beyond repair. Ignatus had to use his power of last resort if there was any hope of retrieving Irridia from the darkness of evil. It was a forlorn hope, but it must be tried.

As Irridia performed with an angry waving lopper, Ignatus rolled over and secreted Igloodool from his wrist glands. It was a weapon of last spurt. Only a royal Iglood was endowed with this special substance.

He flicked it onto her outer casing. She hadn't noticed it or could avoid it; such was her vision blinded by rage. The small droplets were a burning sensation from hell. Stunned by the excruciating pain, she howled like a banshee, generating fear in all those who heard it. In anger, Irridia was the most frightening performer. Finally, Ignatus managed to stand up and, in sympathy, screamed a similar frightening response. They were like a larynx symphony top line act. The valley shook and shuddered. No, it wasn't the Irrid army passing wind – that would have been worse. The Murmur almost choked in fright on his own wind. The three Murmettes faded away to a gentle breeze. The fighting lulled to a stop. The eyes of hatred and lopping behaviour all froze. Only the two frenzied voices engaged in any form of combat.

Irridia was wailing from the effects of the Igloodool goodness eating at her insides. She was trying to resist its changing capabilities. Ignatus was calling the ancient fathers for support. The winds swirled from the heavens as Ignatus absorbed their strength. Irridia had fallen foul to her only combat flaw, Igloodool substance from an ancient Iglood. It wasn't a death sentence, but life changing, returning her to her past, the one she had abandoned.

'I'm not going back,' she moaned.

Ignatus stood as tall as a tower block.

'Accept the change. It's irreversible.'

'Never,' she vehemently protested.

'Then Irridon is over. I call on the great ancients to fill me with power to return the valley to goodness.'

'You always were a spoiled youngster, you glob of Iglood glue. No wonder I had you banished, hopefully forever. I didn't know that my future foe would be my own son. I never expected to see you again. You have ruined my plans for a rotten future.'

'So, it was you who banished me,' whimpered Ignatus, as if someone had stolen his last lolly.

'Yes. You were in my way for control of the Valley of

Triplock. Nothing appealed more to me than the aphrodisiacal qualities of power, my power. You were an inconvenience.'

'But mother.'

'I'm not your mother. That person left a long time ago.'

'You can be saved.'

'No, I can't.'

With a loud, thundering crash, a huge vortex opened up in the sky operating like a massive vacuum cleaner. The Murmur had seen his plans ruined and his vow to destroy Irridia was put into action. He had craved power over land-based life forms and Irridia was his tool of possibility to make it happen. The Murmur didn't possess the power to defeat the Igloods, but a disgruntled royal with the right tuition could. Now it was time to exact revenge for her failure.

Ignatus was aware of the howling winds from above and knew it was show time at last with the winds of Evil that had dogged him throughout the valleys. Not one blow-hard wind had ever tried to be helpful. The Murmur headed straight toward Irridia. Ignatus wasn't giving up just yet.

The Murmur swooped down and hovered over Irridia. His concentration was solely to lift her from the ground and dispense her forever for her failure to make him all powerful. She began to be sucked into the huge hole created. The sky began to close over. It still remained the unfriendly cool and moist climate all Irrids had known during their lifetime. The landscape was still a foreboding horror, an inkblot on a nice canvas. In the kerfuffle of battle with Irridia, all combat had ceased. Limp loppers hung loosely by the combatants' side like washing hanging on a line. All eyes were focused on the howling event before them. The Irrids were leaderless and watched as their beloved leader was being caught in an updraft. They were powerless to act.

Ignatus cupped both knees with his hands and spun dizzily, creating another huge updraft which had everyone hanging onto their clothing. He was plucked off the ground as a speck of dust travels when disturbed, to form another footprint in the sky. Storm clouds celebrated the contest by hurling thunderous abuse and advice at Ignatus. Thunder and lightening lit the sky in a kaleidoscopic light display. The Murmur had engaged his mists and winds to destroy Ignatus instead of Irridia. He loved a battle. However, the powers of an ancient Iglood with the moral support of all ancients had no equal.

Ignatus fired his lazer frayzers as he rotated at high speed. The lightening bolts were diffused. The thunderclap argument was lost as he rose further into the atmosphere. The carpet blanket of cool, moist, lousy mist that had covered Irridon since the Great Split was slowly being dragged upwards, protesting at the rough treatment of banishment. Sunlight began to reappear and creep over the landscape once again. It felt that it had been banished too.

The Murmur, who had sent his evil mists to smother other valleys and rule land-based life forms, was now being sucked into a void. Ignatus opened his mouth wide enough to inhale all the clouds until none were to be seen. The Murmur had ceased to murmur. Ignatus had one almighty sneeze and just as Grunt and Davidia had dealt with the Evil Mist, he spat out the all-offending Murmur and his cohort mists, never to be seen again.

'Gee, that felt good,' he said to himself.

The Irrids, who had never seen the sun before, surrendered in fear. This allowed the transformed Irrids to hug and wrist-rub the balance of the hated fighting force.

Ignatus floated down like a deciduous tree leaf, fluttering

on the wind, afraid to land to become leaf litter and compost. He landed delicately and exhausted after his epic battles. Total confusion reigned. The Irrids had lost the zest to lop off limbs. The sun beat down like a scolding teacher. Plants woke up and were teased into growth. Irridia lay lifeless on the ground.

'This is wonderful,' the trees chorused. 'We can grow and leave our stuntedness behind.'

The running flow burped a few bubbles as it ran over rocks. In time, the flight life forms would also return.

'Cease fighting,' boomed Ignatus. 'This land is free again.'

By that light's end, the Irrid army had been converted into the path of goodness. Surprisingly, they regained their original life forms. Many recognised relatives that had been turned into Irrids, but had never known each other in that life form.

Grunt turned his attention to the still, beautiful life form of his mother. The Igloodool substance had returned her to goodness; however, her struggle with her reluctance to accept the change, had damaged her life functioning components. Her body was damaged beyond repair. A feint pulse filtered through her body. Ignatus sat down next to her. He was once again looking at an ancient Iglood. There was no badness left. He sat silently, allowing his body to shed his own wet matter.

All throughout the valley the landscape had a new feeling of growth. The domino effect of freedom rippled through the five valleys that Grunt (Ignatus), Davidia and Batbit had travelled through on their quest. They also became released from the evil demons that plagued each of them.

Batbit was now visible in the light. He zoomed about with a new freshness for flight.

'Spread the message into Triplock that there are no further threats,' said Ignatus.

He dashed off like a ten-force gale, feeling released and reinvigorated. Over the Waterfall of Wetness he flew. Imagoodshot raised his propulsor and flighter for skewered bat.

'Don't shoot, it's me,' called Batbit. 'It's over. Ignatus has saved the valley.'

'Irridia. What of Irridia?' King Iglandus wanted to know.

'She's lost,' replied Batbit. 'She is with Ignatus right now. You had better hurry, this light might not last long for her.'

Sadness spread over the king's face.

'Oh, well, maybe it's for the better.' He wasn't convinced though.

The king and the Igloods advanced into Irridon. They also hadn't set eyes upon the valley since the Great Split. Its secession from Triplock was over. The two valleys could now be rejoined as one.

At the sight of Ignatus and Irridia sitting together, the king rushed over.

'How is she?' he asked.

'I fear the stress was too much for her,' replied Grunt.

'Isn't she beautiful?'

A soft murmur emanated from Irridia. Her body moved slightly. The king leaned down closely. She opened one eye just long enough to recognise the king. Irridia's face smiled like an angel. A finger moved for a final touch and with a last, gasping effort, burped goodbye. Her life forces had left her. The king was mortified as he felt the loss of her passing. The past was much stronger than the present,

'Is Mr Grunt, er, Mr Ignatus, safe?' Davidia wanted to know. 'Miss Percival wants to know too.'

'Yes.'

'Miss Davidia, would you like to fly over the Waterfall of Wetness? You can climb up on my back,' said Twirp.

Davidia climbed aboard and snuggled tightly into the flying, feathered blanket. The views were breathtaking. She was thrilled with the ride. No hot air balloon could perform this well. Up and over the Waterfall of Wetness they zoomed.

'Mum and dad haven't taken me in an aeroplane yet, but this is much better,' said Davidia, enjoying the rush of fresh breeze against her cool cheeks, which were separated by a grin. The landscape below was dotted with many life forms that could look forward to a different, positive future.

Batbit followed.

'There's Mr Grunt,' Davidia yelled excitedly.

Twirp landed carefully. Davidia jumped down and ran to Ignatus and they shared an emotional hug.

'I'm glad you're safe. We heard lots of strange noises and didn't know where anyone was. Did you have an argument with your mum? My mum and dad never let me argue. It was "be seen and not heard." Sometimes I talked,' she giggled.

Ignatus looked down at his tiny friend, in the frayed, yellow dress. Like Davidia, it had not lost any of its brightness. He reflected briefly on their short time together and the adventures and smiled with the knowledge of the ancients at how helpful she had been. She was a true friend. Nearby, he noticed a small, tired, black item hanging upside down on a tree branch. It was an exhausted Batbit, who hadn't the strength left for a shriek. Ignatus walked over and picked him up. Nothing was said. They each looked at the other and nodded.

'My destiny has now been shown to me. I know who, what and where I am. Let's all return to the Valley of Triplock. My work here has been done.'

'Is that your mum?' Davidia continued, 'She's asleep.'

'Yes,' was all Ignatus could respond with.

Ignatus now had a new responsibility and his time as the round ball known as Grunt was definitely over.

'Where do you think she is?' Ignatus asked his father.

'In a better place, son, in a better place.'

'What do you think, Davidia, are you staying with us?'

Ignatus turned around just in time to see Twirp and Davidia fly overhead. He waved as they became a speck in the sky.

The lands of Triplock, and what was once Irridon, flourished under the rule of Ignatus. Batbit rejoined Mrs Batbit and they feasted on the fattest, thickest and juiciest of insects and ceased squabbling over the best cave roof-hanging spots.

11. HOME AGAIN

Who left the window open? It's cold outside. A dark, cold, mist beckoned Davidia to come out and play. It rattled the window-pane with small twigs and swirling debris. The window swung back and forth trying to wear down its hinges. Cold air rushed in like an unwanted gate crasher. The attic had a frosty feel to it. Davidia was sound asleep in the odd shaped chair. Her yellow, cotton dress hung softly on her. The wind was perform-ing at its optimum nastiness. Miss Percival just stared into space. The cold wouldn't affect her.

It was too much for the poor suffering window. One hinge gave way. Bang! The window slammed into the house. Davidia awoke with fright.

'Who's there?' she said, trying to sit straight. 'Where am I? I must have fallen asleep. What's that wind doing?'

Davidia had slept for one hour whilst the outside winds howled, creating miserable road conditions and an unpleasant day for anyone to enjoy. She looked hard at the window and wondered whether she had been near it. She stood up and walked toward the banging window. It still seemed unhinged and couldn't be shut.

'It's too cold out there,' said Davidia to herself. 'I'm playing inside today. Miss Percival, what would you like me to read to you? I won't read those two lettered books; they send you to sleep.'

'Davidia,' called Dan. 'I hope you haven't opened the window up there.'

Dan could hear the banging sound.

'No, I haven't. They are all closed,' she fibbed. She tried to shut it, but it was obstinate in its damaged condition. She tied the inside latch to the windowsill lock holder with the pink ribbon from the box she had opened earlier.

'There, that will do it. I hope it stays shut otherwise …,' her thoughts trailed off.

'Mum and dad will be home shortly,' Dan called out.

The attic became very quiet. Davidia had another look at the two books left neatly next to the odd shaped chair. She lent over and picked up one, then the other. They behaved exactly like two ordinary little reader books should. She smoothed her hands over them. Their touch was soft. Nothing unusual happened.

'I wonder,' she said out loud. The walls echoed back, 'we do too.'

Davidia dropped both books in surprise. The attic certainly felt like it was a magical place.

'Miss Percival. You sit there and I will read you a story from one of the other books from that pile.' Soon the room was very quiet except for the sound of a small voice reading to Miss Percival.

'Davidia, Davidia,' she heard her father call out. She grabbed Miss Percival and ran quickly downstairs to greet him. The attic door slammed shut behind her. The doorknob twisted tight so that the next person who wanted entrance had to ask permission from it.

Many years passed. Davidia now had two children of her own. Petra, who was twelve, and Steven, who was fourteen. They were both growing so quickly that time seemed to swallow their existence. Are they really that age? Where did all that time go? When I was Petra's age I had that magical place to enjoy with Miss Percival. Would it still be there? Davidia became restless knowing that her childhood experiences were innocent, fun and many years ago. The old attic in the parents' home held a magical feeling for her and before her children reached the age of disinterest – and that's what daggy parents do – she wanted them to experience a little of her childhood. The children were on the verge of a magical goodbye to their impressionable youth as they prepared to battle teenage years with their "I know all" attitude.

She yearned to see the family home one more time. Her parents had sold the house whilst she was at school and had moved elsewhere. The house held her childhood experiences of long ago, but her memories had moved with her.

'Children. Would you like to go on an adventure?'

'Down to the mall, mum?' Petra enquired.

'Great. We can buy that new video game. It's Mongo Juice The Mincer,' answered an excitable Steven.

'That's not quite what I had envisaged. I want to visit my old home and show you both where I lived as a child.'

'Boring.'

'I'll do you a deal. You come and humour me with a visit and we'll do both those things you mentioned.' Bribery, a tool within a parent's armoury of encouragement for getting their own way, still had an effect. It was a win for everyone. Petra and Steven slumped their shoulders. Their faces of enthusiasm looked as if they had been put through a strainer.

'If we have to, we have to,' replied Petra, not quite at the level of excitement expected.

'Right then. Tomorrow it is.'

That night, Davidia trawled through her childhood thoughts about the unpleasant looking Grunt and the valleys where they almost met their doom. That adventure had been relived many times when she was asleep. She often dreamed of a repeat, but it was never the same.

Next morning, the car became cantankerous and refused to start. Steven was a budding mechanic and immediately noticed the problem.

'Mum. That's the front door key you have placed in the ignition.'

Davidia wasn't fully concentrating. The day had a nervous edge to it. After a change of keys and muffled laughter, they were in motion. The drive was a quiet affair, with each person filled with the "adventure" ahead of them. Petra and Steven had tuned out with their Ipods stuck in their ears. Davidia was slightly apprehensive, but didn't know why.

It was a bleak day as she drove down her old street. She stopped the car short of the driveway and could see the silhouette of the old house in the distance. The attic still dominated the front façade. A miserable mist hung about like a bad smell, reducing driving visibility to a dangerous level.

'Where's the dream home, mum?' chorused two youthful voices.

'It's further down the street.'

'Why have we stopped here?' asked a curious Petra.

'I don't know. It's hard to see.'

'Is that where Nan and Pa lived too?' they asked, 'and Uncle Dan.'

'Yes. We all lived there.'

'Cool.'

The house hadn't changed in appearance except for the bubbled paintwork, entangled garden and the attic, which was its dominating feature. It seemed to be pleading for restoration. Davidia had obtained the key from the local real estate agent. He thought that she was a prospective buyer and gave her the usual diatribe about "location, location and location". Davidia didn't wise him up because his spiel was so well scripted, it was a shame to waste it, so she listened to the attributes some copywriter had penned about her old home. The house was actually due for demolition to make way for a condominium, a modern term for large terraces of flats. Perhaps he thought Davidia was a developer. The street held strange emotional feelings for her.

'It looks like a dump,' said Petra.

Steven, who didn't like anything untidy, piped up. 'You didn't live there, did you mum?'

'As a little girl, I loved playing in the attic. It was my favourite place, my secret hideaway and my special place with Miss Percival.'

'Miss Percival is in her special place now, mum, my bedroom,' said Petra, who shared her space with her many dolls.

The car stopped. The engine choked, hoping it wasn't turned off. The street felt creepy.

'Come on,' she encouraged.

The concerned look on the two children's faces needed removal and replacement by a smile.

'When we go inside, I will take you to my special place.'

They both beamed with expectation, wondering where that was.

Davidia placed the key in the front door lock. It resisted. She angrily gave it a vigorous twist. The door seemed to say,

'Okay I was only joking by not opening.' The front door finally creaked open like it was attached with arthritic hinges. The floors were dirty and dusty. Footprints were left as a reminder for people to be able to retrace their steps for a quick exit, if needed.

'It's filthy in here,' said Steven. 'Who'd want to play in this mess?'

A group of spiders observed their movements. They didn't mind a messy home.

They went up the old stairs to the attic door. Funnily enough, as Davidia took hold of the doorknob it didn't speak. Had she expected it to?

'Are you going to let me in?' she said out loud. The children wondered who she was talking to.

'Are you alright, mum? We heard you speak to something.'

'It's nerves, that's all.'

She turned and tugged at the ungrateful doorknob until it gave way.

'You didn't trick me this time.'

Inside the attic, she found that it hadn't changed any. The window suddenly rattled with swirling debris. Davidia jumped in shock at the sound. Her heart rate tried desperately to cause a panic. Who was trying to take her outside?

'What was that, mum?' Steven had heard a sound.

'Imagination. For a moment, I thought I was somewhere else.'

There, open on the table at the final page, was an old, dog-eared storybook with the letter P. Nearby was another book with the letter S. She took a closer look and wondered who she was looking at. There was a little girl and a strange looking creature. They seemed familiar. A black dot in the corner brought a smile to her face. It wasn't a dirt speck, was it? Then she remembered a small flying creature. In the corner was the odd-shaped chair covered in years of dust. She cleared a space on the floor at the foot of the chair and suddenly realised how important her children were. Had she been doomed forever to live in Triplock, she would never have experienced the pleasure of motherhood. Why did she feel so strongly that her adventure was "real"? Her body tingled with the cold.

'You aren't sitting in the dust, are you mum?' Petra didn't want her pretty, yellow dress to get dirty.

'I'm sitting in the chair,' said Steven.

Davidia suddenly became breathless.

'Mum. You're as red as a beetroot.'

Steven was perfectly safe. He sat awkwardly in the chair. Davidia relaxed slightly. She remembered that when she sat there as a child, weird events began happening.

'Are you okay, Steven?'

'It's a bit small and hard on my bottom, but otherwise I like it. I don't even mind the dust.'

'When I was about twelve, I discovered that chair in a box tied with pink ribbons. I sat in it just like you did. That's when the Rock of Yocklaw appeared.'

'What's that?'

'I think it was a fantasy place, but it was so real, I actually felt I was there.'

'From here, you went where?'

'Out of the window on a day, quite like today. Did I ever tell you the story about the Rock of Yocklaw and the Prince of Triplock?'

'No, mum.'

'Perhaps it was time I did.'

There was an almost deathly silence. Only the sounds of the annoying winds buffeting the window-pane interrupted the serenity of the room. The ambience of sweet rose scents swarmed around them.

'Ignatus, is that you?' flashed through Davidia's mind. 'Ah! That was the smell.'

The three family members stayed alert, whilst two listened intently, sitting in Davidia's secret place.

'Once there was …'